P9-DDW-919

ALSO BY ANDREW VACHSS

FLOOD

STREGA

BLUE BELLE

HARD
CANDY

HARD CANDY

a novel by
ANDREW VACHSS

ALFRED A. KNOPF

NEW YORK

1989

THIS IS A BORZOI BOOK
PUBLISHED BY ALFRED A. KNOPF, INC.

Copyright © 1989 by Andrew Vachss

All rights reserved under International and Pan-American Copyright
Conventions. Published in the United States by Alfred A. Knopf, Inc.,
New York, and simultaneously in Canada by Random House of Canada
Limited, Toronto. Distributed by Random House, Inc., New York.

Grateful acknowledgment is made to Famous Music Corporation for
permission to reprint an excerpt from "The Ballad of Charles Whitman"
by Kinky Friedman. Copyright © 1973 by Ensign Music Corporation.
Reprinted by permission.

Library of Congress Cataloging-in-Publication Data
Vachss, Andrew H.
Hard candy : a novel / by Andrew Vachss.
p.   cm.
ISBN 0-394-57791-4
I. Title.
PS3572.A33H37   1989
813'.54—dc19   89-45272   CIP

This book is a work of fiction. Names, characters, places, and incidents
either are the product of the author's imagination or are used fictitiously,
and any resemblance to actual persons, living or dead, events, or
locales is entirely coincidental.

Manufactured in the United States of America
FIRST EDITION

They don't give medals on this planet
for courage in urban combat.
But there are silver stars shining in the sky
that the astronomers can't explain.

ALMA HENRY

BESSIE MYRICK

MARY SPENCER

HARD
CANDY

1

CITY VULTURES never have to leave the ground.

I was standing on the upper level of the Port Authority Bus Terminal, waiting in the November night. Back to the wall, hands in the empty pockets of a gray raincoat. Under the brim of my hat, my eyes swept the deck. A tall, slim black youth wearing a blue silk T-shirt under a pale yellow sport coat. Baggy pants with small cuffs. Soft Italian shoes. Today's pimp—waiting for the bus to spit out its cargo of runaways. He'd have a Maxima with blacked-out windows waiting in the parking lot. Talk about how hard it was to get adjusted to the city—how he was the same way himself when he hit town. He'd be a talent scout for an independent film producer. If the girl wanted, he'd let her stay at his place for a few days until she got herself together. Projection TV, VCR, sweet stereo. A little liquor, a little cocaine. High-style. The way it's done, you know. Another black guy in his thirties. Gold medallion on his chest under a red polyester shirt that would pass for silk in the underground lights. Knee-length black leather coat, player's hat with a tasteful red band. Alligator-grain leather on his feet. Yesterday's pimp—waiting his turn. He'd have an old Caddy, talk his talk, make you a star. A furnished room in a no-see hotel down the street. Metal coat hangers in his closet that would never hold clothes.

You could go easy or you could go hard.

Two youngish white guys, talking low, getting their play together. Hoping the fresh new boys getting off the bus wouldn't be *too* old.

A blank-faced Spanish kid, black sweatshirt, hood pulled up tight around his head. Felony-flyers on his feet. Carry your bags, ma'am?

A few citizens, waiting on relatives coming back from vacation. Or a kid coming home from school. A bearded wino picking through the trash.

The Greyhound's air brakes hissed as it pulled into the loading port. Night bus from Starke, Florida. A twenty-four-hour ride—change buses in Jacksonville. The round-trip ticket cost $244.

I know—I paid for it.

The man I was waiting for would have a letter in his pocket. A letter in a young girl's rounded handwriting. Blue ink on pink stationery.

Daddy, I know it's been a long time, but I didn't know where you was. I been working with some boys and I got myself arrested a couple years ago. One of the cops took my name and put it in one of their computers. He told me where you was, but I didn't write for a while because I wanted to have some-thing good to tell you. I'm sorry Sissy made me run away that time without even telling you goodbye like I wanted. I wrote to her but the letter came back. Do you know where she's at? I guess she got married or something. Anyway, Daddy, you'll never believe it, but I got a lot of money now. I'm real good at this business I'm in. I got a boyfriend too. I thought you could use a stake to get you started after you got out, but I didn't want to mail no cash to a prison. Wasn't that right?

Anyway, Daddy, when you get ready to come out, you write to me at this Post Office box I got now and I'll send you the money for the ticket up here. It would be like a vacation or something. And I could give you the money I have saved up. I hope you're doing okay, Daddy. Love, Belle.

The slow stream of humans climbed down. Hands full of plastic shopping bags, cartons tied together with string, duffel bags. Samsonite doesn't ride the 'Hound too often.

He was one of the last off the bus. Tall, rawboned man, small eyes under a shock of taffy-honey hair. Belle's eyes, Belle's hair. A battered leather satchel in one hand. The Spanish kid never gave him a second glance. A cop would, but there weren't any around.

I felt a winter's knot where my heart should have been.

His eyes played around the depot like it was a prison yard. I moved to him, taking my hands out of my pockets, showing them empty. He'd never seen me before, but he knew the look.

"You're from Belle?" he asked. A hard voice not softened by the cracker twang.

"I'll take you to her," I promised, turning my back on him so he could follow, keeping my hands in sight.

I passed up the escalator, taking the stairs to the ground floor. Felt the man moving behind me. And Max, shadow-quiet, keeping the path clear behind us both.

2

THE PLYMOUTH was parked on a side street off Ninth Avenue. I opened the driver's door, climbed in, unlocked his door. Giving him all the time in the world to bolt if he wanted to try it.

He climbed in next to me, looked behind him. Saw a pile of dirty blankets.

"No back seat in this wagon?"

"Sometimes I carry things."

He smiled his smile. Long yellow teeth catching the neon from a topless bar. "You work with Belle?"

"Sometimes."

"She's a good girl."

I didn't answer him, pointing the Plymouth to the West Side Highway. I lit a smoke, tossing the pack on the dash. He helped himself, firing a match off his thumbnail, leaning back in his seat.

I turned east across 125th Street, Harlem's Fifth Avenue, heading for the Triboro Bridge.

"You all got nothin' *but* niggers round here," he said, watching the street.

"Yeah, they're everyplace."

"You ever do time with niggers?"

"All my life."

I tossed a token in the Exact Change basket on the bridge and headed for the Bronx. The Plymouth purred off the highway onto Bruckner Boulevard, feeling its way to Hunts Point. He watched the streets.

"Man, if it's not niggers, it's spics. This ain't no city for a white man."

"You like the joint better?"

His laugh was short. Ugly.

I motored through the streets. Blacked-out windows in abandoned buildings—dead eyes in a row of corpses. Turned off the main drag heading toward the meat market. Whores working naked under clear plastic raincoats stopped the trucks at the lights. We crossed an empty prairie, tiny dots of light glowing where things that had been born human kept fires burning all night long.

I pulled up to the junkyard gate. Left him in the car while I reached my hand through a gap in the razor-wire to open the lock.

We drove inside and stopped. I got back out and relocked the gate. Climbed back inside, rolled down the window. Lit a smoke.

"What do we do now?"

"We wait."

The dogs came. A snarling pack, swarming around the car.

"Damn! Belle's *here?*"

"She's here."

The Mole lumbered through the pack, knocking the dogs out of his way as he walked, like he always does. He came up to my open window, peered inside at the man in the front seat.

"This is him?"

"Yeah."

He clapped his hands together. Simba came out of the blackness. A city wolf, boss of the pack. The beast stood on his hind legs, forepaws draped over the windowsill, looking at the man like he knew him. A low, thick sound came out of the animal, like his throat was clogged.

"We walk from here," I told the man.

His eyes were hard, no fear in them. "I ain't walkin' *anywhere,* boy. I don't like none a this."

"Too bad."

"Too bad for you, boy. You look real close, you'll see my hand ain't empty."

I didn't have to look close. I knew what he'd have in his satchel— they don't use metal detectors on the Greyhound.

The dirty pile of blankets in the back of the Plymouth changed shape. The man grunted as he felt the round steel holes against the back of his neck.

"Your hole card is a low card, motherfucker." The Prophet's voice, low and strong for such a tiny man. "I see your pistol and raise you one double-barreled scattergun."

"Toss it on the seat," I told him. "Don't be stupid."

"Where's Belle? I came to see Belle."

"You'll see her. I promise."

His pistol made a soft plop on the front seat. The Mole opened his door. The man got out, the Prof's shotgun covering him. I walked around to his side of the car. "Let's go," I told him, my voice quiet.

We walked through the junkyard until we came to a clearing. "Have a seat," I said, pointing toward a cut-down oil drum. Taking a seat myself, lighting a smoke.

He sat down, reaching out a large hand to snatch at the pack of smokes I tossed over to him.

"What now?"

"We wait," I said.

Terry stepped into the clearing. A slightly built boy wearing a set of dirty coveralls. "That him?" he asked.

I nodded. The kid lit a smoke for himself, watching the man. The dog pack watched too. With the same eyes.

The Mole stumbled up next to me, the Prof at his side. The little man supported himself on a cane, the scattergun in his other hand.

"Pansy!" I called out. She lumbered out of the darkness, a Neapolitan mastiff, a hundred and forty pounds of power. Her black fur gleamed blue in the faint light, cold gray eyes sweeping the area. She walked toward the tall man, a steamroller looking at fresh-poured tar. "Jump!" I snapped at her. She hit the ground, her eyes pinning the man where he sat.

I looked around one more time. All Belle's family was in that junkyard. All that was left, except for Michelle. And she'd already done her part.

The Prophet handed me a pistol. "Here's the sign—now's the time."

I stood up.

"They got the death penalty in Florida?" I asked the man.

"You know they do."

"They got it for incest?"

His eyes flickered. He knew. "Where's Belle? Let me talk to her!"

"Too late for that. She's gone. In the same ground you're standing on."

"I never did nothin' to you . . ."

"Yeah, you did. I don't have a speech for you. You're dead."

"I got people know where I am."

The Prophet smiled at him. "Motherfucker, *you* don't even know where you are."

"You want the kid to see this?" I asked the Mole.

Light played on the thick lenses of his glasses. "He watched *her* die."

I cocked the pistol.

He kept his voice low. Reasonable. "Look, if I owe, I can pay. I'm a man who pays his debts."

"You couldn't pay the *interest* on this one," I told him.

"Hey! I got money, I can . . ."

"I'm not the Parole Board," I said. The pistol cracked. He jerked backwards off the oil drum. I fired twice more, watching his body jump as each bullet went home.

The Prophet hobbled over to him. The shotgun spoke. Again.

I looked at the body for a dead minute.

We bowed our heads.

Pansy howled at the dark sky, grief and hate in one voice. The pack went silent, hearing her voice.

I didn't feel a thing.

3

AFTER THE COPS took Belle off the count, I thought about dying too. Thought about it a lot. The Prophet told me the truth.

"If there's something out there past this junkyard, she'll be waiting for you, brother."

"And if there's not?"

"Then what's your hurry?"

"I feel dead inside me," I told the little man with the hustler's soul and the lion's heart. The man who helped raise me inside the walls. Everyone called him the Prof. I thought it was short for Professor—he knew and he taught. But Prophet was the true root. A man who sees the truth sees the future. He showed me both—showed me how to be a man.

Or whatever it is that I am.

"You know what to do with it," he told me.

I knew. Survive is what I knew. What I know. The only tune I know how to play.

Down here, we have rules. We made them ourselves. Feeling dead inside me—that was a feeling. It wouldn't bring Belle back to me—wouldn't get me closer. But making somebody dead . . . that was a debt.

Belle's father. The maggot who made her older sister into her mother. He loaded her genetic dice. She never had a chance. Her mother died so she could run, and she ran until she died.

I was holding her in my arms when she went, torn to pieces by bullets she took for me. She looked it in the eye when it came for her.

4

BELLE DIED in the spring. I went cold through the summer. Waiting.

Her father was in a prison in Florida, finishing up a manslaughter bit. I did some checking—learned they'd cut him loose in late October.

Michelle wrote the letter, copying Belle's handwriting from a poem the big girl once tried to write.

If her father had any family left to spend Thanksgiving with, there'd be an empty chair at the table.

But the cold was still in me.

5

I SLIPPED MY PLYMOUTH through Chinatown, heading for Mama's. The car didn't feel the same since Belle left. I couldn't make it sing the way she could. Her Camaro was cut up into a thousand pieces in the Mole's junkyard. Her body was in the ground. She left her clothes at my office, her life savings stashed in the hiding place in my garage. I burned the clothes. Kept the money. Like she would have wanted.

It was the fourth day I'd made the run past Mama's, checking the dragon tapestries in the window. One red, one white, one blue. Mama's a patriot. But not a citizen. None of us are.

The blue tapestry had been up for days. Cops. The newspapers said the porno theater had been blown up by some extremist group. The searchers found enough evidence to drop Salvatore Lucastro— drop him hard. His snuff-film business was as dead as the little girls he made into movie stars. Sally Lou was looking at a bunch of life sentences, running wild. Some flowers can only grow in the dark. The local badges had a bad attitude. They weren't surprised that the *federales* snatched the evidence. They knew Sally Lou's ass was going to be RICO'd. Continuing Criminal Enterprise. But there was supposed to be something left for them. A couple of bodies. I left pieces of one all over a construction site in Times Square. Took the other one with me to the junkyard. Put it through the recycling program: it turns freaks into dog shit.

That was months ago. By now, the cops knew they'd never find the bodies. But they knew where to find me.

It played the same way it had for the last few dead months. The cops would come around, ask their questions, make their threats, go away.

When they got tired of sending around the hard boys, they sent McGowan.

"I thought we had a deal," he said, his cop's eyes sad and hard at the same time. A good trick. Pimps can do it too. He and his partner, Morales, they had let me run a massage parlor in Times Square with police cover. The perfect bait for a maggot who took his pleasure in women's pain. Blood-orgasms. I was supposed to leave them something when I cleared out, but I took it with me. And left it in a junkyard.

"I don't know what you're talking about."

"Yeah you do. You think you walk away from this, you're wrong. I don't give a good goddamn about another collar. You know that. But you're on the list now. I don't know how you made the shooter disappear, but they found pieces of that karate freak all over the lot."

The karate freak who'd crippled the Prophet to send me a message.

"What karate freak?" I asked him.

"You want to play it that way?"

"I'm not playing."

"Not anymore you're not," he said, getting up to leave.

6

THE WHEEL spun too many times. They'd always be them—I'd always be me. Some cops went bad. I couldn't go good.

I stayed low to the ground for months, waiting for the Greyhound to deliver Belle's father. Didn't get a parking ticket, didn't bet on a horse. Lived like Gary Hart should have.

There was nothing else to wait for.

7

IT PLAYED the same way with Max too. He'd sit across from me, make the gesture for "Why?" I'd shrug my shoulders. Who knows? He never pushed it past that.

Mama knew why. Maybe she'd told Immaculata, I didn't know. But she'd never tell Max.

Only the white tapestry was in the window. I pulled into the alley behind the restaurant, just past the Chinese characters neatly marked on the wall. I didn't bother to lock the car.

I went through the back door, barely glancing at the collection of thugs pretending to be the kitchen staff. Took my table at the back.

Mama was saying goodbye to a customer at the front by the cash register. She didn't put her heart and soul into it—the customer had only bought food.

She came back to where I was sitting, waving her hand at the waiter. He knew what to do.

I got up as she approached. Thick glossy hair tied in a rigid bun at the back of her head, plum-colored sheath covering her from neck to ankles, same color nail polish and lipstick. Dignified, not sexy. Mama never got older.

I bowed to her by way of greeting. "Cops all gone?"

"They come back soon."

"I know."

"Something else happen. Soon enough. Police get tired easy."

"Yeah."

The waiter brought a steaming tureen of hot-and-sour soup. Mama filled my bowl first, then hers.

We ate the soup in silence. She filled my bowl again. I finished it. Shook my head no at her unasked question. The waiter took the bowls away.

I lit a smoke. "It's done," I told her.

"All finish now?"

"Yeah."

She bowed slightly. "Soon, be yourself again?"

I tried a smile, watching her face. She knew a three-dollar bill when she saw one.

"Max on his way."

I didn't say anything.

"Time to stop all this, Burke. Max your brother."

"You think I don't know that? It's not my fault. I did the right thing."

It didn't even feel right saying it.

I felt Max behind me. I didn't turn around. Lit a cigarette as Mama bowed to him. She went back to the front desk. He flowed into the booth across from me, watching my face the same way he had ever since he came back from Boston. Where Mama had sent him on a phony mission to clean up some problem she was supposed to be having with a street gang shaking down one of her joints.

Max the Silent doesn't speak. He can't. He was a free-lance warrior until he met Mama. I met him in the jailhouse—he brought me to Mama when we got out. I took a fall that was part his years ago, when the wheels came off a sting we'd put together. I was there when he met his woman, Immaculata. His baby daughter, Flower, was named for another baby—a baby who never lived to grow up. A baby a chubby little blonde fought a death-duel to avenge. Flood was her name. She loved me and she went back to Japan.

I used to dream about her coming back.

I don't have any more dreams.

He didn't ask me today. The waiter brought him a bowl of fried rice and a pitcher of ice water. I watched him eat, smoking another cigarette. I wasn't hungry.

The waiter took the rice bowl away. I got up to split. To go nowhere. Max pushed his hand toward the tabletop, like there was a delicate bubble of air he was holding to the surface. Stay for a minute.

I sat back in the booth. He pointed to the empty place next to me. Floated his hands before me into a kung fu dragon-master opening. I nodded my head. Yeah, a karate-fighter. So?

He pointed a finger to himself—weaved his own hands in an answering gesture.

I nodded again. The man wanted Max. Wanted to challenge him to a duel.

He pointed at me again, made a gesture of dismissal. He flipped a chopstick between his fingers—snapped it like a dry twig. Right again. I'm no *karateka*—no match for a master.

Max took a sip of water, his eyes pinning me. He waved his hands again, another challenge. Shook his head no. Held up his hand like a traffic cop. Shrugged his shoulders. No big deal. Max the Silent didn't fight for fun. He'd just walk away. It wasn't an ego thing.

He spread his hands in the "why?" gesture again.

It didn't matter anymore.

I jerked a thumb to my right, indicating the challenger. I pointed at Max, put my hands on the table in front of him, two fingers down from each fist. Men walking. I had them approach each other. Stop. One finger pawing the air before the other. Turned one hand and had the fingers walk away. Felt his eyes on my hands. I pulled one hand off the table, flattened it into a wall, slammed it down in front of the two fingers walking away. No. You *can't* walk away. His eyes lifted to meet mine. I took the hand that had been a wall and brought it to my chest. Made the sign of rocking a baby. Pointed to him. *Your* baby. I lifted one hand gently to where the baby's head would have been, watching my brother's face. Held his eyes as I slashed a finger across the child's throat. The *karateka*'s ante in the death-game. *Somebody* dies. "I can always make a man fight," the maniac told me.

Max locked my eyes, making it not true in his mind. But he knew. I heard a sharp crack. The water glass popped in his hand. Blood flowed across the knuckles.

My brother bowed slowly to me. And then he was gone.

I lit another cigarette. Mama came back to the booth. A waiter made the blood disappear.

"You tell him, yes?"

I didn't answer her. She left me alone.

8

WEEKS WENT BY like that. Slow, gray time. Like being inside. I stayed where I was, not even waiting. McGowan's partner took his shot too. Morales, a thickset Puerto Rican. He got right to it, bracing me in the basement poolroom. I was pushing the balls around the green felt by myself when he walked in. Took a seat and watched me for a while, not saying anything. The stick artists ignored him—the salesmen moved away from our area. There's rooms upstairs you can rent by the hour.

He tilted his hat back, small dark eyes like bullet holes in his head. Watching.

I stroked the bright orange five ball into the corner pocket. The cue ball reversed itself on the short rail and slapped into a cluster of balls, scattering them.

"Nice shot," Morales said.

I chalked my cue. Nudged the four ball into the same pocket.

"You're a good shooter, I hear."

I tapped the thirteen, sliding it toward the opposite corner. Chalked my cue again.

"Funny game, pool," he said. "You shoot a ball, you do it right, and it just disappears right off the table."

I banked the ten ball into the side pocket.

He got up, poked through the racks of standing cues, found one that suited him.

"Let's you and me play a game," he said, sweeping the loose balls together into the triangular rack. Nine balls.

"Five and ten?" I asked him.

He tilted his head toward a dirty hand-painted sign on the near wall. No Gambling.

"It wouldn't be," I told him.

His lips curled. He didn't pretend it was a smile. "One money ball—a dime on the nine?"

I nodded. He reached in his pocket for a coin, started to toss it on the table.

"Do it," I said, sitting down.

Morales broke the balls the way he'd like to break mine. With a hard, straight-ahead slash. Lots of power, no stroke. The balls scattered, running for cover. The three dropped in. He power-slammed the one ball, not even thinking about running the table. A slugger—no finesse. When the dust settled, there were still eight balls on the green cloth.

He sat down, watching. I tapped the one ball down the long rail, leaving myself a clear shot at the two. Dumped it in. I kissed the cue off the four ball into the nine. The yellow-and-white striped ball went home. Morales got up to rack the balls. I raised my eyebrows at him.

"Put it on my tab."

I flicked my eyes to the No Gambling sign.

His face went dark. He took a deep breath through his nose, remembering why he was there. Tossed a crumpled ten-spot on the table. I picked it up, smoothed it out. Left it lying on the rail.

I made the nine ball on the break.

Morales put another ten down on the rail. Racked the balls.

I broke again. Two balls dropped. I lined up on the one.

His voice was light, hard-cored. Honey-coated aluminum. "Upstate, when you come in on a homicide beef, you know what they say about you?"

"Tough luck?"

"They say you got a body. Nice, huh? Some punk snuffs an old lady for the Welfare check, he struts around the block saying, 'I got a body.' You ever hear that one?"

"No."

I ran the rest of the table. Morales put a twenty down, taking back one of the tens. He racked the balls. I chalked my cue. Lit a smoke.

"We met once before, remember?"

"No."

"You remember my name?"

I locked his eyes. "Something with an 'M,' right? Miranda?"

"Smart guy. You got a body, Burke?"

My eyes never left his face. "You guys have one?" I asked.

"See you soon," he said, walking away.

I put his money in my pocket. Went back to pushing the balls around the table.

9

I DIDN'T NEED the cop's cash. There'd been a fifty-grand bounty on the Ghost Van. A killing machine for baby prostitutes. Pimps put up the coin—it was bad for business. Marques Dupree made the offer in a parking lot. Take the van off the street and collect the money. It was supposed to be a four-way split: me, the Prof, the Mole, and Max.

Then it went to hell. A *karateka* who called himself Mortay was bodyguarding the van. The freak was a homicide-junkie. He fought a death-match in the basement of a porno circus. The players liked it even better than watching pit bulls or cockfights. And after that he walked through Times Square, frightening even the hard-core freaks. But the whispers stayed on the street. Max the Silent. The life-taking, widow-making wind of death, as the Prof named him years ago. Max could beat this Mortay.

The freak wanted Max. I tried to talk to him and he raised the stakes. Max fights him or Max's baby goes down.

I dealt Max out. Called in my chips. One of Mortay's boys was gunned down in a Chelsea playground. By El Cañonero, rifleman for the UGL, the underground Puerto Rican independence group headed by my compadre Pablo. Another was dog food. Belle dealt herself in. The van was scrap metal. And Mortay himself—they'd need a microscope to find the pieces.

I had a lot of bodies. And the cold ground had Belle's.

I didn't have to look for Marques. He called Mama—left frantic messages all over the city. Couldn't wait to put the cash in my hand.

I split it with the Prof and the Mole. The junkyard-genius would take care of Michelle. Belle left a stash behind—that was mine too.

Bail money. For a jail I couldn't walk out of.

10

By THE TIME summer left the city, I thought the heat would leave me alone. But even months later, there was no place to go.

I was in a bar off Times Square. Sitting with the Prof, waiting for Michelle. I got up to get the Prof a brew. The place was packed, music screaming so loud the heavy metal clanged. The whole joint was about as much fun as chemotherapy. I bumped into a stud hustler on my way back to the table. He muttered something. I kept moving.

Michelle slipped her way through the crowd. Wearing a white beret, deep purple silk blouse, white pencil skirt, spike heels to match the blouse. An orchid in a sewer. She kissed me on the cheek, her big dark eyes wary.

"How you doing, honey?"

"The same."

The stud hustler I had bumped came over to our table, thumbs hooked in a bicycle chain he used for a belt. Pretty boy. Short spiky haircut. He leaned forward, eyes on me. His buddies behind him a few feet.

"You made me spill my beer."

His voice sounded tough. The way a worn-out car with a bad muffler sounds fast.

I threw a five-dollar bill on the table. "Buy another."

"How about an apology?"

I felt a tiny pulse in my temple. I crumpled the bill in my fist, tossed it onto the dirty floor.

Muscles flexed along the surface of his bare arms. "Get up!"

Michelle lit one of her long black cigarettes. Blew smoke at the ceiling. "Sweetie, go back to whatever you were doing, okay?"

He turned on her. "I don't need no fucking he-she telling me what to do."

Two dots of color on Michelle's cheeks.

The Prof turned his air conditioner on the heat. "There's no beef, Chief. Take the five and slide."

"You got nice friends," the hustler said. "A cross-dresser and a midget nigger."

The Prof smiled. "I'm a thief, boy. I may pull a little vic, but I don't suck dick."

The hustler's face went orange in the nightclub lights. "Let's go outside," he suggested to me, pounding a fist into an open palm.

"He don't have the time, sonny," the Prof answered for me.

"It won't take long."

One of his friends laughed.

The Prof wouldn't let it go. "Yeah it would. About ten to twenty years, punk. Even if they let it slide with manslaughter."

I pushed back my chair.

"Burke!" Michelle snapped.

The place went quiet.

"That's you?" the hustler asked. His voice was a strangulated hernia.

"You know the name, you know the game," the Prof answered for me.

"Hey, man . . . it was a joke. Okay?"

I sat there, waiting. He backed away. He didn't bump into his friends—they were gone.

It wasn't just the cops who knew I had a body. And whose body I had.

II

ON THE STREET outside the bar, Michelle grabbed my arm. "What the fuck is *wrong* with you?" She wheeled on the Prof. "And what about you? You turning back the clock twenty years? This idiot's back to being a gunfighter and you're his manager, right?"

"My man's in pain, lady. Give us some play, back away."

Michelle's eyes glittered, hands on hips. I put my hand on her arm—she shrugged it off.

"This isn't *like* you, baby. You're making me nervous."

"It's okay," I said.

"It's *not* okay. You want to go back to prison? Over some stupid argument in a bar?"

"I'm not going back to prison. Just take it easy. We'll drive you home."

She turned and walked away, heels clicking hard on the concrete, not looking back.

12

THREE MORE dead days later, they took me down. Right off the street. The Prof spotted them first.

"Rollers on the right," the little man said under his breath.

"Probably behind us too. Call Davidson," I said. I tossed my cigarette into the gutter, slipped my right hand into my coat pocket to make them think I might not go along nicely, and slid away to draw them from the Prof. I quick-stepped it along Forty-fifth Street, heading west toward the river. Feeling the heat. Unmarked cop car running parallel to me in the street. Spotted a gay-porn movie house. Heard car doors slam as I slid my money through the slot for a ticket. They wouldn't want to follow me inside. Two slabs of beef shouldered in on each side, pinning my arms, pulling my hands behind me. Cuffs snapped home. They spun me around. A cop I hadn't seen before sang their song.

"You're under arrest. You have the right to remain silent. Anything you say can and will be used against you in . . ."

They patted me down before they shoved me into the blue-and-white that pulled to the curb.

Nobody said a word on the ride downtown.

They left me alone in a holding cell for an hour or so. I didn't ask to make a phone call. I did that once, when I was a kid. Just to be doing it—I had nobody to call. Now I knew better. On both counts.

They brought me into the interrogation room. Two detectives I never saw before shouldered in behind me. Street cops. Wash-and-wear suits, bad haircuts, sidewalk shoes. They looked alike. Same size, same weight. Same eyes.

"You want a smoke?" the first one asked.

"How much are they?"

The second one grunted. "On the house," the first guy said.

I nodded. He tossed a pack on the table, pushed a dull metal Zippo across to me. I rolled my thumb carefully across the surface of the lighter, held it up to the light, slid it back to him. The second guy laughed. Threw a book of paper matches at me. I lit a cigarette.

"You want to make a statement?"

"About what?"

"You're busted. Homicide."

I blew smoke at the ceiling.

A knock at the door. The second guy opened it. The new guy was flashier. Younger. Nice suit, silk tie, dimple under the knot. Spent money on his haircut. Mirror shine on his black loafers. Even had tassels on them. The B Team. He took the seat across from me. The street-sweepers stood in the background.

"I'm Detective Lieutenant Swanson. And you're . . ."

"Under arrest."

One of the street cops snorted. The lieutenant gave me a hard look. "I thought you had more sense than that. What's it gonna get you, pal? You know the score. You don't give up your prints, we can hold you forever. You stand for the prints, your rap sheet falls on you and the judge is gonna remand your ass. You're looking at a few months on Rikers Island even if you beat this."

"I already gave you my prints."

One of the rollers laughed. The lieutenant looked unhappy. "Don't play games, okay? You know how it works. We got some homicides, we got a building blown all to hell in Times Square. We got feds taking fucking bows with their big score. We want ours, okay?"

"What's yours?"

"You tell me, pal. It *could* be you. It don't have to be. Understand? You got something to trade?"

I ground out my cigarette.

The lieutenant looked at his watch. Two gold bracelets on his wrist. "Last chance," he said.

I lit another smoke.

"Don't you even want to know who you killed?"

I blew smoke in his face.

He pushed his chair back. "Book him," he snapped to the two street cops, walking out the door.

This time all three of us laughed.

13

IT WAS ONE in the morning before they brought me downtown for arraignment. The Lobster Shift: they run arraignments twenty-four hours a day in Manhattan. Seven days a week. I spotted Davidson in the front row, dressed like he was going to face a jury, wide-awake. I waited for my name to be called.

Wolfe was arguing with the judge. If she was standing up at a night arraignment, the defendant must be some major degenerate. She was standing by herself at the counsel table, ten pounds of paper spread out in front of her, a guy who looked like a bouncer in a waterfront bar just behind her. Her voice was soft, but it carried.

"Twenty-nine counts, Your Honor. Twenty-nine *separate* counts. Seven complaining witnesses. That's seven *children*. The People respectfully request that the defendant be remanded until trial."

The defendant was sitting straight up, facing the judge. Well-dressed, dignified. Looked outraged to be in such a place. His lawyer was an older man, beautiful shock of white hair falling almost to his shoulders, church deacon's voice.

"Your Honor, if I may be heard. *Doctor* West is a prominent member of the community. A man without a *scintilla* of a criminal record. A family man, whose wife and children are shocked by these obviously false allegations. The People's request for a remand is simply outrageous. I assure you we intend to fight these scandalous charges on the *merits*, and we are contemplating the appropriate civil remedies against the parents of these obviously misguided children. I'm sure this young lady means well . . ."

"Don't patronize me, you pompous clown!" Wolfe's voice lashed out.

"That will be enough," the judge said, looking at Wolfe.

"From who?" she snapped back.

"From *both* of you. The Court has heard enough. Bail is set at one hundred thousand dollars."

The white-haired lawyer smiled.

"Application to surrender his passport, Your Honor"—from Wolfe.

"Your Honor, I really don't think . . ."

"Granted," said the judge.

One of the fancy lawyer's assistants walked over to the clerk to make the bail arrangements as they brought me forward for my turn. The white-haired lawyer walked up to Wolfe. "My client . . ."

"Tell him to go play with his nitrous oxide," Wolfe snarled at him. She looked up as Davidson stepped in next to me. A lovely woman, tall and shapely, her dark hair drawn back from her face, streaks of white like wings sweeping through it. Our eyes met. She said something out of the side of her mouth to the heavyweight who was with her. Swept her papers into a big briefcase and walked away. We all watched her leave, spike heels clicking on the old marble floor.

The heavyweight stepped in next to me, barrel chest against my shoulder. "You got money on the books?" You go down broke, you stay broke. Wolfe knew what you have to do to get cigarette money inside jail. And she didn't want me doing it. The kind of law enforcement they never taught her in the DA's Office.

I nodded. He left to follow Wolfe, covering her back like he always does.

I shook hands with Davidson. "You didn't make a statement," he said, making one of his own.

The ADA who took Wolfe's place was a young guy. Tired-looking.

Mustache too big for his face. The B Team detective was standing next to him, looking more like a lawyer than anyone else there.

The judge stared down from the bench. I stared back—I'd seen him before. One of those "why not the best?" political appointees who climbed the ladder using Preparation H for lip gloss. "Gentlemen . . . any point in discussing this?" He wasn't talking to me.

The ADA started to approach the bench.

Davidson stayed where he was. "No" is all he said.

The ADA went back to his stand. "Judge, the charge is Murder Two. The defendant has an extensive criminal history, including the use of firearms to commit violence. He has no roots in the community, and there is a significant possibility he will flee before trial."

Davidson's face was already red. "What trial? There isn't going to *be* a trial, Judge. This was a pretextual arrest, and the People know it. Or they *should* know it. This case won't survive the Grand Jury. I examined these so-called papers I was handed an hour ago," he barked, waving the yellow-backed sheaf that signaled Felony. "My client is alleged to have killed one Robert Morgan, whoever *that* is, several *months* ago. Period. I don't see a *hint* of what this arrest was based on: no statements, no evidence . . . we aren't even told how this person allegedly died . . . was he shot, stabbed, stomped, poisoned . . . what? My client was arrested on the street. If he was going to flee, he's had enough time to circle the globe, much less leave New York. Where's the connection between this Robert Morgan and my client? Where's the motive? Hell, where's the *body*?" he sneered, looking directly at the detective. Telling him he knew.

The judge was unmoved—he only jumped for state senators on up. "Mr. Gonzales?" he asked the ADA.

"Your Honor, Mr. Davidson knows he can file discovery motions and learn the substance of the People's case. This is an arraignment, not a trial."

"Probable cause!" shouted Davidson.

"We don't need probable cause for an arraignment!"

"You need it for a damn *arrest*!"

"Gentlemen! Approach the bench, please."

I couldn't hear what they were saying. Davidson kept shoving his husky body at the ADA, his face turning as dark as his beard. The ADA kept shrugging his shoulders, tilting his head toward the detective. The judge called the detective up front. Listened, a flat, skeptical look on his face.

Davidson came back to the counsel table. Whispered "Three days" under his breath.

The judge swept the tables with his eyes. "The defendant is remanded for three days. Three days, Mr. Assistant District Attorney. During which time there will *either* be a felony hearing *or* this matter will be presented to the Grand Jury. Is that clear?"

"Yes, Your Honor."

"And if it is not, the defendant is to be released on his own recognizance, by agreement of the People. Yes, Mr. Gonzales?"

"Yes, Your Honor."

"Next case."

I shook hands with Davidson again. They took me away.

14

WHEN THEY CAME to my cell the next day and told me I had a visit from my lawyer I knew it wasn't Davidson. That wasn't the way he worked.

They brought me into a private room. Toby Ringer stepped in. Toby's a Bureau Chief in the Manhattan DA's Office. A stand-up guy, killer trial lawyer, homicide specialist. He plays the game square. I don't know how he's kept his job this long, but he'll never be a judge. Neither will Wolfe.

He offered his hand. I took it. And the three packs of cigarettes he pulled out of his briefcase.

"You know why I'm here?"

"No."

"The arrest won't stand up. We all know that, okay? Nobody thinks you smoked this Robert Morgan. Somebody dropped a dime, but the word is that he won't testify no matter what. But we do know Morgan was tied in with the Ghost Van, and we know the Ghost Van's gone. Couple of more guys gone along with it. You know the story."

"So?"

"That was your work, Burke. It's all over the street. Wall-to-wall. The word is you're a gun for hire now. Contract hitter."

I dragged on my smoke.

"I don't think that's true either, okay? But whoever blew up Sally Lou's operation, he left a big fat hole. And the wiseguys are stacking up to fill it. It was his time, anyway."

I looked a question at him.

"Yeah, there was a contract out on him. Four big guys have been hit in the past few months. And the Italians are getting real nervous. They can't figure out who's moving on who."

I shrugged.

"Yeah, right. Why should you care? Here's why *we* care. They're scared, Burke. So they went to the well. Dead bodies. And more coming. Wesley's back to work."

The little room went dark in the corners.

"That's who we want, Burke. Wesley. That's why I came out here. To give you the message."

"You bring any cheese with you in that briefcase?"

He took a breath. Snorted it out. "Save the speeches, hard guy. We all know you're not a rat. I'm telling you this for your own good."

"Sure."

He leaned across the desk, his voice a clean, sharp whisper. "Sally Lou, he was just a pain in the ass. The wiseguys—they could've just warned him away. But he got himself some muscle. Guy named Mortay. A very, very bad guy, I'm told. So bad he wanted a match with Max the Silent."

Nothing moved in my face. Toby didn't waste his time watching. "This Mortay, he went to see one of the big guys. In the middle of the night. Right past the guards, past the dogs, past the alarms. Woke him up in bed. Broke his forearm with one finger. Told him to stop playing with Sally Lou. They went to Wesley."

I watched Toby, waiting.

"Mortay was on Wesley's list, Burke. And Mortay's not around. Way I hear it, you're Wesley's competition now."

I went back to my cell.

Rikers Island. Even when summer's over, just as hot as Hell is supposed to be. I said Wesley's name in my mind and turned my cell into a refrigerator.

15

I DIDN'T GET any more visitors. They let me out when they were supposed to. I caught a cab back to the city. Switched to a subway, walked the last few blocks to my office. Pansy was right where she was supposed to be too—on guard. She made a growling noise in her throat, so glad to see me she vibrated. Doing a five-day bit wasn't any big deal to her, but she hadn't liked the food any better than I had. I opened the back door and she lumbered up the iron stairs to the roof. I folded the heavy sheets of vinyl I leave spread over a section of the floor into a giant garbage bag and tied it closed with a loop of wire. Opened the back window to air the place out. I had a system for leaving dry dog food and water for her when I had to be gone for a while, but depositing her loads was always a problem. That's what the roof was for. I took an aerosol can of pure oxygen from the bathroom and emptied it into the room she had used. It wasn't the worst thing I'd smelled in the past few days.

16

I took a shower. Shaved. Opened the refrigerator and gave Pansy a quart of vanilla fudge ice cream. She snarfed it down while I made myself some rye toast. I fed it into my stomach slowly, sipping ginger ale. Scratching Pansy behind her ears the way she liked. Talking softly to her—praising her for protecting our home while I was gone. Working on calm.

Changed into a dark suit, a pale blue shirt, and a black tie.

Davidson's office is in midtown, a rifle shot from Times Square. The receptionist was a light-skinned black woman with a severe face. When her smile flashed, her face turned beautiful, then went back to business. She goes to law school nights, waiting for her time to come. I gave her the name Davidson and I agreed on. She buzzed back, got the word, told me to go ahead.

The meeting didn't take long. "What they got is a bad bust," he told me. "An unsolved homicide wouldn't make them that crazy, so it's something else running. You know what it is?"

"Maybe."

"Any chance . . . ?"

I knew what he meant. "No," I told him.

"If they need us back in court, I'll get a call."

"Okay. We're square for now?"

"Yeah."

I shook hands and walked out. Davidson would do his piece, but he was a lawyer. For him, survival was a Not Guilty verdict. The jury of my peers was still out.

17

IT STAYED that way for a while.
Hard looks. Role-playing. I felt Wesley's chill but it never got close to
the bone. I drifted back to the anchor. Calmed down. Davidson said
the murder charge would stay open, but they'd never press it. I
worked the perimeter, nibbling. Some good scams were cooking all
over town, but I didn't see my way in.

Another college kid killed his parents. Said "Dungeons and Dragons" made him do it. A creature killed a woman because she tried to
leave him after twenty years. He told the cops she was his. His daughter.
A beast slaughtered his girlfriend, raped and killed her teenage daughter, stabbed his seven-year-old son in the heart, and set fire to the
apartment. The little boy lived. Identified him at the trial. The jury
acquitted him. He went to court and demanded custody of the boy.
The Transit Authority set up bulletproof token booths so they couldn't
be robbed. Anyone who's done time knows what to do about that—
you fill a plastic bottle with gasoline, squirt it through the slot, toss in
a match, and wait for the clerk to open the door for you. One of them
couldn't get the door open. A youth worker confessed to sodomizing
more than three dozen boys over a ten-year period. The judge wanted
to sentence him to a speaking tour. Gunfire crackled like heat lightning
on streets where the franchise to distribute rock cocaine was disputed
by teenage robot-mutant millionaires.

18

IMMACULATA SAT across from me in the last booth. Max's woman. Mama was at her front desk with the baby, bouncing the plump little girl on her lap, telling her how things worked.

"It's okay now," Immaculata said, voice thick with something I didn't recognize.

"Sure."

"Max understands. He was just . . . hurt. That you left him out."

"I had to."

"I know."

"Yeah, you know."

"Burke, why be like this? You made a judgment . . . it was your call to make. It's over."

"But you think the judgment was wrong."

"It was just an ego thing, yes? It's hard to believe this man would have killed our baby just to make Max fight him."

I looked up. Her eyes were veiled under the long lashes but it didn't help. She couldn't make it stick.

"I have to stand with Max," she said.

I bowed, empty. Her eyes were pleading with me. "You still have your baby," I said.

She put her hand over mine. "You still have your brother."

The pay phone rang in the back. Mama walked past, the baby balanced on one hip.

She came back in a minute. Handed the baby to Immaculata, slid in next to her.

"Call for you. Woman say old friend."

A honeycomb of tiny bubbles in my chest. Flood. How could she have known now was the time?

It must have shown in my face. Mama's voice was soft. "No" is all she said.

I lit a cigarette, biting into the filter. The little bubbles in my chest popped—a tiny string of explosions, like baby firecrackers.

"Woman say old friend. Need to talk to you. Very important."

I looked at Mama. Her lips curled, short of a sneer. "Always important. Woman say to tell you Little Candy from Hudson Street. You know her?" Mama asked, handing me a slip of paper with a telephone number.

I nodded. It didn't matter.

19

MAX WENT everywhere I went. Behind me, not with me. Guarding my back. Protecting me from a ghost. His warrior's soul screaming for combat to make it right. Too late for the battle.

We were on a pier near the Yacht Basin, waiting for a buyer to show up. The buyer had advertised over an electronic bulletin board, using the modem on his personal computer. He wanted a little girl. No older than ten. White. Someone he could love. He'd have ten grand with him. To prove his love.

Max took a restaurant napkin out of his pocket, a felt-tip pen from mine. Drew a rising sun, touched his heart gently. Pointed at me, turned the finger around to include himself. We could go to Japan. Find Flood. Bring her home.

I shook my head. She was home. So was I.

The headlights of the buyer's car flashed. Once, twice. Max merged into the shadow next to my Plymouth. I walked over to the buyer's car, a beige Taurus station wagon. The driver's window whispered down, air-conditioned breeze on my face. It didn't make sense for that time of the year until I saw the fat man inside. Ice-cream suit, straw hat, sweating.

"Mr. Smith?" he asked in a pulpy voice.

"That's me," I assured him.

"She's with you?"

"In the car," I said, tilting my head to show him the direction.

I stepped aside to let him out. The light went on inside the station wagon when the door opened. Empty. He took a black attaché case off the seat next to him.

"She's still a little dopey," I said, walking beside him.

"No problem."

I lit a cigarette, the cheap lighter flaring a signal to Max.

"She's inside," I told the fat man, patting the Plymouth's trunk.

"Let's see."

"Let's see the money."

He popped open the briefcase on the trunk lid. Clean-looking bills, nicely banded. And a small plastic bottle with a spray top, some white handkerchiefs, plastic wristbands—the kind they give you in the hospital.

"Got everything you need, huh?"

"Hey, look, pal. This kid isn't for *me*, okay? I'm a businessman, just like you. In fact, you got any more where this kid came from, you just let me know. I got customers waiting."

His fat body slammed into the back of the Plymouth as Max took him from behind—a paralyzing shot just below the ribs, a lightning chop to the exposed neck as he went down. Vomit sprayed onto the Plymouth.

I ripped open his shirt. No wire. Pulled his wallet from an inside pocket, stripped off his watch, passed up the rings, snatched the briefcase. And left him where he was.

It didn't make the morning papers.

20

THE GILT LETTERS on the pebbled-glass door said "Simon J. Rosnak—Attorney at Law." Max and I stepped inside. The girl at the front desk was a cunty brunette with sparkle-dust for mascara and the kind of mouth that would make you throw out the postage meter so you could watch her lick the stamps.

"Can I help you?"

"I want to see Rosnak."

"You have an appointment?"

"No."

"Well, Mr. Rosnak isn't in yet. If you'll leave your name and number . . ."

"He's in. I don't have time." I glanced down at the console on her desk. None of the lights were lit.

"You can't . . ."

I walked past her. "Call a cop," I advised her, leaving Max behind to keep her company.

I found a carpeted hall, followed it to the end. Rosnak was sitting at an old wooden desk, reading some kind of ledger. He looked up when he saw me, a tired-looking man in his forties.

"What?"

"I need to talk some business with you."

"I don't know you. Speak to Mona. I'm busy."

I sat down across from him. Lit a smoke. There was no ashtray on his desk. "I need to speak with you," I said, calm and relaxed.

"Look, buddy, this isn't a supermarket. I don't know who sent you here, but . . ."

"You represent Johnny Sostre?"

"That's not your business."

"Attorney-client privilege, huh?"

"You got it."

"Only one problem. You're not an attorney."

His eyes tracked me. Camera shutters. Waiting.

"You're not an attorney," I said again. "You went to law school, but you dropped out in your last year. You never took the Bar. You've been running a sweet hustle, representing wiseguys. They know you're not a lawyer. You try the case, do the best you can. You win, they walk. You lose, they wait a couple of years, then they discover the truth, right? You get exposed. They file an appeal. And the court lets them walk. Ineffective assistance of counsel, they call it. Never fails. Josephs did the same thing a few years ago."

He watched me, waiting.

I tapped cigarette ash onto his desk. "Only problem is, you got to have perfect timing. This scam works just one time, no repeats. You got . . . what? Ten, fifteen clients now? Got half a dozen guys already upstate doing time. You get exposed at the right time, all the convictions get reversed. And it's a few years later. Witnesses disappear, memory gets soft, people forget, evidence gets misplaced . . . you know how it works. But you move too soon, it's all for nothing. The DA still has everything he needs, and they just try the cases again. Besides, you're in the middle of a bunch of new cases. They discover the truth now, and you're out of business."

He leaned forward. "The people I represent . . . you know who they are?"

"Yeah."

"You know they wouldn't like this kind of thing."

"Don't tell them."

I ground out my smoke, waiting.

He raised his eyebrows.

"One time," I told him. "One time only. Fifty large, and I'm gone."

"You're crazy."

"But not bluffing."

He fumbled with some papers on his desk. "I need some time."

"This is Tuesday. Friday, you get the cash. I'll call, tell you how to drop it off."

I got up to go. Looked down at him. "I'll save you some phone calls. Burke."

"Who's Burke?"

"Me."

Friday, the juicy brunette took a cab to Chinatown at lunchtime. She got out, and the crowd swallowed her up. When she caught another cab, she didn't have her pocketbook with her.

21

I WAS AT Mama's when a call came in. Julio. I called the old gangster back at the social club he uses for headquarters. His dry snakeskin voice sounded like a cancer ward.

"You did me a service once, I don't forget. So this is a favor, Burke. You stung Rosnak. He went crying to the boys. I squared it, okay? There's no comeback on this one. But give it a rest—stay out of our business."

I let him feel my silence. The phone line hummed.

"You hear what I'm telling you?"

"Sure."

"You found out some things. Okay, a man's entitled to make some money, he finds out some things. You made enough money. Stick to citizens."

I hung up.

22

THERE WAS money out there. The city was a boom town. Drugs, not oil. The prospectors drove triple-black Jeeps, wore paper-thin Italian leather, mobile cellular telephones in holsters over their shoulders. Music in their brain-dead heads: Gotta Get Paid. Gold on their bodies, paid for with bodies on the ground. Babies got killed in the crossfire. Children did the shooting. Cocaine was the crop, in countries whose names they couldn't spell. And here, crack was the cash. Named for the sound it made when it hit the streets.

"Gold on their wrist, a pistol in your fist," the Prof rapped, trying to pull me in. Easy pickings. It wasn't for me.

I couldn't let it go. I read a copy of the Penal Law Davidson gave me. Incest. The legislature put it in the same class as adultery. I guess they thought a kid should Just Say No.

23

I MET MICHELLE in Bryant Park, next to the Public Library right off Times Square.

"I'm going away for a while," she said.

"Okay."

"To Denmark, Burke. I'm going to have it done."

"You got enough cash?"

"Yes. I've been saving for a long time. You impressed?"

I nodded.

"It has to be. I'm not having my boy grow up an outlaw, Burke."

"You're going to take him from the Mole?"

"I wouldn't do that. He's ours, not just mine. I know that. But that's no life for him. I want him to be something."

"The Mole's something."

Her hand on my forearm, lacquered nails shining in the late autumn sun. "I know, baby."

I lit a cigarette.

"I won't be any different," she said.

"I know."

"But *you* are."

I didn't say anything.

"You don't want me to go, say the word."

"Go."

"You can get me the papers?"

"A passport?"

"And . . . later . . . I want to adopt Terry. Make it legal."

"Why?"

"Why? You know what I am. Trapped all my life in this body. I can change that. Be myself. The boy . . . I don't want him to grow up like . . ."

"Like me?"

"I love you, Burke. You know that. I'd never walk away from you." She kissed my cheek, walked away.

24

ONCE I COULD always find something on the sweet side of the edge I lived on. It was gone. Even in prison, there were some things you could laugh at. That was then. The Plymouth drifted back to Mama's. I pushed a cassette into the slot. Janis Joplin. Pure estrogen filtered through sandpaper. Begging some man to take her pain, twist it into love. Throwing her soul at a barbed-wire screen until it diced.

I heard Belle's little-girl voice. "Rescue me."

She'd asked the wrong man.

25

"SHE CALL AGAIN," Mama greeted me.

I looked a question at her.

"Woman say her name Candy, remember? Little Candy from Hudson Street. Very important."

"Nothing's so important."

Mama's eyes were black, small hard dots in her smooth round face. "Baby important, okay? Baby safe now."

"I thought . . ."

"Yes. You think, you think what is right. Big girl, you love her, she's gone. High price."

"Too high."

"No. Babies die first, soon no people, okay?"

I put my fingers on each side of my head, holding it like an eggshell with cracks. I wanted to howl like Pansy, grieve for my woman. For myself. Nothing came.

Mama stayed with me. One of the waiters came over, said something in Cantonese. Mama ignored him. He went away. I felt the trembling inside me, but it wasn't my old pal this time. Not fear. I wasn't afraid. Too sad to cry. Nothing left alive to hate.

I looked over at the only woman I had ever called Mama. "Max could have beaten him."

"Maybe."

"I didn't know the answer, Mama."

She tapped my hand to make me watch her face. See the truth. "You don't *know* the answer, you must *be* the answer."

"Who said that? Confucius?"

"I say that," she said.

When she got up, she left a piece of paper in front of me.

26

I USED A pay phone off Sutton Place. Not my neighborhood, but the best place to call from. The feds wouldn't tap these phones—they might net somebody they knew. I looked at the slip of paper Mama gave me. Seven numbers, a local call. I pushed the buttons, working backward from the last digit. Mama writes all numbers backwards—she says it's Chinese bookkeeping.

She answered on the third ring. In a throaty low purr sweet enough to kill a diabetic.

"Hello, baby."

"You called me?"

"Burke? Is that really you?"

"It's me."

"You know who this is?"

"Yeah."

"Can I see you?"

"Why?"

"I have something for you."

"Nothing I want."

"You remember me?"

"Yes."

"Then you know I've got something you want."

"Not anymore."

"Yes, yes I do. I got something you want. Love or money. One way or the other."

"No."

"Yes. You wouldn't have called otherwise. I know you. I know you better than anyone."

"You don't know me."

"Come over and listen to me. I won't bite you. Unless you want me to. Friday afternoon."

I didn't say anything.

She gave me an address.

I hung up.

27

I DROVE BACK to my office. My home. Let Pansy out onto her roof. Lit a cigarette and looked out the window, feeling the airborne sewage the yuppies called a river breeze.

I think her real name was Renée. Or Irene. She always called herself Candy. I couldn't bring her face into my mind but I'd never forget her. She was just a kid then. Maybe thirteen years old. But you could run Con Ed for a year on what she *wanted*.

She didn't have what she wanted then. None of us did. So we fought young animals just like us—fighting over what we'd never own. We *called* things ours. Our turf. Our women. The street forked at the end. Where we found what was really ours. Mine was prison.

Girls like Candy were always around. We didn't have pistols or shotguns then. Just half-ass zip guns that would blow up in your hand when you pulled the trigger. But you could break a glass bottle into a pile of flesh-ripping shards. Squeeze a thick glob of white Elmer's Glue into your palm. Twirl a rope through it until it was coated end to end. Then twirl it again, through the glass. Wait for it to dry and you had a glass rope. When you got real close, you could use half a raw potato, its face studded with double-edged razor blades. Car antennas. Lead pipes. Cut-down baseball bats with nails poking through them. Sit around in some abandoned apartment, drink some cheap wine, pour a few of the red drops on the ground in tribute to your brothers who got to the jailhouse or the graveyard before you did. Toke on throat-searing marijuana. Wait for the buzz. Then you meet the other losers. In a playground if they knew you were coming. In an alley if they didn't. The newspapers called it gang wars. If you made it back to the club, the girls were there. If you got too broken to run, you got busted. And if you stayed on the concrete, maybe you got your name in the papers.

When I went to reform school, she wrote me a letter. A poem, just for me. Signed it that way. "Love, Candy. Just for you." Nobody had ever done anything like that for me. The feeling lasted until I found out it was the words from some song she'd heard on the radio.

Little Candy. A whore in her heart even then.

Just what I needed to cheer me up.

28

HER BUILDING was a co-op in the Thirties, near the river. We watched it for a couple of days, seeing how it worked. The doorman handled both ends of the building. No problem. On Friday, the Prof rang the service bell at the rear. When the doorman left his post, Max and I stepped inside, past the sign that said "All Visitors Must Be Announced." I took the elevator to the sixteenth floor, Max took the stairs. He was there before I was. We walked up five more flights to the top floor. He stood off to the side as I knocked. I heard the peephole slide back. The door opened. "It *is* you," she said.

I didn't know the woman. Candy had been a slim, dark-haired child. Her body hadn't caught up to her hormones then. But I'd never forget her eyes: yellow, like a cat's, tipped at the corners, glowing under heavy dark lashes. This woman looked about thirty—ten years younger than she should have been. Her black hair was as short as a man's, soft and fine, framing her face. Barefoot, she stood as tall as my jaw. Her eyes were a bright, china-doll blue. The woman had an hourglass figure—the kind where the sand takes forever to get to the bottom but has plenty of room to spread out once it arrives. She was wearing a pair of ragged blue-jean shorts and one of those little T-shirts that stop around the diaphragm. Pale flesh covered her stomach, muscle rippled just below the skin when she spoke.

"It's me, for real."

I shook my head. "Who gave you my name?"

"Burke! It's me. You don't recognize me?"

I let my eyes travel over her. "Not a line."

She fluffed her hair, ran her hands quickly over her face, across her breasts, down past her hips, patted the front of her thighs. "It's all new."

"Some things you can't change," I told her, reaching behind me for the doorknob.

"You don't remember me at all," she said, sadness in her voice.

I closed one eye, watching her with the other. Tapped the closed lid. It was the only chance she'd get.

"Oh! Damn! I forgot. Wait a minute."

I didn't move. She put a hand on my arm. Nails cut short, no polish. "Please."

I watched her walk over to the window, tilt her head back, reach into her eyes. Pull something away from each one. "Come here, Burke. Just for a minute . . . okay?"

I went to the window, the carpet soft under my feet. The late afternoon sunlight came through the window. "Take a better look," she said, her voice soft.

The yellow cat's eyes watched me.

"Contact lenses." A little girl's whisper, giggling at soft conspiracies. Candy.

29

THERE WAS a white phone on a glass table near the couch. One of those Swedish designer jobs, big round numbers in four grids of three. I left her standing by the window, picked up the receiver, and dialed the number of the pay phone on the corner. I scanned the joint while the phone rang—it looked like the waiting room in an expensive clinic. The Prof answered. "Call you back in fifteen minutes," I said, and hung up.

I sat down on the couch. Lit a cigarette, watching her. Thinking how I should look through the place first. But it didn't feel like a trap. And a woman who could change herself into something new could hide a microphone anyplace.

"What do you want?" I asked her.

She came to the couch, sat at the opposite end, curling her legs under her like a teenager.

"Maybe I just wanted to see you."

"Write me a letter."

She shook her head slightly, a fighter shaking off a punch. "I was just a kid."

I shrugged.

"You're still angry with me?"

"I'm not angry with anyone. I don't know you."

"But . . ."

"I remember you. It's not the same as knowing you, okay?"

"Okay."

"What do you want, Irene?"

"I haven't been Irene for a long time. That's one of the things I changed."

"What do I call you?"

"Whatever you want. That's me—I can be whatever you want. There's all kinds of candy."

"That's what you do now?"

"That's what I do."

I looked her over again, seeing it. "You got a closet full of wigs too?"

Her smile flashed. She scissored her legs off the couch, held out her hand to me. I grabbed her wrist instead, my thumb hard against the nerve junction. She didn't seem to notice. I left my cigarette burning in the ashtray. She led me down a carpeted hall, stepped into a room nearly as big as the living room. One wall was floor-to-ceiling mirrors. "My closet," she said.

One shelf was wigs, carefully positioned on Styrofoam heads. Blondes, brunettes, redheads from soft rose to flame. Every style from flower child to Dolly Parton. A wall of cosmetics: lipstick with all new, gleaming, fresh tips, standing in rows like large-caliber bullets . . . blusher, body powders, eyeliner, prefitted fingernails, polish, false eyelashes. Makeup table with a round padded stool, tiny row of frosted light bulbs surrounding another mirror, this one three-paneled.

The far wall looked flat. She slid back a panel. Fur coats. Fox, ermine, sable, mink, leopard. Others I didn't recognize.

Another panel. Cocktail dresses, formal gowns, yuppie go-to-business outfits. Leather miniskirts. Dresses from silk to cotton. Jumpers and pinafores.

Another section was shoes. Lizard-skin spike heels, black leather boots from ankle to mid-thigh, shoes trimmed with rhinestones, jogging shoes, little girls' shoes with Mary Jane straps, sandals.

Rows and rows of built-in drawers. She opened them smoothly, stepped aside, gesturing with her hand like a wrongly accused smuggler sneering at a customs agent. G-strings, silk panties, bikini briefs, garter belts, teddies, camisoles, cotton panties in a dozen colors. Panty hose still in the original wrappers. Stockings from fishnet to sheer. Push-up bras, front-opening bras, bras with holes for nipples to poke through, bras with straps that crossed over the back. Red, black, white, and a pastel rainbow.

There was another panel to the wall. She slid it back. Riding crops, handcuffs, lengths of thin steel chains, a leather-handled stock, leather straps at the end, like a shortened cat-o'-nine-tails. Leather belts, from spaghetti straps to thick slabs. Something that looked like a black rubber sweatshirt. Dog collars. A leather face mask, laced up the back, the mouth a zippered slash. Hairbrushes, Ping-Pong paddles, some foam-padded, others covered with sandpaper. Rings, clamps, vibrators. Dildos, from pencils to sausages. A bullwhip of braided silk.

"Seen enough?"

Her eyes were a challenge. My face was flat. I nodded.

She held out her hand again, turning it so I could hold her by the wrist. The next room down the hall was a teenage girl's bedroom: Heavy Metal posters on the wall, fluffy quilt on the big bed, stuffed animals, pink telephone. A leather-bound book next to it. It said "My Diary" on the cover in gold. Bathroom off to the side.

Three more bedrooms. A single working girl. A movie star. The last one had a black leather psychiatrist's couch in one corner. Rings bolted into the floor. The walls were lined in dark cork.

She took me back into the front room. My cigarette had burned itself out. I let go of her wrist—lit another one. She walked out of the room. I picked up the phone, hit the * button, watched the thin slash of liquid crystal fill up with the same number I had dialed before. The Prof answered. "Okay so far," I said. Hung up again.

She came back in again. "You think of a name for me yet?"

"There's lots of names for it."

"Money is the name for it. Nothing's changed."

"I haven't got any money."

"Yes you do, bounty hunter. I know what you do. But it's not your money I want. It's money I have for you—something I want you to do."

"There's nothing I want to do."

She took off her top. Her breasts stood out hard as white marble. "Silicone. The very best—envelopes, not injections." She licked her lips. "Collagen. Here too," she said, patting her seamless face. She stood, dropping the denim shorts to the floor in the same motion. "This is mine," patting her butt. "Hard work. Three times a week on the machines." She took a deep breath through her nose—her waist wasped. "I can do more crunches than a bodybuilder. Six days a week." The soft patch between her legs was dark, gleaming, heart-shaped. "Electrolysis. Once a month," she said, holding out her arms for me to see.

"You don't miss a trick."

"Don't be nasty, Burke. I'm proud of you—you got what you wanted. Can't I do it too?"

"What did I want?"

"You think I don't remember? A name. You got a name now. The whole street knows your name. After Mortay . . ."

She caught me looking at her, felt the chill. "I'm sorry. I know better. Don't say anything. I know the rules. There's something I need you to do—something you know how to do. And there's money. A lot of money. Just think about it, okay? And call me. You have the number. I'll come wherever you want . . . tell you what I need."

I stood up. "One more call," I told her. She shrugged, walked over to the window, naked in the light. The glass had a faint orange tint. One-way. I picked up the phone, dialed 958-2222. A recorded voice spat back a phone number. Ma Bell's black box telling the phone repairman that he was working on the right account. It wasn't the number I had called her on. I said "Okay" into the phone and hung up.

She came over to the door with me. "Whatever you want. *And* the money," she whispered. "Call me." Her lips flexed like she was going to kiss me. Saw me watching her face and pulled the punch. The door closed behind me. I took the elevator to the fourth floor, met Max on the stairwell. I pushed an imaginary button with my finger. We split

up at the bottom of the stairs. When the doorman went to the back
to answer the buzzer I walked out the front door.

30

I DROPPED the Prof off at the edge
of the Village, turned the Plymouth toward Chinatown. Max spread
his hands, asking me "What?" I shrugged. I pulled over to the curb
when we got near the warehouse where Max had his temple. His face
was a mask, staring out the windshield to some other place. His hand
dropped on my forearm, a leather-colored bone sculpture, a ridge of
horned callus raised along the chopping edge, the first two knuckles
enlarged, a white slash across the back from an old razor scar. He
wasn't going to move. I turned to see what he wanted.

The mute Mongolian took his hand from my forearm, tapped two
fingers against my chest. Where my heart would be. He put his fingertips together, elbows extending in a straight line. Slowly opened
his fingers, tilted his face up. Sunlight? I looked a question at him.
He went through the whole thing again. He wasn't getting through.
A thick finger drew a cross in the dust on the dashboard. I watched.
He put an arrow at the top of the cross. A compass? He extended the
right-hand line of the cross all the way to the end of the dash. East?
He made the gesture again. I nodded. The Rising Sun. Japan. I said
her name. Flood. His hands came together in a prayerful gesture.
Pointed at me. At himself. Extended his arms in a child's gesture of
an airplane banking through the sky. We could go to Japan. Find her.
Bring her back.

I shook my head. No. Again.

He bowed slightly. The way you do before the fight starts. Opened
the door and he was gone.

31

WHEN I GOT to the junkyard, Terry let me in. "They're fighting," he said, leading the way back to the bunker.

The Mole was a sodden lump, seated on one of the cut-down oil drums he used for chairs. Elbows on his knees, chin in his hands. His coveralls were so dirty they worked like camouflage—his dead-white face looked suspended in air, light shifting on the thick lenses of his glasses as he followed Michelle's swooping circles around him. She was wearing a white raw silk coat that reached past the tops of her black boots. A black cashmere turtleneck sweater and black slacks that puddled over the tops of the boots. Long strand of pearls around her neck. Her hand flicked them back and forth as she snapped at the Mole. Simba sat next to the Mole, head cocked, ears flared. Fascinated.

She whirled as we came into the clearing, hands on hips.

"Stay out of this, Burke."

"I came to see Mole," I told her.

"You'll see him when I'm finished with him."

"Mom . . ." Terry started.

All the hardness went out of her face. "This doesn't concern you, sweetheart. You know the Mole and I argue sometimes. Soon as we're finished, I'll let you take me out to dinner in town, okay?"

The Mole's head swiveled toward me. "She wants to have the operation."

"Mole!"

"You think the boy doesn't know?"

It went quiet then. I lit a cigarette, waiting. Terry went over to Michelle, took her hand. "It's okay, Mom."

She kissed him hard on the cheek. Pulled away from him. Walked right up to the Mole, leaned into his face. "It's me. I waited for this. I know I kept talking about it, but now's the time."

"It's dangerous."

"It's *not* dangerous. You think this is like a coat-hanger abortion? They know what they're doing."

His head swiveled to me again. "She wants to be a citizen."

"I know."

"None of you know."

The Mole's eyes were liquid pain behind the glass. "You can't live out there, Michelle. It's not for you."

"You just don't want to lose Terry. How selfish can you be, Mole? You want him to spend his life in this junkyard? Never go to school?"

"I go to school, Mom," the kid said quietly.

"Oh, sure you do, honey. I'm sure you know all about tapping telephones and beating burglar-alarm systems. Maybe someday the Mole will teach you how to blow up buildings."

The Mole's head came up. "Tell her," he said, his voice rusty. He didn't use it much.

Terry tapped Michelle's hand, making her look. "Mom, I study physics. And chemistry. And math. I do. Ask me anything. Burke got me the textbooks for all the first-year courses at college. Mom, I *already* know the stuff. Mole is the best teacher in the world."

"And what are you going to do with all this knowledge, baby? Go to med school?"

"I don't want to go to medical school."

"No, you want to live in a junkyard with this lunatic. Well, you're not."

"Mom . . ."

"Don't 'Mom' me, Terry. You want to end up like Burke? You like the idea of going to prison?"

"The Mole doesn't go to prison."

"Ask him why. Ask your *teacher* why he didn't go to prison."

"I know why, Mom. I know Burke took the weight for him that

time in the subway tunnel. Mole told me all about it. That's what family does."

"That's what good *criminals* do, honey."

"That's the rules."

She grabbed the boy by his shoulders. Shook him roughly. "I know all about family. My biological parents taught me very well. They weren't family, so I picked my own. And we picked you. All of us, not just the Mole. You're not growing up in the underground. You're not going to spend your life like this."

Tears ran down the kid's face but his voice was steady. "I lived with them once. The citizens. Remember, Mom? Remember how you found me?"

Michelle dropped to her knees in the junkyard, clutching the boy's legs, crying. He patted her head gently, whispering to her. The Mole moved away. I followed him.

"It's not safe" is all he said.

"The operation?"

"The boy. He can't live out there. Maybe Michelle could. Go back and forth all the time. It's not right to split him like this."

We walked through the twilight, jagged shadows spiking from the cannibalized cars. I moved between two of the cars. Stopped short when I heard a snarl. A white pit bull was lying against an old Cadillac, tiny squealing puppies nursing underneath her. Even Simba stepped around her.

"I never saw a pit bull here before. I thought they were all dog fighters."

"Terry found her. They were fighting dogs on the other side of the meat market . . . you know just past where the trucks pull in?"

"Yeah."

"She lost a fight. They left her there to die. We fixed her up. Now she's part of the pack."

"Like Terry."

He didn't say anything for a while. I lit another smoke. We made a wide circle, giving Terry and Michelle plenty of time.

"The boy knows Hebrew too," the Mole said, defensively.

I dragged on my cigarette, remembering the boy's Bar Mitzvah. The kid already knew how to blow up buildings.

32

WHEN WE got back to the clearing, Michelle was perched on the Mole's oil drum, a fresh blanket beneath her. The boy was sitting on the ground, her hand on his shoulder. They were waiting for us.

The Mole went into his bunker.

"I'm still having the operation," she told me, defiance lancing through the fear in her voice.

I bowed.

A half-smile played across her lovely face. She patted Terry's shoulder. "Sweetheart, just tell me you don't want to be like Burke—that's all I ask."

"I want to be like Mole."

"Honey, the Mole's a genius. I'd never take that away from him. And he's a wonderful man in many ways. I know he's taught you a lot. And I know he loves you, although I'm sure he's never told you."

"He told me. He said he was proud of me."

"I know, baby. But . . . to live like this. You'll be a man soon. The Mole . . . I mean, you want to live out here? Never have a girl of your own?"

"I'll have a woman, when I'm ready. A mate. Like the Mole said. A man has to have a mate."

"But the Mole . . . he doesn't . . ."

"Mom, I thought *you* . . ."

It was the first time I ever saw Michelle blush.

33

WE WERE crossing the Triboro Bridge before Michelle spoke. "You think the Mole feels that way about me?"

"You know he does. Always has."

She lit one of her long black cigarettes. "He never said . . ."

"Neither did you."

I hooked the East Side Drive, high-rise lights flashing past us. "You miss her?"

"I'll always miss her."

"Belle's dead, baby. You know who I mean."

The Plymouth sharked its own way through the light traffic. "Sometimes," I said.

34

I PULLED UP outside Michelle's hotel. "You working tonight?" she asked.

"No."

"Take me to the Cellar."

"Who's playing?"

"Who cares? If we don't like it we can split."

"Okay," I said, turning the wheel to slip back into traffic.

"Hold it! Where're you going?"

"You said . . ."

"Honey, I've been in a *junkyard*. Park this car, wait downstairs in the bar. I'll be changed in a minute."

Right.

35

THE BAR had one of those giant-screen TV sets suspended in a corner. I ordered a vodka and tonic, telling the barmaid not to mix them. Sipped the tonic.

Some pro football game was about to start. Three guys in pretty matching blazers were talking about it like they were about to cover a border dispute in the Middle East. "This is going to be a war," one of the white announcers said. The black announcer nodded, the way you do when you hear irrefutable wisdom. The guys along the bar murmured agreement. Sure, just like the War on Drugs. If it was really going to be a war, one team would blow up the other's locker room. The Mole was right—we could never be citizens. Where I was raised, there's no such thing as a cheap shot.

"What do you see as the key to this match-up?" one of the announcers asked.

The guy he asked said something about dee-fense. Chumps. The key is the team doctor. The only war in pro football is chemical.

The barmaid leaned over to ask me if I wanted a refill, her breasts spilling out of the top of her blouse. I thought of Candy and her silicone envelopes. What's real?

Michelle tapped me on the shoulder. She'd changed to a red-and-black-striped skirt that pinched her knees close, the hem just peeking out under a black quilted jacket with wide sleeves. Her hair was piled on top of her head, most of the makeup gone. She looked fresh and sweet. I left a ten-dollar bill on the bar and a cigarette burning in the ashtray. Nobody watched us leave—it was kickoff time.

36

I was going through the motions. Playing out the string. Not waiting for full bloom, like I had been all my life. Full bloom had come to me. Just for a visit.

Jacques called me at Mama's. He's a gun dealer, runs a sweet little operation out of a rib joint in Bed-Stuy. I found a pay phone, called him back.

"I have a client for some of my heating units, mahn"—his West Indian accent singing over the line.

"So why call me?"

"This client, he's one of those Haitians, mahn. Spooky, you know. All that zombie-talk . . ."

"Yeah." There's an army of Haitians between Brooklyn and Queens, waiting for the day when they take back their land from the Tonton Macoutes. They don't fear the living, but Papa Doc's spirit still frightens their children.

"I don't travel, mahn. You know this. And they don't come to my place. I need a traveling man."

"I'm not doing any deliveries."

"Of *course* not, mahn. You know how this works. You go there, they pay you. You call me. I tell them where to pick up the units."

"And I wait with them while they send someone to do the pickup?"

"Sure."

"How much you paying hostages these days?"

"Oh, mahn, do not speak like this. Nobody going to cause trouble. These are not drug dealers, you understand?"

"Sure."

"Let us do business, mahn. Good business for me, good business for you."

"How good?"

"Couple of hours of your time, say . . . five?"

"Okay."

"Yes?"

"I'll see you in a couple of days," I told him, hanging up.

I heard the surprise in Jacques's voice. A deal like this had to net him six figures, and I was going cheap. But I had a secret he didn't know about. I didn't give a fuck.

37

I LEFT THE Plymouth just off the West Side Highway near Forty-second and walked over to Eighth Avenue to catch the E train for South Jamaica. A young white dude was sprawled on a bench, chuckling over something he was reading in a magazine. I put one foot on the bench, lit a smoke, took a look over his shoulder. An article about how to make your car burglarproof.

I dropped underground, fishing a token from my pocket. A young black woman dressed like a nun was sitting just past the turnstiles, a flat basket full of coins in her hands. Her face was calm, eyes peaceful.

"Help the homeless?" she asked.

"Say something in Latin first."

"Fuck you," she said, her voice soft.

Everybody's got a pimp.

I caught my train. A huge black guy got on at Queens Plaza. Walked up and down the car announcing that this was *his* train. He was a combat-trained Vietnam vet and nobody was going to pull any stuff on *his* train—all the passengers could feel safe with him. Took off his cap and went up and down the row, collecting contributions for his program. Right across from me was a young Oriental, a folded copy of the *Times* in one hand, a small dictionary in the other. The black man collected some change from the lady a couple of seats down from me, checked my face, passed me by. The guy next to me looked like a lab rat. He threw some coins. When the collector strolled back up the other side, I watched the Oriental. The black guy shoved his cap right in the Oriental's lap. The Oriental was stone-faced. The black guy was covering his newspaper with the cap, not moving. The Oriental reached into the cap, took out a handful of change, jingled it in one fist, watching the black man. The black man pulled his cap back. The Oriental tossed the change into it.

The black guy moved on, into another subway car. Maybe he really was a Vietnam vet.

I rode the train nearly to the end of the line. Walked up Sutphin Boulevard, looking for the house Jacques had described to me.

Three young blacks were watching the traffic from a topless white Suzuki Samurai. The driver stared through the windshield, his passenger watched the street. Another draped a casual hand over the padded roll bar to watch me approach. The passenger got out to sit on the hood, cradling a cellular phone in a white leather shoulder bag. Ten pounds of gold around his neck, brand-new orange leather sneakers on his feet. Wearing a white leather jacket with layered lapels. I kept coming, hands out where they could see them. The driver reached under the dash. The largest one climbed out of the back. Three gold rings on his right hand, welded into a slab across the knuckles. He put his hand to his cheek. I read "Stone" in raised gold letters. The one with the cellular phone took off a pair of dark shades, raised his eyebrows, tapped his nose. I looked through him, went on past. Crack dealers, not hiding it. Nujacks, they called themselves. Flashing. The way a fuse does before it reaches the dynamite.

They were marking out territory in the wrong neighborhood. This turf belonged to a Rasta posse. The last crew from Brooklyn had ended up extremely dead. That's the only War on Drugs going down around here.

I found the house. Knocked four times on the side door. Stepped into a basement. Nobody said a word in English—a couple of the men muttered in something that sounded like French. They pointed to a suitcase. Opened it. I looked inside, counted. They pointed to a phone. I called Jacques.

"It's me. They got one twenty-five."

"New or used?"

"Used, not in sequence. But I got no blue light with me, pal."

"That's okay, mahn. Put them on."

The guy who pointed at the suitcase listened to Jacques, said something to the others. They went out through a different door than the one I'd used. I sat down to wait. I'd told Jacques that the cash *looked* good, but I wasn't vouching for it. If it was funny money, I was taking the same risk he was—my five grand would come out of the suitcase.

I sat down to wait. Put my hand in my pocket for a smoke. The guy waiting with me said, "Easy, easy." I took it out real slow. I had the match to my cigarette before I realized the guy wasn't talking to me.

It was less than two hours later when they came back.

I hit the street with the suitcase. Before I got to the corner, a dark sedan pulled over, flashing its high beams on and off. The window came down. An Island voice said, "Burke?"

I got in the back. It took off smooth and easy. At the next corner, an identical car pulled in front of us. There'd be another one behind. I didn't look. We stopped at a light on Queens Boulevard. A guy in the front got out of the car carrying the suitcase. He handed it over to the car in front, got back in as the lead car took off in a squeal of rubber.

They dropped me off in Times Square. Handed me an envelope. I walked to the Plymouth by myself.

38

I WALKED BY myself a lot then. The court case was pending, but not hanging over my head. Davidson was right—if I didn't do something stupid, I was okay.

I didn't feel okay.

After a few more dead days, I called Candy.

39

SHE OPENED the door, wearing an apricot sweatshirt that came down almost to her knees, face sweaty, no makeup. No contact lenses either, yellow cat's eyes patient.

The apartment looked the same. Fresh rosebuds in a steel vase on the coffee table. The air smelled sharp, ionized. Like after a hard rain.

I sat on the couch. She curled her legs under her, wrinkled her nose when I lit a cigarette. I waited.

"I have a daughter," she said.

I dragged on the cigarette, watching the glowing tip.

"You don't seem surprised."

"I don't know you."

"I know you. You're the same. So am I."

"Okay."

"She's almost sixteen years old. Always had the best. The very, very best. Designer clothes, dance lessons, private schools. The last school she went to, they even had a rule about boys in the rooms. You had to have one foot on the floor at all times."

Candy's mouth curled—her laugh didn't come from her belly.

"Imagine that, huh? I was older than her before I knew people fucked lying down. Remember?"

I remembered. The dark stairwell at the back of the building where she lived with her mother in a railroad flat on the top floor. Candy standing one step higher than me, her back to me, her skirt bunched around her waist. I remembered taking down a drunk in an alley just past a waterfront bar with two other guys from the gang. Thinking my share of the loot would buy her a sweater she wanted. And me another few minutes on those stairs.

"Her name is Elvira. Pretty name, isn't it? I wanted her to have everything I didn't." She waved her hand, taking in the sterile waiting room to her office. "That's what I started all this for."

I watched her lying eyes, waiting.

"A few months ago, she ran away from school. She's staying with this cult. Over in Brooklyn. I don't know much about it . . . even what it's called. The man who runs it, he's called Train. I don't know how he got to her. I went there once. They wouldn't let me speak to her. I told them she was underage, but they must know something about me. Maybe she told them. Call a cop, they said."

I lit another smoke.

"I want her back. She's mine, not theirs. She's too young for this. She needs help. Maybe even a hospital. She . . ."

I cut her off. "What do you want from me?"

She tilted her chin to look up at me. "Get her out of there. Get her back."

"I don't do that stuff."

"Yes you do. You do it all the time. It's *what* you do. What you used to do before . . ."

I looked a question at her.

She pointed a finger at me, crooked her thumb. "Bang bang," she said softly.

I shook my head.

"All you have to do is *ask*, okay? Just go there. See the man. *Ask* him to let Elvira go with you."

"And if he says no?"

"Then I'll do something else."

"Do something else first."

"No! I want to keep my life. Just the way it is, okay? Just ask him."

"Why should he go along?"

"It doesn't matter. He will. I know he will."

I got off the couch, walked over to the window. It was dark outside, lights spotting the building across the street. Nothing was right about her.

"Say the whole thing," I told her.

"You go there. You ask him for Elvira. He gives her up. You bring her to me."

"He says no?"

"You walk away."

"No more?"

"No more."

"What kind of cult is this? They have the girls hooking, begging, selling flowers, what?"

"I don't know."

"How do you spell this guy's name? Train."

"Like a subway train."

I lit another smoke. "You said you'd pay me."

"I said I'd give you whatever you want."

"Money's what I want."

"Tell me the price. I'll have it here for you when you get back."

I smiled.

She didn't. "Half now, half when you come back."

"Five now."

She padded out of the room on her bare feet. I punched the redial number on the white phone, memorized the number that came up on the screen, hung it up gently before it could ring at the other end.

Candy came back in, handed me a thick wad of bills wrapped in a rubber band. I put it in my coat pocket.

"Here's all I know about him," she started, curling up on the couch again.

40

I DID IT RIGHT. Habits die hard. Like the woman I loved. The building was an old meat-packing plant in the shadow of the triangle formed by Atlantic and Flatbush, on the edge of the gentrification blot spreading east from Boerum Hill. A nonprofit corporation owned it. Four stories. The ground floor was a loading bay for trucks. The front-facing windows were new, vinyl-trimmed. The sides were flat-faced brick. The back windows were covered with iron bars. Front door was steel, set a few inches into the frame. The City Planning Office had the records. The place had been gut-renovated four years ago. The top floor had a domed skylight.

Traffic was light in and out. Most of the visitors were young. White. Empty-handed.

I went to see a guy I know. An ex-cop who doesn't pretend he's honest. For three hundred bucks, he told me the place had six separate phone numbers and two pay phones.

"You want the numbers, the toll calls?"

"How much?"

"A grand gets you the numbers, and one month's bill for each number."

"I'll let you know."

Four cars registered to the corporation. Two vans, a station wagon, and a Mercedes sedan.

Five hundred bought me an IRS scan. The corporation called itself Mission 999. It declared almost three hundred grand last year in contributions, none larger than a couple of thousand. The guy I paid told me that it had never been audited.

I had a picture of Elvira. Pretty little brunette in a school uniform. Looked about thirteen. Smiling a school-picture smile.

It made me think of something. Something that wouldn't come to the surface.

41

I TOLD MAX about the deal. Sitting in my booth in the back of Mama's restaurant, I drew a picture of the house. Max kept tapping the paper, not satisfied until I drew in every detail I could remember. He curled his fingers into a tube, held it to one eye, flicked a finger across the opening at the end. I shook my head—I didn't need photographs of the place. When I was finished, I handed the drawing to Max. He lit a cigarette, took a deep drag, let the smoke bubble slowly out his nose as he concentrated.

He ground out his cigarette. Reached down, gestured like he was pulling a plant out by the roots. I shook my head again. We weren't going to snatch the kid. I took him through the whole bit again. And again. Finally he nodded.

42

THE NEXT morning we parked a couple of blocks from the building. Walked the rest of the way. Calm and quiet. I knocked on the steel door. Waited. Max stood next to me, just off my shoulder, centered inside himself, ready.

A young guy just past his teens opened the door. Wearing a blinding white karate gi, black belt loosely tied at his waist, black headband.

"Can I help you?"

"I want to talk to Train."

"Your name?"

"Burke."

"Wait here, please." He closed the door gently. No sound reached us from inside.

It wasn't a long wait. "Please come with me," he said.

The door opened into a long, narrow room. Kitchen sounds to one side. Young people moving around, serene looks, quiet smiles. "This way," he said, turning toward a staircase.

We followed him to the second floor. Sounds of a postage meter, telephones chiming. More people moving around. Nobody gave us a glance.

Another flight. Quiet. All the doors closed. The guy in the karate outfit never looked back.

He opened a door at the top of the last flight. Stood aside, sweeping a hand to show us in. A room the size of a basketball court. Wide-board pine floor, scrubbed so hard it was almost white. The walls were eggshell, the single row of windows blocked by thin aluminum blinds, slanted to make horizontal bars across the floor. The skylight threw an oblong slash of bright light into the center. A teardrop-shaped blob of concrete was placed at the center of the light. The guide led us to it. The center was hollowed out, red and white pillows arranged in the core to form a chair.

"Please wait," he said. He walked across the room, tapped on a door at the far end, came back, and stood next to us. A rainbow formed an arc over the concrete chair. I flicked my eyes to the skylight, catching a glimpse of a long arc-shaped prism suspended by a thread from the ceiling.

The far door opened. A man came through at the head of a wedge, three men on each side of him. Medium height, dark hair. Barefoot, loose faded cotton pants. He was bare-chested under a flowing white silk robe.

"I am Train," he said to me, ignoring Max.

"Burke."

"Get chairs for our guests," he said to nobody in particular. He sat down, one man on each side of his chair. The other four came back carrying one of the concrete blobs between them. I saw where hand-holds had been cut into the sides. They put the chair down. Went back and returned with another. Nobody spoke. The four men came back, each carrying two black pillows. They arranged the pillows in the hollow of the chairs. I took the chair closest to the windows. Max swept the room with his eyes, sat down next to me. One of the men put a metal bowl between our chairs. The four chair-carriers walked out. Train spoke to me from between his two remaining guards—their eyes tracked me. Nothing serene in them.

"You wanted to speak with me?" His voice was mellow-calm, almost polite.

I reached into my coat, watching his eyes. They stayed calm. I took out a smoke, fired it up, dropped the match into the metal bowl.

"You have a girl here. Elvira. Her mother wants her back."

"Is that your message?"

"Half of it. I'm here to take her."

"Just like that?"

I shrugged.

"Do you want to know *why* she's here?"

"No."

"Or how she got to us?"

"No."

He closed his eyes. Held his hands to his temples like he was waiting for a message.

"Are you a private detective?"

"No."

"What if she wants to stay?"

"She's underage. It's not her choice."

"Everyone makes choices."

"Everyone tries."

He put his fingers to his temples again. "Can we discuss this?"

"What's to discuss?"

"I'm interested in people. Why they do things. It helps me do my work."

I dragged on my cigarette.

"Are you interested in a proposition?"

"Enough to listen to it."

He leaned slightly forward. "I'm interested in you. Why you would do something like this. An hour or so of conversation. Just you and I. We'll talk. You'll answer my questions. And I'll answer yours, if you want. A dialogue. I will have to prepare the girl. You'll come back tomorrow. She'll leave with you. Fair enough?"

My face stayed flat. "Even if you don't like the answers I give you?"

"Yes."

I made a sign to Max. He flowed to his feet, approached the man sitting across from us. Train didn't move. The guards stepped in front of him. Max kept coming. I couldn't hear what Train said, but the guards parted when Max closed in. He took one of Train's hands in his, turned it over, examining it. Stepped back, nodded to me.

Train's eyes flickered in the artificial rainbow. "What was that about?"

"My brother is leaving now. I'll talk to you. Like you said. I'll come back tomorrow. For the girl. Like you said."

"That doesn't answer my question."

"Yeah it does. You keep your word, there's no problem. You don't, my brother comes back to see you. He'll know you when he does."

Train shrugged. Max stepped away from him. Stood behind his own chair. Thrust his fingers into the handholds and lifted the concrete blob off the ground. The only sound in the room was the whistle of air through the Mongol warrior's flat nose.

That wasn't like Max. Muscle-flexing. Maybe none of us would be ourselves again.

He gently lowered the chair to the floor. Bowed to Train. Walked to the door we used to enter the room. The guy in the white karate outfit stepped in his way, looking to Train for a sign. By the time Train shook his head, the guy was on the floor, face a black shade of red, holding his ribs gently so they wouldn't cut into his lungs. And Max was on the other side of the door.

I lit another cigarette. "Let's have that dialogue," I said to Train.

43

THE TWO guards helped the guy in the white outfit to his feet. Went out the same door, leaving us alone. Train put his hands to his temples again.

Silence.

"What do you call yourself?" he finally asked.

"Burke."

"Not who, what. You say you're not a private investigator . . . you're not a lawyer, not a doctor . . . all of us are something. You're . . ."

"Waiting."

His eyes stayed calm. "A dialogue. As we agreed."

I nodded my head forward, acknowledging. "I'm just a man. I guess you could call me a contractor."

"Could you explain?"

"I make contracts with people. I promise to do something for them, they promise to do something for me."

"Pay you money?"

"Sometimes."

"And other times?"

"It depends. I need certain things. Just like you or anybody else. I do my work to get those things. It's not always money."

"Are you for hire, then?"

"Only by people who know me. Or know my people."

"This girl you want . . . her mother hired you?"

"Yes."

"And you know her?"

"Yes."

"Do you ever work as a bodyguard?"

"No."

"Why not?"

"It's not what I do. A bodyguard does his job by getting hurt. Or dead."

His lower lip flickered. "And you're afraid of getting hurt?"

"Or dead."

The concrete chair was comfortable. I lit another cigarette. Train shifted his weight, leaning forward, elbows on knees. "Do you feel safe? Here, with me?"

"No."

"Why is that? Your . . . *brother*, you called him . . . seems very powerful. Is that why you brought him?"

"He's gone," I pointed out.

"That confused me. It seems that you told him to go as a gesture of faith. As I told my men to leave. We are the only ones here. Are you afraid of me?"

"Not especially."

"Then . . . ?"

"I'm sitting in this chair. Your chair. It could be stuffed full of low-yield explosive. Wired for electricity. Sitting under a sniper's rifle . . . like that."

"But you don't think so."

"No. I don't think so."

"Would you feel more comfortable if we switched chairs?"

"No. It doesn't matter."

"Are you armed? You have a weapon with you?"

"No."

He leaned back in his chair. "Have you ever been arrested?"

"Yes."

"In prison?"

"Yes."

"Were you innocent?"

"Which time?"

A smile came and went so quickly I couldn't be sure I'd seen it. "Do you mind if one of my people joins us for a minute?" he asked.

"Why?"

"She has a special skill. Something that would help our dialogue."

I shrugged.

"You sure you don't mind?"

"We have a contract."

"Ah . . . yes." He snapped his fingers, a brittle crack in the empty room. The door behind him opened and a woman stepped through. Long, thick dark hair gathered into a heavy braid hanging down the front of a pale violet robe. She stood next to Train, her eyes on me. Big eyes, tropic skin, a slash for a mouth. Dark polish on her nails. "This is Reba," he said.

I lit another smoke. Train rested the fingertips of one hand on the back of the woman's wrist. She was a statue.

"Have you ever taken a lie detector test?"

"Sure."

"Did you pass?"

I felt the ghost of a smile, thinking about it. "The cops never tell you."

"I will."

I raised my eyebrows, waiting.

"Reba has the gift. You know how a polygraph works, yes? Galvanic skin response, heartbeat, pulse rate?"

"Sure."

"Reba does that. With your permission . . . ?"

"Okay."

The woman walked toward me, stepping out of the robe without moving her arms. She was naked, barefoot. I kept my eyes on Train as she crossed the room, the violet puddle of silk at his feet. She came to the right side of my chair, dropped to her knees, her breasts spilling against my forearm, pinning it to the chair. Her right hand slipped inside my jacket, unbuttoned my shirt, hovered over my heart, gently came to rest. I felt two fingers of her left hand against the back of my neck. My eyes flicked to the right. The dark hair disappeared over her shoulder, smooth line of her back down to the swell of her butt, the soles of her feet were callused, deeply arched.

"You know how it works," he said. "Just answer yes or no."

I dragged on my cigarette, flicking the ashes with my left hand.

"Have you ever been in prison?"

"Yes."

"Have you ever killed anybody?"

I just looked at him, no expression on my face. He went on as if I'd answered.

"Have you ever broken the law?"

"Yes."

"Are you a professional assassin?"

"No."

"Do you pay taxes?"

"Yes."

"Did Elvira's mother hire you?"

"Yes."

"Did you ever hear my name before you spoke to her?"

"No."

"Do you mean me any harm?"

"No."

"Have you ever met Elvira?"

"No."

"Are you working for anyone now besides the woman who says she is Elvira's mother?"

"No."

I tossed my cigarette into the metal bowl. I let my eyes follow the arc of the smoke, swept them back across Train's face, let the sweep carry me to the right. A clear droplet of sweat ran down Reba's spine. Her head came up, lips against my ear. "You told the truth," she whispered. Her hand came away from my heart, brushed smoothly across my crotch as she rose to her feet. She walked over to Train, her back gleaming with sweat. His eyes shifted up to her face as she passed. She went through the door without picking up her robe.

Train's hand went back to his temples. "What do you think of my security here?"

"What security?"

"I don't understand."

"Security against break-ins? Telephone taps? Firebombing? What?"

"Oh, I see. I mean my personal security . . . say, if somebody wanted to injure me."

"Seems easy enough to me."

"How so?"

"I walked in here with my brother. We wanted to do it, you were a dead man once you came in the room."

He dismissed the possibility with a wave of his hand. "Forget that. What if you wanted to kill me without getting into the house."

"You ever *leave* the house?"

"Sometimes."

"That'd be the time."

"How?"

"There's too many ways to even talk about. Shooting, stomping, stabbing . . ."

"What if I had bodyguards. *True* bodyguards."

"Bullet-catchers?"

"If you like."

"So somebody pops you from a rooftop. Or blows up a car with everybody in it."

"If I stayed in this house?"

"Set fire to it, you'd come out quick enough."

Train rotated his head on the column of his neck, working out the kinks from sitting so stiffly. A glaze over his eyes. Maybe it was the rainbow. Finally, he nodded. "Do you know what we do here?" he asked.

"No."

"Do you care?"

"No."

"When we were talking before . . . about assassinations? You seem to be saying that if someone wants to kill you, there's nothing you can do about it . . . no way you can protect yourself. Is that right?"

"No."

"What *can* you do, then?"

"Hit them first."

He bowed his head over clasped hands. Like he was praying. Looked up. "You are a man of your word. I will honor our contract. Come back tomorrow. Anytime after seven o'clock in the evening. The girl you call Elvira will be ready to leave with you then."

He snapped his fingers again. The door behind him opened. One of the guards came out. I got to my feet. Bowed to Train and walked to the door I'd come in, the guard at my heels.

The street was dark as I stepped outside. I didn't look back.

I found the Plymouth, started the engine, waited.

The door opened. Max slipped inside. Shook his head. I hadn't been followed.

44

BACK AT the restaurant, I explained what had gone down to Max. His face didn't change, but I could feel the sadness. Wishing Train had refused me the girl. I made the sign of a rifleman on the roof, watching Train through a sniperscope. Max pointed his finger at me, questioning. I shook my head. I left the symbol of the rifleman in place with my left hand, walked the fingers of my right hand up behind it. Knife-edged the right hand, chopped at the symbol, flattened my left hand. Max pointed at me again. Did Train want us to do the job? No.

I didn't know what he wanted. We'd pick up the girl tomorrow and it would be over.

45

I FOUND THE PROF working the Living Room—what the army of homeless humans who live in the tunnels and work the corridors call the arena-sized waiting room at Grand Central. He was propped against the wall by the gourmet bakery, a thick blanket beneath his legs, single wooden crutch standing next to him, a paper plate half full of coins in front of him. I bought him a large cardboard cup of black coffee. Hunkered down next to him, back to the wall. Street people stopped by the Prof's station, talking their talk, dealing their deals. Cops strolled past, eyes working from the ground up. Drugs moved in and out faster than the trains. It felt like being back on the yard in prison.

"You know a guy named Train? Over in Brooklyn."

He sipped his coffee, buried inside a winter overcoat that tented around his shoulders, running it through his memory bank. "It doesn't scan, man."

"He's got some kind of thing going. Like a cult, only . . . I don't know. Woman asked me to bring her kid home from there."

"Runaway?"

"I don't think so. The deal was, I just *ask* him, okay?"

"Ask him hard?"

"No. And just once."

"If it's like you say, what's the play?"

"He asked *me* the questions."

"Show me a piece."

"Mostly about his security system . . . did I think it was good enough."

"For what?"

"To protect him, I guess. I thought he was trying to hire a bodyguard at first, but he never really asked."

"He want a favor? Don't he know you only play for pay?"

I lit a cigarette. Told the little man about the lie detector Train used, the karate-man he had at the door, the layout of the house.

I wasn't watching his face but I could feel him nod. The words came out of the side of his mouth. "I ain't read the book, but I'll take a look."

I left him at his post.

46

I CALLED CANDY from a pay phone in the station.

"He said okay."

"You have my girl?"

"Tomorrow night. I'll bring her to you."

"See? I told you . . ."

I hung up.

47

A DOLL-FACED young girl was working the exit ramp to the subway at Forty-second Street. Soft brown hair in pigtails down the sides of her face, body buried in a quilted baby-blue jacket.

"Mister? Can you help me? I'm trying to get together enough money to go home."

"Where's home?"

"In Syosset—on Long Island."

"That's where I'm going. Come on, I'll give you a ride."

She bit her lower lip. "Twenty bucks."

"What?"

"Twenty bucks. And you can ride me wherever you want, okay?"

Before I lost Belle, I would have taken her with me. Called McGowan.

I walked out into the street.

48

THE NEXT DAY it was dark enough by seven, but we gave the night a couple of hours to settle in. I went to Train's place alone. A different guy let me in. I followed him upstairs. Took my seat. Waited.

The door opened and they all walked in. Train was with them. The woman who said I had told the truth came in last, leading a girl by the hand. A short, slender little girl wearing faded jeans with a rip above one knee. A pale green T-shirt with "Zzzzap!" across the chest, plastic strap of an airline bag across one shoulder, denim jacket in one hand.

"Do you know this man?" Train asked the girl.

She shook her head no.

The lie detector opened her robe. She was naked beneath it. Took the girl inside, hugging her close, looked over her shoulder at Train. Nodded.

"This is who you asked for," Train said to me.

"If you say so."

"You don't know her?"

"No."

"But you've seen a photograph . . . had her described to you?"

"Sure."

"And?"

"I can't tell." The girl's yellow cat's eyes watched me.

"Do you want to ask her any questions?"

"No." I lit a cigarette. "If she's not the right girl, I'll bring her back."

His lower lip twisted. Hands went to his temples. The lie detector opened her robe. The girl walked over. Stood in front of me. "Let's go," she said, slipping one arm into her jacket.

I stood up. Nobody moved. She followed me to the door. The new guard stepped aside. We walked down the stairs by ourselves. Opened the front door and stepped outside. She didn't look back.

49

SHE WALKED beside me to the Plymouth. I unlocked the passenger door for her. As she swung her hips into the front seat I slipped the airline bag off her shoulder. She didn't react. I closed the door behind her, walked around behind the car, unzipping the bag, rooting through it with my hand. Nothing in there that could hurt you unless you swallowed it.

I climbed inside, handed her the bag. She put it on the floor, groped inside, came out with a cigarette.

"Can I have a light?" Her voice was soft, like she was asking me for something else.

I fired a wooden match, held it out to her. She wrapped both hands around mine, lit the smoke, eyes on me. "Your hand feels strong."

I wheeled the car down Flatbush Avenue, heading for the Manhattan Bridge. Turned right on the Bowery, heading uptown.

"My mother sent you?"

"That's right, Elvira."

"Nobody calls me that."

"What do they call you?"

"Juice," she said, flashing a smile. "You think that's dumb?"

"Kids have funny names."

"I'm not a kid."

"Fifteen, your mother said."

"My mother is a liar. She always lies."

I shrugged.

"What if I don't want to go back?"

"Talk to her about it."

"I'm talking to you."

"You're talking to yourself."

I pulled up at a red light on First Avenue. She snapped her lighted cigarette at me and ripped at the door handle, shoving her shoulder against the passenger door. It didn't budge. I picked her cigarette off the seat, tossed it out my window. She pushed her back against the car door, watching me, breathing hard through her mouth.

"You think you're smart—you're not so smart."

"Just relax."

"Will you *talk* to me?"

"About what?"

"Just talk to me. I'm not a package. Not something you just deliver."

"Yeah you are."

"Look, you can keep me in this car, okay? But you have to bring me in the house too."

"I can do that."

"Oh yes. You're a hard man. Momma only likes hard men."

"It's just a job."

Streets passed. Her breathing got calm again. "Can I have another smoke?"

"Sure." I handed her the little box of wooden matches.

"You don't trust me?"

"Why would I?"

"Because I'm not like my mother. I *never* lie. Never, ever. If I tell you I'll do something, I'll do it."

"And so you're telling me what?"

She drew on the smoke. "I'm telling you I want to talk to you. Just for a couple of minutes. Pull the car over . . . anyplace you want . . . just talk to me. Then when we get to my mother's, I'll walk in with you just like I was supposed to. No trouble, no screaming, nothing. Okay?"

I made a right turn on Twenty-third, found an empty slot facing the river under the East Side Drive. An abandoned car, stripped to its shell, was on my right, empty space on the left. I slid down my window, killed the ignition. Lit a smoke. "Let's talk," I said to the girl.

Her smile flashed again, knocking the pout off her face. "What's your name?"

"Burke."

"Are you my mother's man?"

"No."

She shrugged out of the denim jacket, arching her back so her breasts poked at the T-shirt. "Is this what you do?"

"What?"

"Deliver packages."

"Sometimes."

"You like it?"

"It's work."

"But do you *like* it?"

"If I liked it, people wouldn't have to pay me to do it."

"Sometimes you get paid for what you like to do. Like a whore who loves to fuck."

I shrugged. I had never met one.

She took a drag on her cigarette. Handed it to me. I tossed it out my window.

"It's real dark here."

"You're all done talking, we can leave."

"You want me to shut up?"

"It doesn't matter. We have a deal, right? We talk, then I take you home."

"You mean you take me to my mother's."

"Whatever."

"If you wanted me to shut up, you know the best way to do it?"

"No."

"You put something in my mouth. You want to put something in my mouth?" Her voice was bad-little-girl teasing. She knew how to do it.

"No."

"Yes you do. I can feel it." Her hand snaked toward my lap in the darkness.

I grabbed her wrist.

"All done talking?"

"What's the matter, Mr. Burke? You never went back to your girlfriend with lipstick on your cock before?"

"Lipstick, yeah," I told her. "Not bubble gum."

"I'm old enough."

"Not for me."

The car was quiet for a couple of minutes. "I'm done talking," she said, her voice soft and flat.

She didn't say another word until I pulled up outside Candy's apartment building.

"This is it," I said.
"I know."

50

"Does the doorman know you?" I asked her.
"Sure."

He waved us in as soon as he saw her face. Never looked at mine. She was quiet in the elevator.

The door swung open before I had the button depressed enough to ring the bell. Candy.

"Come in here," she said to the girl, not looking at me.

Elvira walked past her to the couch, dropping her bag on the floor like the maid would get it in the morning.

Candy walked over to me, reached up and put her hands on my shoulders. "Thanks, baby," she stage-whispered. The girl was sitting on the couch, watching her mother's back. Waiting for the truth.

I gave it to her. "Where's the money?"

Her fingers bit into the top of my shoulders, eyes lashed at me. I waited.

She whirled, heels tapping on the parquet floor. Elvira put her fingers to her chin, like she was considering something important. Her mother came back into the living room, stopped two feet in front of me. Handed me an envelope. I put it into my coat.

I heard the door click closed behind me.

51

I GOT BACK into the Plymouth, started the engine. Lit a smoke. The door opened and Max slid inside. I handed him Candy's envelope, pulled out into traffic.

He tapped my shoulder. Holding a slab of cash in each hand. Nodded. All there. He put one hand in his pocket, the other in mine. We'd split the front money too.

I spun my finger in a circle, tapped the back of my neck. Anybody follow us?

The blunt-faced Mongol tapped one eye. Shook his head no. But then he shuddered his shoulders like he got a chill. Something. Something you couldn't see.

I checked the rearview mirror, moving through traffic. Max didn't spook at shadows. I pointed north. He nodded. Anyone following us to the junkyard would stick out like a beer drinker at a Jim Jones picnic.

We crossed the Triboro, turned into the jungle. Nothing behind us. I whipped the Plymouth into a tight U-turn, pointed back the way we came. Max lit a smoke for himself, one for me.

Half an hour later it was still quiet. The cops don't have that much patience. I took another route back downtown, dropped Max off near the warehouse, and headed back to the office.

Pansy was glad to see me.

52

I FELT BETTER when I got up the next morning. Not good enough to bet on a horse, but like something bad was over. It was still early enough to risk using the phone in my office. My phone is just an extension run from the collection of deservedly unknown artists who live downstairs. They don't know about it—neither does Ma Bell. They probably wouldn't care if they did know—they don't pay their own bills.

"Any calls, Mama?"

"No calls. You come in today, okay?"

"Anything wrong?"

"Someone leave note for you."

"So?"

"Talk later," she said, hanging up.

I took a quarter-pound slab of cream cheese out of the refrigerator, dropped it in the bottom of Pansy's bowl, covered it with her dry dog food. "I'll bring you something good from Mama's," I promised her.

53

MAMA WAS at the table almost before I sat down. She handed me a cheap white business envelope, the top neatly slit open. The note was typed:

Burke: Be by your phone at 11:00 tonight. Don't have anybody take a message. Be there yourself. Wesley

I drew a narrow breath through my nose. Let it out. Again. Feeling the fear-jolts dart around inside my chest, looking for a place to land. I lit a cigarette, holding the note against the match flame, watching it turn to ash. Wishing I'd never seen it.

"You see him?"

"A boy. Street boy. Around five o'clock this morning."

"He say anything?"

"Not see me. Push this under the front door, run away."

"You opened it?"

She bowed. It was okay. I knew why she told me to come in. She never met Wesley, but she knew the name. Every outlaw in the city did.

"Burke? What you do?"

"Answer the phone when it rings," I told her.

54

I SAT THERE quietly while Mama went to call Immaculata. To tell Max the devil was loose. Wesley never threatened. He *was* terror. Cold as a heat-seeking missile. He took your money, you got a body. Years ago my compadre Pablo told me about a contract Wesley had on a Puerto Rican dope dealer uptown. The dealer knew the contract was out. He went to a Santeria priestess, begging for voodoo heat against the glacier coming for him. The priestess took the dealer's money, told him Chango, the warrior-god, would protect him. She was an evil old demon, feared throughout the barrio. Her crew was all Marielitos. Zombie-driven murderers. They set fires to watch the flames. Ate the charred flesh. Tattoos on their hands to tell you their specialty. Weapons, drugs, extortion, homicide. The executioner's tattoo was an upside-down heart with an arrow through it. Cupid as a hit man.

The priestess called on her gods. Killed chickens and goats. Sprinkled virgin's blood on a knife. Loosed her death-dogs into the street looking for Wesley.

The dealer hid in her house. Safe.

Blazing summer, but the kids stayed off the streets. Winter always comes.

A UPS driver pulled up outside the apartment house where the priestess kept her temple. Her Marielitos slammed him against his truck, pulling at his clothes. Eyes watched from beneath slitted shades. They took a small box from the driver, laughing when he said someone had to sign for it.

They held the box under an opened fire hydrant, soaking the paper off. One of the Marielitos held the box to his ear, shaking it. Another pulled a butterfly knife from his pocket, flashed it open in the street, grinning. They squatted, watching as the box was slit open. Looked inside. They stopped laughing.

They took the box inside to the priestess. A few minutes later, the dope dealer was thrown into the street, hands cuffed behind his back, duct tape sealing his mouth. He ran from the block.

They whispered about it. In the bodegas, in the after-hours joints, on the streets. They said the priestess found the hand of her executioner inside the box, the tattoo mocking her. Chango was angry. So she found a better sacrifice than a chicken.

The cops found the dealer a few blocks away, a tight group of four slugs in his chest, another neat hole in his forehead. Nobody heard shots.

55

Max came into the restaurant. Sat across from me. Made the same gesture of getting a chill through his back he'd made when I'd asked him about being followed. Now we knew. Gold tones shot through his bronze skin—the warrior's blood was up. He showed me a fist, stabbed his heart with his thumb. I wasn't dealing him out of this one. Max tapped my wristwatch. Shrugged. I knew what he meant: why wait? I shook my head, held an imaginary telephone receiver up to my ear. If Wesley wanted to come for me, he wouldn't play games. It had to be something else.

Max folded his arms across his chest. I wanted to wait, he was waiting with me.

I told Mama I'd be back before the call came through, catching Max's eyes. No games—I'd be there.

56

Pansy tore into the gallon of meat and vegetables Mama had put together for her. No MSG. I closed my eyes and lay back on the couch. Watching the smoke drift toward the ceiling. Wondering how long it would be before the office got back to its usual filthy state. The way it had been for years until Belle hit it like dirt was her personal enemy.

Wesley. We'd once worshiped the same god. But only Wesley had been true.

It had been a long time.

57

I WAS BACK at the restaurant before ten. "Max still here," Mama told me. "In the basement."

There's a bank of three pay phones past the tables, just outside the kitchen area. One of them is mine. People call, Mama answers. Tells them I'm not in, takes a message. It's worked like that for years.

The phone rang at ten-thirty. I looked at my watch. It wasn't like Wesley to be cute. I grabbed the phone.

"Yeah?"

"You answer your own phone now?" Candy.

"What?"

"I have to see you."

"I'm busy."

"I know what you're busy *with* . . . it's about that. You want me to talk on the phone?"

"I'll call you when I can come."

"Call soon. You don't have a lot of time."

58

AT ELEVEN the phone rang again. I picked it up, saying nothing.

"It's you?"

"It's me," I said to the voice.

"We need to talk."

"Talk."

"Face to face."

"You know where I am."

"Not there."

"Where, then?"

"Take the bridge to the nuthouse on the island. Pull over as soon as you get in sight of the guard booth. Midnight tomorrow. Okay?"

"Want me to wear a bull's-eye on my back?"

"I don't care what you wear, but leave the Chinaman at home."

"What's this about?"

"Business," Wesley said, breaking the connection.

59

I FELT LIKE calling a cop. It passed.

Max didn't like any of it. When he gets like that, he acts like he can't read my hand signals. Everything takes longer.

None of our crew ever messed in Wesley's business. We didn't work the same side of the street. Max knew the myth; I knew the man. They both played the same. Finally, I got through to Max: if Wesley wanted me, bringing him along would just add another target. I played my trump card. Religion. Our religion. Revenge. If Wesley hit me, Max would have to square it. He bowed in agreement. I could always talk him into anything.

And I wasn't going alone.

60

IT WAS ABOUT eleven when I pulled out of the garage the next night, heading for the East Side Drive. If the cops stopped me, they'd get license and registration from Juan Rodriguez. I had a Social Security card too. Juan always pays his taxes and his parking tickets. They wouldn't find dope and they wouldn't find a gun. Pansy made a sleek black shadow in the back where I had pulled out the lower seat cushion, growling to herself. Glad to be along. "Keep your voice down," I told her. "You're supposed to be a surprise."

I took the East Side Drive to the exit for the Triboro, paid the toll, and hooked the turn onto the short bridge for Randalls Island. Followed the signs to Wards Island, then to the Kirby Psychiatric Institute. Home to the criminally insane. The Plymouth trolled under the maze of connecting ramps running above us. I spotted the guard booth about a quarter mile ahead. Behind the booth was a network of state institutional buildings, the size of a small town. Huge sewage disposal plant to my left. Everything Wesley needed.

I pulled over, sliding the Plymouth a few yards off the road. Killed the lights. Flattened my hand in front of Pansy's snout to tell her to stay where she was. Left the door wide open. Lit a smoke.

He came out of the night like he must have come the very first time. Wearing military fatigues in dark gray with black camouflage splotches. Dull black jungle boots on his feet, a soft hat in the same camo-pattern pulled down to his eyes. Black slashes below his eyes. Hands covered in dark gloves, held where I could see them. His voice was like his clothes.

"You came alone?"

"My dog's in the car."

"Call it out."

I snapped my fingers. Pansy bounded off the seat, landing next to me on all fours, head tilted up to watch Wesley's groin. If she fired, she wouldn't go higher than that.

My eyes shifted back to Wesley. To the Uzi in his hands, held tight against the strap around his neck. "Tell it to get down," he said, the barrel pointed between me and Pansy, ready to squirt us both into chunks of dead flesh.

I made the sign and Pansy hit the deck.

"Why's the dog here?"

"What d'you care? She can't talk."

"Put her back in the car. And lock it."

I pointed to the car. Pansy jumped into the back seat. I slammed the back door. Put my key in the lock and twisted it, left and right. Stood aside as Wesley tried both doors, Pansy's huge head looming behind the glass, tracking him. The second twist of the key had popped the trunk. If I called her, she'd come out that way.

"Go ahead," he said, pointing into the underbrush. I followed a narrow dirt path, feeling him behind me. We came to an abandoned pickup truck, rusting to death, its nose buried in one of the I-beams holding up the overpass.

"Sit down," he said.

I hoisted myself up to the pickup's open bed, legs dangling. "Can I . . . ?"

He held his finger to his lips. I counted to fifty before he spoke again.

"Yeah, you can smoke. I know you not carrying."

I took one out, bit hard into the filter to stop my mouth from trembling. Fired it up, cupping the flame. Wesley stood facing me, legs spread, hands behind him. The Uzi was gone.

He didn't look like much. If you didn't know, he could walk up to you—you wouldn't know him till you felt him. The same way cancer works.

"Why am I here?"

"You totaled a freak. Mortay."

I waited. A tiny gleam of white at his mouth. Wesley's smile. "You think I'm trying to get you to confess? Working for the Man?"

"I know you, Wesley. You don't ask questions."

"Yeah I do. I always ask who. Never ask why."

"Okay."

"We go back a long way, Burke."

"This a reunion?"

"You know what I do. Ever since I got out the last time. They give me a name, I do my work. This Mortay, he was off the rails. He had to go. I was tracking him when you went nuts and blew him up."

Toby Ringer had told me the truth. Belle died for nothing. If Wesley was tracking Mortay, all I had to do was wait. All for nothing. "I didn't know," I said, working to keep my voice from cracking. I never said truer words.

"They don't want to pay me," he said. Like God was dead.

"So?"

"So I don't work for them anymore." His body shifted slightly. I thought about the Uzi. Dismissed it—on the best day of my life, I wasn't fast enough. "You got in the way with that freak. You fucked things up. That's one time. It happens. But now the word's all over the street—you're in business. My business."

"I'm not—that's not me."

"I know. You're a hijacker. A sting artist. You got *friends*." His dead man's voice made the word sound like a perversion.

"What's your problem?"

"Train. You know him."

"Yeah."

"He's on the spot. He has to go down. You've been sniffing around. Either you're working for him or you're looking to take him out."

"No. I had a contract. I pulled a girl out of his joint."

"I saw that."

"That's it. There's no more."

"You know what he does?"

"No."

"Don't find out."

I lit another smoke, watching my hands near the flame. They didn't shake. Wesley took you past fear.

"Wesley, I got no beef with you. You know that. You want to know something, ask me. And let me go."

"You know why I wanted you out here? You're a fucking nut-case yourself, Burke. You got this Jones for kids. I know about the day-care center too. Out in Queens. Why didn't you use the Chinaman on Mortay?"

"He wasn't around."

"Something about a kid, right?"

I just watched him.

"Yeah, you're bent. Remember when we were coming up? Learning the rules? You don't work with drunks, you don't work with dope fiends, you don't work with skinners, right? You don't work with *nobody* who's off the track. Now it's you—you're off the track."

Tracks. I was a kid again in my mind. In a subway tunnel. Me and Rupert facing each other. Chins on the tracks, bodies spread out behind. The rest of the gang waited off to the side. I heard the rumble of the train, felt the track tremble under my jawbone. Watching Rupert. Last one off the tracks was the winner. Sixteen years old. Don't mind dying. I read my tombstone: Burke Had Heart. Better than flowers. Rupert's face a few feet from mine. He'd offered a knife fight, I bumped the stakes with the train tracks—the tunnel. No matter what happened, I'd have a name. It wouldn't hurt, I told myself. The train roared at us, coming hard, a hundred-ton mindless life-taker. Light washed the black tunnel. Rupert jumped back. Me! My legs wouldn't work. Hands grabbed my ankles, jerked me off the track, cracking my jaw. The train shot past.

That night, on the roof, Candy took my cock in her mouth for the first time.

"I was the last off the track," I reminded him.

"Yeah." A robot's voice. He knew the truth. Even when we were kids, Wesley knew the truth. He'd been there. His hands on my ankles. If he hadn't pulled after Rupert jumped back, I'd still be there. "Train's a dead man. My dead man. You get in the way again, you go with him."

"I'm not in the way."

His face moved closer, watching mine. No psychiatrist could read his eyes—you can't take a census when there's nobody home. I held his gaze, letting him in. See the truth, monster. See it again.

He stepped back. "You're not good enough," he said. Not putting me down, just saying it. "You still do that trick? Where you memorize something without writing it down?"

"Yeah."

He said a number. "You call this number. Anytime. Let it ring three times. Hang up. Do it again. Then you wait by the number I have for you."

"I don't need to call you."

"Yeah you will. I know how things work. You used to know too."

He put his gloved hands together, looking down at the temple they made. "Kids . . . what fucking difference does it make, Burke?"

Once I thought it did. Prayed to that god in the orphanage, in the foster homes, in reform school. Somebody would come. Be my family. I found my family in prison. Prayed to another god. Belle in my mind. *Rescue me.* Sure. The first god ignored me. The second came close enough for me to have a good look. "It doesn't make any," I said to him.

"You're a burnt-out case," the monster told me. "You're done."

"Okay." Nothing to argue about.

"Train's safe for a bit. I'll get to him. But first I got a whole lot of Italians to do."

"Do what you have to do—I'm not in it."

His eyes were tombstones. With no date of birth and no epitaph. "I know how things work. You'll get a call, hit man. Then you call me, got it?" The Uzi came into his hands again. "Stay where you are for a few minutes."

He didn't make a sound moving off past the pickup, away from the Plymouth.

I sat staring into the darkness. Counting the years. Lit another smoke. It was snatched out of my hand. Max the Silent held it to his own lips.

61

DRIVING HOME, Max was full of warrior's fire. Full of himself. He grabbed my wrist, tapped the face of my watch, shrugged his shoulders. Sneered. "Anytime," he was saying. Anytime we wanted. Max would cancel the undertaker's ticket.

Too many boxes inside too many boxes. If Max could roll up on Wesley in the dark, I wasn't the only burnt-out case on the set.

I dropped Max off and headed back uptown.

62

I FOUND THE PROF in an after-hours joint by the river. He caught my nod. I waited outside for him. The little man hopped in the front seat, tossing his cane into the back. Pansy's snarl swiveled his head.

"Get down, hound. You ain't bad enough to try me."

Pansy made some noise I hadn't heard before. Maybe she was laughing.

I left the motor running, jumped into an all-night deli and ordered three brisket sandwiches on rye, hold everything. In the car, I threw the bread out the window, squeezed the brisket into a ball the size of a melon. Tossed it back into the pit. Pansy made ugly sounds as she finished it off. She ventured an experimental whine, trying for seconds. Saw it wasn't playing with the home crowd, and flopped down to grab some sleep.

I nosed the Plymouth back down to the waterfront, found a quiet place and pulled over. The Prof fired a cigarette, waiting.

"I saw Wesley."

"*Damn!* Up close?"

"Close as you are right now."

"You ain't dead, so you came out ahead."

"Yeah."

"What'd he want?"

"The freak. The freak who wanted the duel with Max. Wesley was on his case. Way before we started."

"So . . ."

"Yeah. If we'd just gone to ground, holed up, it would have passed."

"You couldn't've known, brother. No man knows Wesley's plan."

"I know."

"He knows the freak is dead. He has to know. Fuck, even the cops know. So what's he want?"

"He wants to get things straight. Says the freak was on his list. A contract, right? And the guys who hired Wesley, they don't want to pay."

"That ride is suicide."

"Yeah. Wesley said he's going to be doing a whole lot of Italians soon."

"Who cares? Let him do a few for me while he's at it. They ain't us."

I lit my own smoke. "He gave me the name of another guy he wants. The same guy I took that little girl from a couple of days ago."

"So?"

"So he doesn't want me in the way. He thinks I'm working his beat now. Hitting for cash."

"Oh."

"I think I squared it."

"You must've, man. With Wesley, you fuck around, you're in the ground."

"You think he's crazy?"

"Not middle-class crazy, bro'. Wesley, he's not . . . he ain't got but one button, and he pushes it himself."

I looked out over the water toward Jersey. "Wesley said I was a burnt-out case. You think that?"

"Wesley's the coldest dude I ever met. But that don't make him the smartest."

"What's that mean?"

"Like Michelle said, man. You not being yourself. Ever since . . ."

"I'll be all right."

"Who says no, bro'?"

"Wesley . . ."

"Wesley. Whatever my man's got, they ain't got no cure for. It's like he's got a couple of parts missing. He *looks* like a man, but he's something else."

"Something . . ."

"Else. That's all I can call."

"You don't come like that stock from the factory."

"Don't get on it, Burke. I didn't know Wesley when he was a kid."

"I did."

"Burke, if you *not* crazy, you putting on a great act." The little man lit a smoke. Drew it in slowly, taking his time. Like you do when you got a lot of it to spare.

"This is the one true clue, brother. Wesley, he's the Mystery Train. Nobody knows where he's going, but everybody knows where he's been."

"I . . ."

"You got no case, Ace. I don't know nobody who ever walked away from a meet with Wesley. He's telling you something. Something just for you. Listen to the lyrics, brother."

I threw my smoke out the window.

Time passed. Wesley said I was off the track. And the Prof was saying that's where I needed to be. Out of the way.

"You got it handled?" he asked.

I nodded, thinking about kids.

63

I DIDN'T EXPECT ANYTHING to happen soon. Wesley ran on jailhouse time.

Survive. That's what I do. The biggest piece of that is waiting. Knowing how to wait. Before Belle, I was the best at it. Drifting just outside the strong currents, keeping out of the pattern. Moving in on the breaks, never staying long. In and out.

But if you just stayed in your cell—that was a pattern too.

64

MAX WASN'T at the warehouse when I pulled in. Immaculata was upstairs, in the living quarters they fixed up above Max's temple. She had a stack of mail waiting for me. One of Mama's drivers handles the pickup from my PO box in Jersey, drops it off every few weeks. Mac bounced her baby on her knee while I smoked and went through the pile.

Anything goes through the U.S. mail. It moves more cocaine than all the Miami Mules going through customs. That's why they invented the "American key." Key as in kilo. A true kilo, European-style, is 2.2 pounds. And the Federal Express cut-off is two pounds.

I work a different kind of dope. Some of the letters were from would-be mercenaries, sending their handwritten money orders to me for "pipeline" information. Child molesters sent cash, seeking the "introductions" I promised in my ads. Freaks ordered hard-core kiddie porn they'd never receive. Let them write the Better Business Bureau. Every so often, someone would answer one of my sting ads: "Vietnam vet, experienced in covert actions. One-man jobs only. U.S.A. only. Satisfaction guaranteed." You hire a hit man through the mails, you find out who first wrote that Silence Is Golden. Blackmailers.

The PO box isn't just for suckers. Anyone out there who knows the game I play can use it for a mail drop. One of the envelopes contained only a single page ripped from a doctor's prescription pad. A blank page except for one word. Shela. She was a high-style scam artist who hated the freaks as much as I did. I never asked why. Whenever she ran across a rich one, she'd pass it along.

I left the money orders in a neat stack for Max to take to Mama's laundry, shrugged into my coat, bowed to Immaculata and the baby.

"Burke . . ."

"What?"

"Max can take care of this thing for you."

"What thing?"

"This man . . . the one you met . . . the one with the machine gun."

"Max told you about that?"

Her lovely dark eyes shone under lashes like butterfly wings. "Do you think that was wrong?"

"I'm glad he has someone to tell."

"You have someone too, Burke. You have us. You know that."

"There's nothing to tell. Wesley's not a problem."

"Not like before?"

"Let it go, Mac."

"That's what *you* must do," she said.

65

I'M A GOOD THIEF. Two words—two separate things. When I had that name, I was out of the loop. Safe. The old rules are the best rules—you dance with the one who brought you to the party.

I made some calls, put the team together.

66

"THIS'LL REALLY work?" I asked the Mole. He was bent over a lab table in his workroom, a pile of gold Krugerrands spread out before him.

He didn't answer. Terry was standing next to him, his little face vibrating with concentration, nose two inches from the Mole's hands.

Michelle was perched on a stool, her sleek nyloned legs crossed, smoking one of her long black cigarettes. Heart-shaped face peaceful. She could have been a suburban housewife watching her husband teach their son how to build a ham radio.

Outside, dogs prowled the night-blanketed minefield of junked cars. Ringed in razor-wire and dotted with pockets of explosives. The safest place I know.

Time went by. The Mole's stubby paws worked tiny probes under a huge magnifying glass he had suspended over the workbench. I heard the clink of coins, saw the red laser-beam shoot from a black box. I picked up one of the Krugerrands, turned it over in my hand. It looked like it was minted yesterday.

"I thought these things weren't allowed in the U.S. anymore. No more trading with South Africa, right?"

The Mole looked up. Hate-dots glinted behind the thick lenses. "No *new* Krugerrands. Illegal since 1984. But it's still legal to trade in older coins if they were made before that date."

I looked at the coin in my hand. Gleaming new. "This says it was minted in 1984," I said.

"It was minted a month ago," the Mole said. "This country always looks the other way for its Nazi friends."

Michelle threw me a warning look. Don't get him started. The Mole was never far from critical mass when it came to his reason for living.

I lit a smoke, patted my brother on the back, willing him to be calm, go back to work.

Soon the Mole pushed back his chair. Pointed at a pile of a half dozen gold coins. "Which one?" he asked.

I took them in my hand. Felt their weight. Held them up to the light. Tried to bend them in half. They were all the same. I tried the magnifying glass. Nothing. Handed them back to the Mole.

He picked out the one he wanted. Handed me a jeweler's loupe. "Look around the edge—where the coin is milled."

It took me a minute, even when I knew what I was looking for. A tiny dark dot standing between the ridges. I gave it back to the Mole.

"Go outside," the Mole said to Terry. He handed me the coin. "Hide it," he said.

"Put it in your purse," I told Michelle.

Terry came back into the bunker holding a transmitter about the size of a pack of cigarettes.

"Find it," the Mole said.

The boy pulled a short antenna from the corner of the transmitter. Hit a switch. Soft electronic beeps, evenly spaced. He moved toward the far wall. The beeps separated, a full second between them. The beeping got more intense as he neared the workbench. The boy was patient, working the room in quadrants. When he got near Michelle, the transmitter went nuts. He worked around her, closing in. When he put it next to her purse, the beeps merged into one long whine. "In there," he said, a smile blasting across his face.

Michelle gave him a kiss. "You're going to take Harvard by storm, handsome."

"Will it work through metal?" I asked the Mole.

"Even through lead," Terry assured me solemnly. I lit a cigarette, satisfied.

"This is the way we're *supposed* to work," Michelle said. "This is us. I'll see the doctor tomorrow."

67

THE DOCTOR wouldn't blink at a transsexual for a patient. He didn't judge his clients, he just wrote their needs on his R_x pad. He sold what the customer wanted, and he didn't take checks. Quaaludes, steroids, amphetamines, barbiturates. That kind of traffic wouldn't make him rich. But the page from the prescription pad told me what I wanted to know: the doctor was selling Androlan, Malogex . . . all the injectable forms of testosterone. Even threw in a supply of needles. There's a new program for child molesters. The shrinks still haven't figured it out—the freaks, they don't *want* to be cured. This new program, it's only for special degenerates. Ones with money. Counseling, therapy . . . and Depo-Provera. Chemical castration, they call it. Reduces the sex drive down to near-zero. Supposedly makes the freaks safe, even around kids. Methadone for baby-rapers. Some judges love it. The freaks are crazy about the program— it's a Get Out of Jail Free card. The maggots do their research better than the scientists and all their federal grants. They figured out that a regular dose of testosterone cancels the Depo-Provera. Gets them back to what they call normal.

Testosterone's not a narcotic. The feds don't check on how much you dispense. The doctor was doing all right. Medicine changes with the times. When I was a kid, the underground plastic surgeons would give you a new face if you were running from the law. Now some doctors will put a new face on a kid—a kid whose face is on a milk carton. It would do until they outlawed abortions again.

Michelle bought such a big supply that the doctor must have figured she was going into business for herself. The word I got was that he'd wholesale the stuff if the price was right. Michelle paid him in Krugerrands. A dozen gold coins, almost six grand.

The doctor lived up in Westchester County. He had two kids—a boy away at college and a fifteen-year-old girl. We watched the Mercedes pull out of the driveway, his wife next to him in the front seat. The girl was already out for the evening. We figured on a few hours.

The back of the house was protected by an unbroken row of thick hedges. Max unscrewed the top of a cardboard tube, the kind you keep an expensive fishing rod in. Pulled out two aluminum poles. They telescoped like car antennas. He cross-latched the two poles with some X-braces, making a ladder. Max went up first, climbing backwards as easy as if he was using a staircase. The Mole followed him, satchel on a strap over his shoulder. I came next—the Mole was no athlete.

It was a short drop to the ground. The windows were free of burglar-alarm tape. The doctor's wife wouldn't like the look. The Mole fluttered his hand—a flag in a breeze. Motion sensors. "Hard-wired," he whispered. "Expensive."

"Can you take it out?" I asked.

The Mole didn't answer, looking through the window with some kind of lens held up to his glasses. "There," he said, pointing.

I saw a wooden box in a corner of the living room. Some kind of dark wood, a slim crystal vase standing on top. A tiny red light glowed near the base.

The Mole fumbled in his satchel. Max braced the pane of glass with his hands as the Mole fitted a tiny drill against the surface. He nodded. Scratched an X on the glass with a probe, fitted the drill point into it. Pressed the trigger. A split-second whine. He reversed the drill bit, pulling it free of the glass. Then he threaded a wire through the hole. Attached the other end of the wire to something inside his satchel. The Mole pushed a toggle switch and the red light on the box inside the house winked out. I could have opened the back door with a credit card.

We left Max on the first floor in case somebody came home. The Mole took the upstairs bedrooms, I hit the basement.

The doctor had a nice little home-office setup downstairs. IRS would approve. I pulled the antenna on the same little box Terry had used to show off for his mother and went to work. It only took a couple of minutes. Second-rate wall safe behind a framed painting of assholes on horses chasing a fox. Amateur Hour. I could have knocked off the dial and pried the thing open in twenty minutes.

It took the Mole less than five. It looked like gray putty he pasted around the edges of the safe. Until you saw the fuse. When he touched it off, we stepped back to watch. A soft pop and the door crumpled.

Our Krugerrands were inside. The doctor liked gold. Canadian Maple Leafs, Chinese Pandas, Australian Koalas. American cash in neat stacks. A small leather loose-leaf book. A Canadian passport. The doctor was prepared—but not for us. We took it all.

68

An AMATEUR steals only when he's broke. I'm a professional—I work at my trade.

It didn't stop the pain, just put it on hold.

I've had bad dreams all my life. But now it was sad dreams . . .

bone-marrow pain. Belle. I never would have left her. Now she wouldn't leave me.

I told Michelle I'd pick Terry up at Lily's. Got there early, looking around. Waiting. Lily came down the corridor at high speed, shrugging out of her parka, long black hair streaming out behind her. "Tell her I'll call her back!" she shouted over one shoulder. She pulled up when she saw me, a busty, glowing woman with a scar over one of her big dark eyes. Lily's old enough to have a teenage daughter, a little heart-breaker named Noelle, but she looks like she's still in college. Noelle's at the age where she's always griping because her mother isn't stylish enough. She tried to get me on her side once.

"Don't you think Mom would look cool with her hair up?"

"Your mother is beautiful, baby. She looks like the Madonna."

"Oh, Burke!" the kid shrieked. "She's not even blond!"

It's not a generation-gap anymore, it's a time-warp.

I waited until she ran up on me. "Hi, Lily."

Her face was reserved, eyes watchful. "Is there trouble?"

"I'm here to pick up Terry."

"Okay." Dubious.

I lit a cigarette, ignoring her frown, moving aside to let her pass.

She wasn't going for it. "She doesn't bring Scotty herself."

"Scotty?"

Her eyes raked my face, looking for the truth. A trained therapist against a state-raised thief. No contest. I knew who she meant. Scotty was the little boy sodomized by a freak who had a feeder deal with a day-care center. The freak took a picture of his fun—took the little boy's soul for a souvenir. The kid never told anybody until he let it slip to the mother of a little girl he played with. The devil stole his soul, so he asked a witch to get it back. Strega. Flame-haired, steel-hearted Strega. I made a promise to her. To never come back. If she and Wesley mated, their child could walk through Hell in a gasoline overcoat.

Immaculata came down the hall, her arms on the shoulders of the pair of ten-year-olds framing her slender body. One kid was black, the other white. Her long nails made bright slashes of color as she emphasized her words, looking for the right chord to play. Her English was perfect, but the Catholic school in Vietnam where she learned it left a few things out.

"Benny, the very last thing on earth you need is *another* model airplane. It would be . . . coals to Newcastle."

She pulled up short when she saw me standing with Lily. Raised her eyebrows in a question. I shook my head.

"Burke, these are my friends. Benny and Douglas."

I shook hands with each of them. Benny tugged at Immaculata's smock.

"What's coals to Newcastle?"

"Cocaine to Colombia," I told him.

A grin flashed. He raised an open palm and I slapped him a high-five. His buddy grinned.

"Maybe you missed your calling," Immaculata said, pulling the kids down the hall with her, leaving us alone.

Lily wouldn't let it go. "You came here to volunteer . . . teach one of our self-defense classes?"

I dragged on my cigarette. Lily wasn't an ex-con, but she had enough patience for a dozen of them. "Can I talk to you for a minute?"

"Come on," she said, charging down the hall to her office. She walked through the open door, tossed her parka on a couch already overflowing with files, plopped herself in a battered old chair next to the computer she only used for video games. She didn't wait for me to work around to it. "What?" she demanded.

"I lost a friend. Somebody close to me."

"How?"

"She was murdered."

"Oh. You know who did it?"

"Yes."

"Is he . . . the perpetrator . . . arrested?"

"No. And he's not gonna be."

"Why?"

I held her eyes until she understood. "And that didn't end it for you?"

"No."

Lily combed both hands through her thick hair, pulling the mane off her forehead. "You don't know about grief, do you, Burke? You pay your debts, it's supposed to be all done, right?"

I nodded.

"Your friend . . . you loved her?"

"Still do."

She watched my face. "And she knew? You told her?"

"Just before . . ."

"That's not too late."

I lit another cigarette, biting deep into the filter, cupping the match to give my eyes a rest from Lily. "She didn't have to die," I said.

"You think it was your fault?"

"It was my fault."

"She was with you? In your life?"

I nodded.

"Then she knew . . ."

I nodded again.

"Burke, listen to me, okay? Some pain's not *supposed* to go away. That's the price. That's what it costs to remember her."

"Aren't you going to tell me to remember the good times?"

Lily's voice was sweet and quiet, but it made you listen. Honey-in-the-rock. "We all know you're a hard man, Burke. If it works so well for you, why did you come here?"

"Nothing works all the time."

"What does that mean?"

"I played all my cards, Lily."

"Then do what you do best."

My eyes flicked up to her face, watching.

"Steal some more," she said, a Madonna's smile so faint I couldn't be sure it was ever there.

69

A PLANE CAN run on automatic pilot, but it hits the ground when it runs out of fuel. Nothing was pushing me. I needed to get back to where I was before. Before Belle. The sands shifted—I couldn't find my own footprints. Throwing antacid tablets into a cauldron of boiling lye. Stealing and scamming didn't bring me any closer. Everything worked. The money kept coming in but there was no payoff.

Even Wesley's fear-jolts wouldn't jump-start my battery.

Dead and gone. Dead and gone.

I called Candy.

70

SHE ANSWERED the door, left me there while she walked away. I knew her this time, even with the blond wig and the violet contact lenses. Much taller in four-inch spikes, ankle straps lancing across the seams that ran down the back of her dark silk stockings. She was wearing a wool minidress in some metallic green color, a heavy black chain around her waist as a belt. Swinging the long end of the chain in one hand, a leopard twitching her tail. Waiting.

I walked as far as the couch, flicking the ashes off my cigarette in the general direction of the ashtray on the end table. She twirled, hands on her hips. "Sit down."

I didn't like the sound. "Don't make a mistake," I told her. "I'm not the trick who just left."

A smile blazed across her face. Perfect teeth, as real as the violet eyes. A sociopath's smile. A woman smiles at you . . . for you . . . it's like a rheostat . . . comes on slow until it hits full boost. Little tiny increments. Different every time. Hers was an on-off switch. She came to me, tilted her seamless face up to mine, tried to bring some feeling into those cash-register eyes, wet her lips. "I'm sorry, baby. I was teasing. Some men like to be teased. I just want to talk your language. What*ever* that is . . ."

"*Dónde está el dinero?*" I said. Thinking of Wolfe. The beautiful prosecutor sitting in her office, a killer Rottweiler at her feet, my rap sheet spread out in front of her. "John Burke, Maxwell Burke, Robert Burke, Juan Burke . . . *Juan?* Say something in Spanish, Mr. Burke." I sang my theme song for her.

Wolfe got it when I said it. Candy lived it. "I promised you a couple of things. You sure you only want the cash?"

"Yeah."

She curled up on the couch, her legs beneath her. I sat next to her, not too close. Her lacquered fingernails played with the buttons on the front of her dress. Opened one. Then another. The black lace bra stopped just above her nipples. "A lot sweeter than when you last saw them, huh? When we were kids. Remember?"

What's real? Candy wasn't a woman before the surgeons did their work. And Michelle, the most woman I'd ever met, even with the spare parts they threw in as a dirty joke.

"I never saw them when we were kids," I told her.

It was the truth. Foreplay was for people with money. People who had doors you could close. Elephants don't fuck the way rabbits do. Predator pressure sets the rhythm.

"You want to see them now?"

"No."

She shifted her hips, moved against me, face in my chest. "Pretend you just got out of prison," she whispered. "You could do all the things you dreamed about every night."

Her perfume was thick, with a sharp underbase, like it came from inside her body. The last couple of times I got out of prison, I knew where to go. What to do. But the first time out . . . it was like she said.

I TOSSED my duffel bag on the bed in the cheap hotel and hit the street. I needed a gun. And a cabdriver who wouldn't get a tip. But first things first. The skinny whore in the screaming-red dress was waiting in a doorway a block from the hotel. Dishwater blond, hard-boned face, yellowish teeth, blue-veined hands, two bracelets on her narrow wrist, junkie's eyes. She was probably young and plump and dumb and sassy when she got off the bus from West Virginia.

"You wanna have a party, honey?"

I looked at her face.

"Ten and two, baby. I french, I do it all . . . come on."

I felt the street. Every doorway had one like her.

She knew it too. "It might as well be me, mister."

Another hotel. Two dollars to the clerk. No register to sign. I followed her up the stairs to the second floor. She put the key in her purse, left it open, waiting. I handed her the ten bucks. Peeling wallpaper, swaybacked single bed against one wall, bare mattress. She took a yellowed sheet from the top of a pile on a straight-backed chair, flicked it open, covered the bed. She never turned on the light. Street-neon washed against the streaked window. She pulled the paper shade down. Reached down to the hemline, pulled the cheap dress over her head. Dark elastic garters at the top of her stockings, joyless little breasts in the dim light.

"You want something special, honey? A little half 'n' half?"

No need.

"Let me look at you, baby. Milk it down for you one time, okay? Can't be gettin' burned; I got me a big habit to support." Reaching over to me, her thumb hard against the underside of my cock. "You all ready to go, huh, baby? I like a man all ready to go. You ain't no kid all charged up on beer, huh?"

Yes and No.

She fell back on the bed, still holding me in one hand, tied us together, rocked back to the base of her spine, grabbed her knees. "Come here, baby. It's riding time."

It didn't take long.

This. Fucking. Nothing.

"I DIDN'T just get out of prison," I told her.

"Just the money?"

"Just the money."

"I know you, Burke. I know you forever." It sounded like a threat.

"We've been through that."

"You're not here just for the money."

"I'm not here at all, you don't tell me what you want."

She took a breath. Her breasts blossomed. "Train," she said.

"What's that mean?"

"Not what you think."

"I don't have time for this." I started to get off the couch. She threw herself across my lap. I reached under the wig to the back of her neck, squeezed. Hard. Pulled her face up to mine. Her eyes were measuring, calculating. "You like that? You want to hurt me?"

My hand came off her neck by itself.

She locked my eyes. Saw the truth. "No, that's not you," she whispered. "Hard man, soft center. I know you. Remember the kitten? I was with you when you found it. In the basement, remember?"

SIMON. He was in the gang with us. A freak. Liked to hurt things. Especially small things. Liked to set fires too. Nobody said anything. Simon was a good man in a rumble, quick with a razor. We weren't running a therapeutic community. The kitten was hanging from a noose made out of a coat hanger, ripped from chin to balls, its guts trailing out all the way to the floor. Making sounds no living thing should make. Candy was with me. We were hurrying down there for the darkness and the sex when we heard the tiny shrieks.

I remembered. I unhooked the kitten. Laid it on the concrete floor. Found a brick. Pounded its head into flat jelly. I didn't know how to stop its pain, so I made it all stop.

I found Simon out on the flatlands that night. Burning something on a spit over a little fire. I didn't want to know what it was. I left him there. When I threw the tire iron into the street it was so slick with pulp that it skidded for half a block.

"I PAID that off."

"Yeah. You kept your name. But I remember. You cried for an hour over that kitten. Cried like a baby. You were shaking so hard I didn't think you'd ever get up. You were going to do the same thing to Simon. Remember how you swore that? And how you told the others it was *your* kitten Simon tortured? Liar! You never had a kitten—you don't even like them."

She sounded like the judge who told me I was a menace to society.

"That never happened," I said, lighting a cigarette. "Your mind is all fucked up."

"I kept your secret. I could have told . . ."

"Who'd listen to a little cunt like you?"

"Anybody who wanted it—and they all did."

" 'Cause they paid?"

"That's the way you tell."

"That's the way *you* tell. That's all you know."

"I know you," she said, the dress sliding off her shoulders.

I got up to leave. She stood before me, stepping into my chest. I remembered the basement. How she watched while I cried. How she never touched me—waiting to see who'd win. It wasn't hard keeping my hands from her body. Just from her throat.

I turned sharply away from her, my shoulder cracked against her jaw.

"You never knew how to hold a woman," she said.

"I know how to hold what matters."

"A gun?" she sneered.

"A grudge," I told her, stepping out of the whorehouse.

71

COLD FIRE inside me. Ugly acid, all the way to my eyes, burning off the haze. I felt them cut through the darkness as I neared my car. Everything in sharp-edged black&white. I wanted to talk to whoever took Belle from me and offered this sociopathic slut in return. Just for a hair-trigger minute.

A lump of shadow against the building wall a few feet from the passenger side of the Plymouth. I stepped forward fast on my left foot like I was going to charge, locked on the pavement, pivoted, and threw myself behind the car, turtlenecking like a gunshot was coming. Heard a grunt, a body slamming into the passenger side. Silence. Steel-palmed hands clapped once, twice. Max.

He was standing on the sidewalk, a body at his feet. His hands went parallel to the ground, palms down, patted the air twice. The body was alive. I knelt down to take a look, Max watching my back.

A small body, wrapped in a Navy pea coat, hooded sweatshirt inside covering the head. Dark gloves. Jeans and sneakers. I pulled the hood away from the face. Elvira, the wolf-child. Eyes closed, face blue-toned in the streetlight. I pinched her lower jaw—her tongue slid out. I looked up at Max. He tapped his diaphragm with two stiffened fingers. Just the wind knocked out of her. I touched the face of my wristwatch. Max's finger made one full circle, flashed his hand open and closed. She'd been waiting over an hour—since I'd parked the car.

I opened the passenger door and we put her into the front seat. I motioned for Max to climb in behind her. He bowed, brought his hands together, and disappeared. He was doing his work, not mine.

72

BY THE TIME I got near the river she was sucking in ragged gulps through her mouth. I hit the power-window switch to give her some air.

"Breathe through your nose. Shallow breaths. In and out. You're okay."

"I'm going to be sick . . ."

I pulled over. Went around to her side and helped her out. She walked toward the water under her own power. I smoked a cigarette while she left her supper in the parking lot.

Michelle had left one of her old street-trick kits in the back of the Plymouth. I gave the girl one of the premoistened towelettes to wipe her face. Handed her the airline-size bottle of cognac. "Rinse out with this," I told her.

I moved the car deeper into the darkness, backing it in against an abandoned pier. Dropped my own window, listening for sounds a human would make. Nothing. I lit another smoke. She still had some of the cognac left, sipping at it, watching me, color coming back in her face.

"What was that?"

"What was what?"

"What happened to me?"

"You set off the burglar alarm."

"I thought I was going to die."

"You could have—you're playing with dangerous things."

"I had to talk to you."

I snapped my smoke out the window, watching the little red dot through my black&white eyes. "So?"

"I have to go back."

"To Train?"

"Yes."

"So go."

"It's not that easy. She'd send you after me again."

"How d'you know?"

"She said so. You work for her, right?"

"Wrong."

"Oh."

I waited. She sipped the cognac.

"You got money?" I asked her.

"I can get some. How much . . . ?"

"Not for me. For cab fare. I'll drop you off near a good corner. Go where you want to go. I won't be coming after you."

She went quiet again. I lit another cigarette. "What's the rest, Elvira?" I asked her.

"I don't believe you," she said in a quiet, subdued voice. "She never tells the truth."

"It's not her talking."

"And I know about you, Mr. Burke."

"Say what you have to say, little girl. I got things to do. And you're not my friend."

"Can I have one of your cigarettes?" Stalling, like a kid who doesn't want to tell you she did something bad.

I gave her one. Fired a wooden match before she could try the dashboard lighter.

She took a deep drag. "I know what you do," she said.

"That right?"

"Yes, that's right. Danielle told me."

115

"I don't know any Danielle."

"I don't know what her street name was. We're not allowed to use street names in the family. She was a hooker. You came and took her away. A long time ago."

"Away from what?"

"Her old man. And you brought her home. To a big house on Long Island. Her father paid you to do it."

I shrugged.

"I know you. I know things you know and I know things you don't know."

Her mother's rap, a few years early. "I haven't heard one yet."

She dragged on the cigarette, a soft glow lighting her face for a second. Calm now. Watching me.

"Her old man's name was Dice. A sweet mac—he never made his girls turn hard tricks or anything. Let them go shopping whenever they wanted. You were waiting for them when they came back to the hotel room. You must've had a passkey or something. You pointed a big gun right in Dice's face. Told him you were taking the girl. There was another guy with you. Big guy—he didn't say anything. Dice tried to talk to you and you started whaling on him with the gun. Danielle said she could hear the bones break in his face. She'll never forget it. You took all her old man's money and jewelry. Then you put her in a car and drove her to Long Island."

I shrugged again.

"Why'd you do that?"

"You think it's right to fuck fourteen-year-old girls?"

"Her father did. The man who paid you the money to bring her back. He *loved* to do it. In the basement. Danielle told me he had a special room for it. She only has one nipple—he burned the other one off. To teach her not to run away again."

I didn't say anything. Shuffling the memory cards. Going right past Dice and the sleazy hotel room. Looking for that address on Long Island. The world was still black&white, but a piece was out of place.

"And Train saved her?" I asked.

"Train saved us all. Men like Danielle's father. Powerful men. They're always after him. It's not that they don't understand. They know. And they hate him. Our family too. They hate us all. And they use men like you to do their dirty work for them."

"How'd he save *you*?"

"You think you're smart, don't you? You think you know everything. You don't know everything. We're saving for a place. Our place. Not in this miserable country. Where we can be free. We're in a war. You make sacrifices in a war. Not everyone will be able to go, but that's all right."

"And you all live in that house in Brooklyn? Raising money for your new country? You sell flowers on the street? Phony magazine subscriptions? Blowjobs in parked cars? What?"

"What*ever* we do, that's okay. It would never be as bad as what people did to us."

"Sure."

"Sure. You don't know. You're a mercenary. That's what Train calls you. You only serve yourself—you have no honor. Your god is cash."

"That house must be pretty crowded, what with Train saving the world and all."

"We *don't* all live in the house. Some of the older ones, the best ones . . . if they show the commitment, prove themselves . . . they work other places. For our family. Outriders. The special people. I'll be one someday."

"Danielle's an outrider?"

"No. She lives with us. Outriders are special. I only met one. She went to prison for seven years for the family. And she never said a word. That was her commitment. That proved her true."

"So how come this family let you go?"

"It was a test. I know it was a test. We have to act for ourselves. Train isn't running a mission or a runaway shelter. It's only for those who are worthy. I had to find my own way back."

"Which is why you're running this game on me?"

"It's not a game. I thought if you knew what we *really* did, you wouldn't bring me back again."

"I don't know any Danielle."

"You know me. Maybe you're a good man inside. You wouldn't fuck me when I asked you. Maybe you really thought Danielle's father was sincere."

"I don't think anybody's sincere."

"Yes you do. My mother thinks she knows you. Maybe I know you better. And you don't know her."

"But you . . . you know a lot."

"Don't mock me. You know why my mother wanted me back?"

"To fuck you in the basement?"

"Bastard! You know what my mother is?"

"Your mother's a whore. She was a whore before you were born."

"No. Danielle was a whore. My mother . . . I was on the street when Train found me. I was turning tricks in cars. Like you said. Cars just like this one. My mother didn't care. I was too old then. Fourteen. Too old. When I was a *little* girl, my mother trained me. I thought ice cream was the stuff that shoots out of men's pricks when they come. My mother would hold my face between her legs while one of her customers fucked me behind. I used to scream right into her cunt. And the pictures. I still shake when flashbulbs go off near me. I had so many daddies. I knew how to make nice for them. My mother taught me. But once these grew"—flicking her hand at her breasts—"I was too old for the games. And my mother . . . she can be fourteen herself. She can be anything a man wants."

"No she can't."

"Oh yes. You don't know her. She can change. Like a demon. You know why she wants me back? To *sell* me. I'm hers, she said. Not Train's. I'd die first."

"So you don't turn tricks for Train?"

"Even if I *did*, it wouldn't be the same. Nothing's just for Train, it's for *us*. All of us. Together. It's my life. She doesn't own me."

"How old are you?"

"Seventeen."

"How old, Elvira?"

"Okay, fifteen. I'll be sixteen soon. I was born on Christmas Day."

I lit another smoke. "I'll take you to that cabstand," I told her.

"And you won't bring me back to her?"

"No, I won't. If you'll do something for me."

A knowing smile on her little face. "Whatever you want." Her mother's voice.

"I'm going to give you a phone number. You call it. In one week. And you meet me where I tell you to. And you don't tell anyone."

"And then?"

"You answer some questions."

"That's it?"

"Yes."

She took a breath. "I'll do it. I keep my word. You'll see. Can't you drive me home yourself?"

"I got things to do," I said to the girl. Danielle never told me about the basement, but she'd said she had a younger sister. I wondered which part was true.

73

THERE WAS nobody I could ask. El-vira was partly right. Candy wasn't a whore. Not a real stand-up, pussy-for-cash whore. I knew one once. Never knew her real name. Everybody called her Mercy. She said she got into the business when she mercy-fucked some poor shlub and he bought her a pearl necklace. She was maybe forty years old. An old lady to me then. "It's show business," she told me. "Mind games. Mystery. There's no old whores, honey. Flesh sags. But money earns interest."

I was sitting in her kitchen, sunlight washing the room. Watching her drink her coffee, listening to her story. Even then, I knew how to listen.

"I just want somebody to talk to him," she said, her voice husky and soft. Thick hair pulled back from her face, held there with a rubber band. Cigarette in her long fingers. A housewife in the morning.

"What do I say?"

"Whatever works. He's an old trick—I've been dating him for years. The difference between a *good* whore and just an experienced one is repeat customers. Now he wants an exclusive, you understand? He wants me to move into an apartment in this building he owns. Be there when he shows up. Hold dinner for him."

I shrugged. "It doesn't sound so bad to me. One trick instead of a lot of tricks. And he'd pay the same?"

"Sure. But when he changes his mind, I'm out. I don't have a pimp—I don't want an owner." She walked over to the sink, her hips churning under the faded bathrobe. Washed out her coffee cup, talking at me over her shoulder. Patted herself on the butt. "This is mine. I rent it out—it's not for sale. Money lubricates me—it doesn't own me."

"You told him?"

"I'm his toy. I do what he wants. It's not inside his head that a toy makes up its own mind. He thought he was my dream coming true."

"I'll fix it," I told her.

When I went back to see her, she had the money ready for me. "He called me," she said. "He won't be coming back."

"That's what you wanted, right?"

"One of my tricks is a champion bridge player. You know how to play?"

I nodded. I knew how to play chess too. And dominoes. Prison.

"This trick, he told me any game you play with a partner, there's a difference between the best result possible and the best possible result. You understand?"

"What I did . . . it was the best result possible, right?"

"Yeah." She kissed me on the cheek. "You're a good man. Solid, keep your word. I thought they didn't make them like you anymore. In a few years, you ever get to Phoenix, you look me up, okay?"

"Phoenix?"

"I'm buying a little motel out near there. My retirement. Been saving for years. You get too old, the mystery wears thin . . . it gets too hard to do the act."

"You'll never be too old, Mercy."

Her smile mocked my lie. She kissed me again. Goodbye.

Candy was a different breed. That didn't mean her little daughter wasn't a liar too.

74

I FELL ASLEEP in my office later. On the couch, the little TV set flickering at the edge of my consciousness, Pansy snoring on the floor next to me. When I woke up it was dark again. A piece of light sat like a candle flame in the corner of the room, reflected from someplace past the window. I didn't move, watching it, letting it take me. Splitting off from this mess, disassociating. It works sometimes—you let go, it comes to you. But only if it's out there.

No use asking questions if you don't care what the answer is.

The cops wouldn't just walk away, but they'd find something else to do.

I blew smoke at the ceiling, wondering if I would.

75

THE NEXT morning, I grabbed a tip sheet from the newsstand and went back to the office. None of the horses spoke to me. I didn't dream about having one of my own one day—the way I used to all the time.

I spent a lot of time thinking about who I could steal from next.

76

I DRIFTED BACK to Mama's. White dragons in the window. She told the waiter something. He brought me a plate of fried rice, beef in oyster sauce. No soup.

"Everything okay now?" she asked, leaning forward, watching.

"Sure."

"You wait for something?"

"You mean . . . here?"

"No. For *something*, okay?"

"I don't think so."

"I think so."

I didn't answer her. After a while, she went back to the cash register at the front.

I was walking out when the pay phone rang. Mama walked past me. I waited.

"Man say tell you watch the papers tomorrow. Sutton Place."

"Anything else?"

"No."

"He say his name?"

"Man who called before. One time. Dead-man sound when he talk."

77

I WAS AT the restaurant before it opened the next day. Mama brought me the four-star edition of the *Daily News*. They put it out on the street by six in Chinatown. I didn't have to search through it. The headline screamed "Bizarre Murder on Sutton Place." A socialite with a WASP name was found murdered by her Wall Street husband when he came home from work around nine o'clock last night. Her name didn't mean anything to me. The newspaper account was short on facts—long on adjectives: grisly, ritualistic, satanic. Hinting at things that only come out on evil nights.

It was too early to call any of the free-lance reporters I know, but I had another solid contact in the press: a West Indian who worked the streets for one of the tabloids. Worked them hard. He'd lost his Island accent somewhere between Newark and journalism school but he was a hard-core risk-taker. He might be on the job.

I found a pay phone on the West Side. I got the reporter's answering machine. "If you know who you're calling, you know what you want to say. Do it when you hear the beep and I'll get back to you."

I heard the beep. "Leave me a message," I said into the recorder.

78

I GOT OFF the street before the citizens took over the city. Let Pansy out to her roof. Gave her some of the food I'd brought back from Mama's. Felt her pleasure as she lit into it, her sadness when it was gone. In another couple of minutes, she forgot about both feelings, back to herself. Lucky dog.

Maybe I'd go away for a while. Cruise out to Indiana, visit my old cellmate Virgil. His daughter was almost ten and I'd never seen her.

I could always see Virgil's daughter.

79

"ANYTHING?" I asked Mama when I called her from the street late that afternoon.

"Come in, okay?"

Max was in the kitchen when I walked in through the back door. He followed me out to my table. Mama sat down next to him, facing me.

"Man call. Black man, sunny voice. Call him at home, seven o'clock tonight."

"That's it?"

Mama's smooth face never changed expression. "Dead man called. Said call him. Hangs up."

I waited.

"Man say his name is Julio. You know him. You call him at his club, okay?"

Julio. Fuck!

"Girl call too. Same girl. Say to call her too. Very important."

"Okay."

"Not okay. Take Max with you."

"To make phone calls?"

"Meetings, yes? All these people?"

"Maybe. Maybe not."

"Take Max."

80

THE BASEMENT under Max's warehouse has a tunnel we cut through to the building next door. Some architects own it. I stepped into their basement, flashing the pencil-beam before my feet. Empty, like always. I hooked the field phone into their lines with the alligator clips. Julio first.

The beef-brain who answered took his time understanding I wasn't going to talk to him first. Julio got on the line, the old alligator's voice down to a whisper.

"I want to meet you."

"Take Marcy Avenue all the way until it hits the bridge that crosses the BQE. Seven-fifteen, okay?"

"Why don't you come here?"

"I don't have time."

"You should make time."

"Take it or leave it," I told him, cutting the line.

81

I RANG THE number Wesley gave me, using the code. Three times. Again. Then Candy. She answered on the first ring.

"What do you want?" I asked her.

"To see you."

"Tell me."

"I'll tell you whatever you want to hear. You know that. There's trouble for you. I can help. You believe me?"

"No."

"Come anyway. Listen for a few minutes."

"I'll come tomorrow. Don't be cute. Don't be stupid."

"The only thing I'll be is here."

82

WE CROSSED the Brooklyn Bridge to Tillary Street, left to Flushing Avenue. Ran parallel to the highway through Williamsburg. The sidewalk was thick with dark-eyed girls. Young Jewish beauties from the Hebrew high school in Williamsburg. Walking in tight clumps, chattering like sweet birds. All the brightness was in their faces—their clothes were too old for the way their hair bounced at the base of their necks, the way their eyes snapped at life. Mothers wheeled babies in strollers. Hassidim with their black stovepipe hats and long coats covered ground with purposeful steps. Laughter was for children. Hebrew writing on the walls, iron bars over the windows. Occupied territory, carved out of other ghettos on all sides.

We hadn't walked a block before we picked up cover. Half a dozen men, plain white shirts, dark suspenders, yarmulkes on their heads. Hands in their pockets. One had a coat over his forearm. Israeli soldiers—different uniforms. A clot of young girls passed us, demure but fearless. They were used to strangers.

The group of men watched me as I dialed the pay phone, not making a secret of it. The reporter was waiting for the call.

"Morehouse here."

"You know my voice?"

"Sure."

"You working on anything?"

"Lots of things, man. This a social call?"

"Maybe a trade. You know the shelter by the meat market?"

"Sure."

"Two o'clock coming. On the far corner?"

"Sure."

83

THE CADILLAC SEDAN stopped on the east side of the short bridge. The old man stepped out of the back. His driver opened the door, stood outside, watching. The pack watched him. I leaned against the stone wall, Max between me and the west side entrance. Traffic rumbled underneath us—tail end of the rush hour.

I let him come to me.

"Who's this?" he snarled, tilting his head at Max.

"What d'you want, Julio?"

"I want to know who this is."

"Fuck you."

"Burke, don't play with me. You got a pass. One time. You know why. Nobody gets two."

"Save it for the Godfather movies, old man. You don't need to know who this is. You had any brains, you'd already know."

"Why's he here?"

"To memorize your face, okay? So don't threaten me."

Max stood as stony as the wall, eyes slitted on Julio. Camera lenses. The old man's driver put his hand in his pocket, restless.

"Tell him to stay where he is, Julio. My brother wants to hurt somebody bad, and you'll do. That guido driving your car, he comes out with a piece and the Jews make him into chopped liver. Look for yourself."

Julio waved his hand as if he'd just seen an old friend. His driver took out a cigarette, kept his hands in sight. The street was empty like it was four in the morning. Except for the pack. One of them walked over to the same pay phone I'd used. Picked up the receiver.

"We can't stay here long," I told Julio.

He took a breath. "Last night, he hit Torenelli's daughter."

"What?"

"On Sutton Place. That was the don's daughter. She broke away from the family. Years ago. Married a citizen. Gives parties to raise money for the homeless, lives in a two-million-dollar co-op, okay?"

"So?"

He moved in close to me, prison-yard whisper cutting, hands shaking. "The husband, he comes home, finds her on the bed. Staked out like a piece of beef, wrists and ankles wired to the corners. With her head chopped off. *Off!* He shoved the head between her legs, you understand? So her face was looking at the husband when he comes in the door."

"Who?"

"Wesley. Who the fuck else? Who else would do that?"

"A freak."

"Sure. A freak who can get past the security in that joint. A freak that don't leave a lousy fingerprint. Not a trace. It was a pro hit. The fucking detectives threw up just looking at it. The husband—he's in a rubber room."

"What's this got to do with me?"

"It's Wesley's work. A fucking message, right? The don said he wasn't going to pay that maniac. He didn't do the job—he don't get paid. Wesley, he says he don't get paid, he's coming for all of us. Crazy motherfucker. He's a hitter. A contract man. He don't tell *us*, we tell *him*. Now he has to go. We can keep the sicko stuff outta the papers for only so long."

The old man tried to fire up one of his twisted black cigars. He couldn't get it lit—it wasn't the wind. I cracked a wooden match in my palm, held the cup for him. He leaned close to take the flame. A sour smell came off him.

"This ain't the first one. He dropped one of the don's boys. One shot, right in the back of the neck. Calls up, says, 'One down.' Like he's going to pick us off one at a time."

"Do whatever you want."

"No, it don't play like that. *You* started this fucking mess, you clean it up, *capisce*?"

"*I* started it? Where d'you get that? You got things mixed up. Wesley just wants his money, right?"

"He was up front with us, we woulda done that, okay? That Mortay—we know Wesley didn't hit him. But there was another guy—one of Sally Lou's boys. Our inside man. To watch Mortay. We had it all wired. The way we got it, you had a meet with Mortay in a playground in Chelsea." His deep-set eyes turned up to watch mine. Waited a beat, went on. "Our guy was along for backup. And *he* gets dropped. From the rooftop. Sniper shot. Somebody working with a silencer and a night scope. That's the murder the cops want you for . . . that's what they busted you on, right?"

It wasn't McGowan or Morales who made that bust. They wouldn't have squawked to the other cops anyway. I felt the gears mesh. The city has a compost heap for a heart—why shouldn't gangsters drop a dime on it—maybe grow some dollars?

"I wasn't there," I said quietly. "The judge cut me loose."

"Yeah, you wasn't there. Okay, I'm easy. But it was Wesley on that roof. Nobody else works like that . . . like a fucking hillbilly in the mountains. That puts you and that maniac together."

I watched him, waiting.

"It's good enough for the don," Julio said.

"Why don't you just pay Wesley the money?"

"Now you got it. That's exactly what we're gonna do, pal. And you're gonna deliver it."

"No thanks. I don't do crossfires."

"You gonna do this one. You don't, the don says to tell you you're on his list too."

"Why? What difference does it make?"

"You think . . . after what that fuck did . . . you think the don's gonna be happy just seeing him dead? He gets his hands on Wesley, it's gonna take that *animale* a week to die."

"I'm not meeting Wesley to hand over money—he'd waste the errand boy—you know that."

An alligator's smile. "I told them . . . Burke's too slick to play the chump. We don't care how it's done. We gotta have Wesley. Do whatever you gotta do. But quick."

"I'll get back to you."

"Don't even think about hiding. There's no place you can go in this town. One phone call and you're locked up again. You know what it costs to have a man hit in jail today?"

"You mean one *more* phone call, don't you?" I said, so close to his face I could see the pores. "Goodbye, old man."

The pack watched him walk to his car. Watched it drive away. Watched me use the pay phone again. Mama's voice was soft and clear. "He called. Say, same time, same place. Tonight."

Max and I walked back to the Plymouth. One of the young men in the pack caught my eye. I got the message. Don't. Come. Back.

I'd heard it before.

84

WE ROLLED back onto the BQE, heading toward Queens. Random loops, in case Julio was going to be stupid. Time to kill. Exited at La Guardia and looped around the airport, taking our time. Dark now, headlight patterns in the mirror. Max was watching, face turned to the rear. He made the "okay" sign as we pulled into the parking lot of one of the airport motels. We smoked a couple of cigarettes, watching the shadows dance. Men in shiny, pointy-toed boots with Cuban heels, light bouncing off thick shocks of heavily oiled hair. Bulletproof vests over tropical-colored silk shirts. Cocaine and money switched partners. They work outdoors now. The DEA has the rooms wired. A few years ago, some local Colombian paid a half million cash for the key to one of the lockers in the airport. He opened it up, the spring snapped, and the explosion took out nineteen people. That was back when the Italians still thought they could keep narcotics in the family. Wesley had the contract on the Colombian—the other eighteen bodies were on the house. The *federales* are still looking for the terrorist organization responsible.

Julio was playing it like Wesley was just a shooter, but he knew better. And he knew I knew.

I ran it down for Max. He already had most of it, from watching Julio. The Mongolian made the sign of a man aiming a rifle. Pulled his hand away from the trigger, knife-edged it, and chopped at his own neck. Pointed to my watch. Let's take him out tonight.

I shook my head no.

His hands asked why.

I shook my head again, pointed at my watch. Not now. Wait. I held my palm over my eyes like I was shielding them from the sun, turned my head from side to side. Something else around.

I couldn't say what.

85

WE CROSSED the Triboro from the Queens side. Worked our way to the junkyard. Hours yet until we had to meet Wesley—I wasn't going to wait in a bar.

I shoved a cassette into the tape player, jamming the bass as high as it would go for Max. He put his fingertips on the speaker on his side of the car.

Judy Henske. "High Flying Bird." And "God Bless the Child." I wondered if they let torch singers into heaven—I couldn't see Henske in a choir.

Sonny Boy Williamson. "T.B. Blues."

The sky looks different from the gutter.

Kinky Friedman and the Texas Jewboys. I'd forgotten he was on the tape. Just a bar singer's voice, but his dark-side poetry was diamonds shining through blood. The Texas Tower song—Kinky's ode to America's favorite sniper, Charles Whitman.

> *There was a rumor*
> *About a tumor*
> *Nestled at the base of his brain*

Maybe the Mole knew.

86

Terry let us in, leading us through the dog pack. Simba was sitting by himself a few feet from the Mole's bunker. His eyes ignored me, tracking Max. Calm, inside himself. Max stepped to the side, hands flowing to a clasp just below his waist. He bowed to the beast. Not in deference—a warrior on another's ground. Simba flashed a lupine grin and strolled off into the darkness.

We went down into the bunker. The Mole was in his chair, lap covered by an artist's pad. The page was covered with sketches of machinery, formulas and equations scrawled from corner to corner. He grunted a greeting, not looking up.

"Would you like some tea?" Terry asked me, making the sign of a cup to the lips for Max. The warrior nodded his head gravely. "You got any ginger ale?" I asked. The kid gave me a look like the Mole does sometimes. Michelle would be proud of him.

We sipped our drinks. The Mole ignored us. Finally, he dumped his calculations on the floor. Terry was waiting with a cup of tea. The Mole nodded his head absently.

"What're you working on?" I asked.

"A computer retrovirus."

"What?"

"Computer virus . . . you reach a certain point and it eats the data, yes?"

"Okay." I knew what he meant. Pedophiles are really into computers, meticulously recording each victim. They have crash-codes built in. The cops try to access the disc and the whole thing goes down.

"There's a way to use the surge-suppressor . . . part of the line conditioner . . . what they plug in to hold the data if there's a power outage . . . you could use that to eat the virus instead of the data."

"I don't . . ."

"Another module. It goes in the line conditioner. Then you drop the power, just a little bit, and the suppressor kicks in, finds the virus, and eats it. And gets out without a trace."

"How long would it take?"

The Mole snapped his fingers. "A thousandth of that."

"Damn."

"I'm still working on it. It's not ready."

I lit a cigarette, leaving the pack on the table in case Terry wanted one. He took out his own—I guess they weren't expecting Michelle.

"Mole, you know anything about tumors?"

"What kind?"

"Brain tumors?"

"Yes."

"Could a tumor make a man kill?"

"It's not so simple," he said. Annoyed at having to explain. "It could make a man mad. Irrational. It couldn't make a man different from what he is . . . just what he does, you understand?"

He watched my face, got his answer. Went on. "Tumor, it's a growth. Different parts of the brain control different functions. A tumor gets in the way. Changes things. Behavior is one of those things."

"Mole, you know Wesley?"

"Only what people say."

"He kills people. That's what he does. I've known him since we were kids. He doesn't have . . . feelings. You understand? He told me once, you want to kill a man sleeping in a house, you don't go in after him, you set fire to the house. Everybody dies. Makes it hard on the cops. The more bodies, the more motives. You can't be *born* like that, right?"

"Everybody's born like that."

"What?"

"Everybody. Humans are born into the world screaming for what they want. They feel their own feelings. They have no pack instincts, like dogs. A baby is a monster."

"So a baby raised by wolves, it would be a wolf?"

"It would be a man who behaves like a wolf."

I dragged on my smoke. I could never keep the Mole talking for long. Terry was watching, focused. Maybe the Mole wasn't talking to me.

"Wesley was always like that," I told him. "He never cried, never laughed. He has no fear in him. Nothing in him at all."

"That's not what you said at first," the Mole replied, his eyes impossible to read through the thick smudged lenses of his glasses. "Babies have all those things. Babies learn to feel past their *own* feelings—that's what we teach them."

"Psychology . . ."

"This isn't psychology. Not a soft science. Animals adapt or they die. That is a biological law. Sometimes things are left over, vestiges. Like the appendix. We don't need it. Eventually, it will disappear from our bodies. Biology . . . it's like what Max does . . . we have to use power, not resist it. Things get left over . . . we are only here for a short time, so we adapt. Or we die."

"Left over . . ."

"Sex. That's left over." Terry shifted his posture, dragging on his smoke. "You know the orgasmic curve . . . different for men than women?"

"You mean it takes them longer to come?"

The Mole's lips tightened primly. "To reach orgasm, yes. Do you know why?"

"The way they're put together . . . I don't know."

"Herd animals, they mate serially, you understand? There's a fail-safe biological response to every genetic code or the organism dies."

"Come on, Mole. Talk English."

Another annoyed look. "A herd of elk. Mating season. The bucks fight it out. And the winner gets to mate with the entire crop of females, right? That's the genetic code. So the strongest, most powerful stud mates with the females and the babies have the best DNA."

"Yeah . . ."

"What if the strongest male is sterile? What if he has a low sperm count? What happens then?"

I glanced at Max. The Mole hadn't moved his hands once, but the warrior watched as intently as the kid.

The Mole answered his own questions. "The herd dies off. So the fail-safe kicks in. When the females are in season . . . when they are in heat . . . the bucks smell it and they start to fight. The winning buck mates with a female, he discharges his sperm, then he moves off to wait for his power to recharge. But the female, she is still in heat. While the winning buck mates with another, one of the other bucks, one of the losers in the fight, he mounts her too. They all do that. If the first discharge of sperm is potent, the genes from the strongest buck make a baby. But if it isn't, the next one . . . or the one after that . . . takes. And they have babies. The strongest babies survive, and the pack lives on. Understand?"

"Okay, but . . ."

"If the females reached orgasm faster than the males, they would pull away. Animals don't commit rape—the females must be willing. The mating wouldn't be completed. The orgasmic curve is longer. Much longer. Long enough for the first buck, long enough for the bucks to follow."

"That's why women take longer to . . ."

"Yes."

"So one day they'll get off as quick as we do?"

Something less than a smile ghosted on the Mole's lips. "Yes. In another half million years or so. You won't be around to see it."

I lit another smoke. Thinking about it. How Mercy said money was her lubricant. "Wesley . . . he adapted?"

"To something. I don't know what."

"How do you know . . . that he adapted?"

"He has many enemies. And he isn't dead."

87

THE PLYMOUTH pussyfooted its way through the maze of twisted little roads. I pulled to the side. Max's door opened. The interior light didn't come on. He vanished.

I parked where I had the last time. Got out nice and slow.

"Go ahead and light your smoke." A voice behind me.

I felt him next to me. Turned to look. His hands weren't empty this time.

"Tell the Chinaman to come out. Listen to my voice. I'm telling you the truth, Burke. You don't call him out, I'll waste you right here. Whatever happens, you're dead."

If this was the movies, I'd have heard the sound of the Uzi being cocked. This was Wesley—I knew it already was. They say Wesley files the safety off his guns. I pulled the white handkerchief out of my coat sleeve. Waved it high above my head in a circle, stopped the circle right in front of me. Max was coming whether Wesley killed me or not—this way there'd be two of us. Maybe . . . ?

Wesley was on my right, the Uzi in my rib cage. Max came forward, making enough noise so we'd hear him. He kept walking. A lumbering, thug's walk, giving no hint of the speed and grace in the thick body. A locomotive that makes its own tracks. He stopped ten feet away, right in front of us.

"Close enough," Wesley said.

I held a palm out to Max to keep him where he was. The Mongolian dropped his left shoulder a fraction. If he went, he'd go to Wesley's left. I pushed my weight against the stubby barrel of the machine gun, ready to lock my elbow over it, hug my death close to me if it came. Wesley was right. Close enough. For Max. I'd go first, but Wesley would be right behind me.

"You wanted to talk?" I asked the monster.

"You think I didn't know the Chinaman was here last time?"

"I didn't know myself."

"I know. That's why you got to walk away. But you knew this time."

"Okay."

"Max the Silent, right? That's him?"

"That's him."

"Looks like a real bone-breaker."

"He's here for me, not you."

"I know. Tell him I got a gun on you."

"He knows."

"So why'd he come out?"

"He's my brother."

"Yeah. That's nice. I had a brother too."

"I never knew that. Where is he?"

"Dead."

Like you, I thought, taking the last puff of my cigarette, tossing it away. "What d'you want, Wesley?"

"You like the job on Sutton Place?"

"Why'd you do it?"

"They owe me money."

"I know. I met with one of them earlier tonight. They want you bad. They're going to get word out that they'll pay. They want me to deliver the cash."

"And blow me up?"

"No. They want you alive."

"That's the way I figured it. It takes the heat off."

"*Off?!*"

"Sure, off. They could have paid me. Like they should've. When I hit the first guy, they got scared. So they put out the word. Hit Wesley, right? Any asshole with a gun could do it, he got close enough. Now it's different. They're spooked. I made shit of the *don*—fucked him where he breathes right in front of everybody. They had an open contract out on me before. Now it's canceled, right? Now it's personal."

"There's more."

"What?"

"They think it was you who did the job in the Chelsea playground. They had the whole thing wired—one of the guys working with Mortay, he was theirs. He's the guy who went down in the playground. Sniper fire from the roof. They dropped a dime on me to put on the pressure."

"The cops think it was me on the roof too?"

"Probably do, by now."

"We both know it wasn't. So you got a sniper in your stable too."

"He was a loaner. From a friend. I can't use him again."

"Okay. They won't dime you for the Sutton Place thing. It won't fly."

"How d'you know?"

"I dress in a nice suit, nice trench coat. Eight-hundred-dollar briefcase, Rolex, diamond ring. I'm a lawyer, right? I tell the doorman I got a package for Mrs. Swanson in 21A. From Mr. Torenelli. He makes the call, I go up. No problem. Maid's day off. I know. Ring the bell, she answers it herself. Starts right in on me. 'I told my father I didn't want to have anything to do with his . . .' I cut her off, tell her I just got a couple of papers in my briefcase for her to sign and I'm out of there. She treats me like a servant, turns her back on me. I close the door behind her, follow her to the living room. Open the briefcase. She's still yakking at me when I hook her in the stomach with a set of brass knuckles. She's out—can't get a breath. Anesthetic nose plugs and she goes right to sleep. I take off my clothes, lay them in the briefcase. Talcum powder on my hands, surgeon's gloves. Carry her to the bedroom. Piano wire until she's spread out. I find a chopping block and a set of those Ginsu knives in the kitchen. All those rich assholes have fancy kitchens. I put the block under her neck, pull her hair back, and take the head off. Half a dozen shots is all it took. Blood spurts out all over the back wall. I stick the head into her cunt, facing out. Say hello to her husband when he comes home. I write the number two on the wall in her blood. That's the polygraph key the cops'll use when freaks start confessing. I take a shower. Pop open the drain. Pour three bottles of that Liquid Plumber stuff down, leave the hot-water tap on. I get dressed, put everything back in the briefcase. I go downstairs, tell the doorman the package is too big to lug through the lobby. Mrs. Swanson wants it through the service entrance. Wants him to handle it *personally*, right? Slip him a pair of twenties. I'll drive around into the back alley with the box, he'll meet me there, take it up to her. I drive out back. He opens the door. I put three rounds into him. Pop, pop, pop. Drive away. The papers don't have that body either. But the cops, they know they ain't looking for a maniac. They ain't looking for an amateur like you either. They know."

His voice wasn't chilly, just flat. Not quite bored.

"Why?" I asked.

"I was going to spook them. Kill a few the same way. Make 'em think a freak was after their women. Get them all together in one place to figure out what to do. And blow the place up. But this is quicker."

"They got your message."

He wasn't listening. "I was going to beat off onto the body but with that DNA fingerprinting they use now . . ."

"Cut it out, Wesley. You don't give a fuck about blood types, or fingerprints either. They drop you for this, you're not going to jail. . . . You just couldn't do it."

"Couldn't do what?"

"Beat off on a dead body. I came up with you, remember? I know what you do for a living, but you're still a man."

"I'm a bomb," the monster said. "I'm tired of this place. When I check out, you'll *hear* the sound."

My body was rigid with the strain. He wasn't going to pull the trigger. I stepped away from him, carefully.

"Yeah, go ahead," he said. "I was going to waste you, I'd take the Chinaman first. Always take the hard man first. That's the rules."

"Look . . ."

"You're not a hard man, Burke. Maybe you was once, but you let things get in the way. There's a way out of this. For you, not for me. I don't care. I'm tired. I got to do Train first. I took the money. And the don. Then I'm gone."

"What's my way out? What d'you want from me?"

"You're the link. Like I knew you'd be, remember I told you? I need a cop."

"What?"

"A big cop. High-ranker. The don's gone to ground. I'll never find him. The cops and the mob, they're all in the same bed. You find out where he's at, I'll do the rest."

"I don't know any top cops."

"You know how to do things. Talk to people, work around. I can't do that. Nobody knows my face, but they can feel me coming."

Survivors can, I thought.

"They'll want to set up a meet, tell me I'm getting my money," he said. "I want my money, right? It's going to take a little bit of time. Use it. When I finish my work, everybody's happy . . . the cops'll have their bodies and you'll be off the hook."

"You can't hit them all. They'll always come for you."

"No. I'm going to kill their seeds. And then I'm going where they can't come after me."

"The Program? You can't . . ."

His voice didn't change. You can't insult a monster. "The Witness Protection Program? I already hit two guys that was *in* the Program. I told you, I'm tired. Don't worry about it."

"Same deal—I call you?"

"Yeah." He looked over at Max. "You think he's close enough to take me out, don't you?"

"He is."

"No he's not," said the monster, as he stepped away from me into the dark.

88

THE MEAT MARKET is a triangular slab hacked out of the West Village with the wide end opening onto the West Side Highway. Before they opened a bigger version in Hunts Point, all the city's butcher shops got their supplies down there. Every morning, way before the traffic stream thickens with citizens bound for City Hall and Wall Street, the streets are clogged with refrigerated trucks. By noon it's pretty quiet. In the evening, some of the city's best steak houses do a booming business. Yuppies can walk there from their million-dollar lofts. When they close, the meat market is home to the army of kids who spend the night selling the one thing they have left. To buy drugs to make them forget what that is.

The shelter is a clapboard shack the kids built out of abandoned packing crates. Scraps of carpeting on the floor, discarded mattresses, sometimes an old broken chair. The street kids drift out of Times Square like vampires being chased by daylight. They made this place for themselves. The cops leave them alone as long as they're back on the street by the time the truckers are gone. Nobody turns tricks in daylight down here. I found more than one runaway there over the years, especially when the winterhawk drops down.

Waiting for Morehouse. An abandoned window fan sat upright in the street, plugged into nothing, its blades rasping as it turned in the night wind.

The reporter's battered Datsun rolled around the corner. Spotted my Plymouth, pulled in behind. We got out to meet him. A dark-skinned man about my height, wearing a khaki jacket over a bulky sweatshirt, unpolished combat boots under a pair of chinos. Subway outfit. He'd been around for a while, but his face was unlined, hair cut close. Morehouse has an athlete's build, rangy. Next to Max, he looked like a stick. He held out his hand, smile flashing. The Island way. He ignored Max—the meeting was with me. The City way.

"This is all on the record, right?" he said. His idea of a joke.

"The Sutton Place killing . . . you cover it?"

"I write a column, man. I can't cover every breaking story."

"That means no?"

"That means I know the facts, but there's no column in it."

"How about this for a lead? Mafia don's estranged daughter snuffed. The number two written in blood on the wall. Head chopped off the body and stuck between her legs. Building doorman found dead. Cops cover up mob connection."

He blew a sharp breath through his teeth. "This is on the street?"

"Not yet."

"So you spoke to the cops. Or the killer."

"I don't just know *how* it went down, I know *why*. Want to trade?"

"Sure. What do *you* want?"

"Torenelli. He's holed up. And he's working with the cops. One of them knows where he is. Probably brass."

"So?"

"That's what I want to know."

"This is deep water, man. Deep and dark."

"Pretend you're back in Haiti." Morehouse had won a journalism award for his coverage of the insanity on that island after Baby Doc fled.

"I have to *live* here."

"It's your choice." I shrugged.

"What do I get?"

"You get the inside story. The why of it all. It wasn't a random murder and it wasn't a sex-freak mob. There's a job war coming down."

"Drugs?"

"No."

"What, then?"

"We have a deal?"

"Sure."

"You first."

"That isn't the way it works, Burke. I give you what I got, you give me what you got. Same time, no taking turns."

"Except you got nothing. Nothing now. You get what I want, let me know, and we'll trade. Deal?"

"You at the same number?"

I nodded.

"Sure," he said, watching the disconnected fan spinning in the street.

89

I DROVE THROUGH the Village streets, working toward Chinatown. Max held his hand out in front of his eyes, rigid as a steel bar, asking a question. I took one hand off the wheel, did the same. My hand didn't tremble. Too many things to be scared of at the same time—my nerves were in a coma.

When we pulled into the warehouse, he made the sign for me to come up with him. Sleep over. I bent my wrists, holding paws in front of my face. Pansy was home—I had to get back. His face didn't change. He knew the beast could get along for days without me. I pointed at my watch, showed him the time I wanted to roll tomorrow. He gestured like he was picking something off a plate, putting it in his mouth. We'd meet at Mama's.

90

I ATE BREAKFAST at my desk the next morning, listening to the all-news station on the radio. An FBI agent was busted for molesting kids. The DEA seized another twenty million dollars' worth of coke at JFK. A group of inmates at Sing Sing were demanding a nonsmoking wing. There was a city-wide hunt for a bank bandit. Thirteen hits—total take under twenty grand. He was probably scared to hit the bodegas—they had more cash on hand, but you couldn't push notes across the counter.

Rye toast, cream cheese, pineapple juice. I made it last. I like to eat alone. By myself. That's the worst thing about prison—even worse than the fear-mist that makes it hard to breathe—no privacy. Nothing to yourself. Even in solitary, the smells come in.

I thought about what Morehouse said. I have to live here too. I'd had this office a long time, but I wouldn't miss it if I had to go.

Flood drifted around in my thoughts. I pushed her back. I thought when I settled up with Belle's father, it would quiet my mind. I could go to Japan, like Max said. Find Flood. Here in the city, a monster was charging toward a machine. I didn't figure out how to get out of the way, I'd find Belle quicker.

91

I CALLED CANDY from the street.

"Buzz downstairs. Tell the doorman you're expecting a package. Two guys'll be bringing it up."

"Now?"

"Yeah."

Max and I carried the giant carton stamped with the brand name of the TV set in big black letters. His sleeves were rolled up, biceps popping with the strain, veins roped on his forearms. I kept my coat on. The doorman took us up in the service elevator, let us out on her floor. I picked up the empty carton by a corner and carried it in one hand as Max faded into the stairwell.

She opened the door while my finger was still on the buzzer. Stepped aside to let me in.

"Where's the other guy?"

"He went back down to the car."

"You brought me a present?"

"It's empty."

"It's the thought that counts."

"Tell me what you want."

She was wearing a red silk slip. Barefoot. Thick brunette wig, yellow cat's eyes patient. "Can we talk in the back?"

I followed her down the hall. The backs of her legs were muscular, hips rolling in a tight round arc. "Any particular room you want?" she asked.

"I don't care," I said to her shoulder. "Where's the kid?"

"Back in school."

She turned into the last room. The only window was masked behind a midnight-blue screen—twilight inside. She tilted her head at a reclining black leather chair in the corner, chrome dish ashtray atop a black tripod next to it. I sat down. Lit a smoke. She propped one leg on the psychiatrist's couch, stood sideways facing me, flexing the muscles in her leg.

"That's the part that goes soft first," she said, patting the inside of her thigh. "Mine're like rocks."

"Great."

"It doesn't do anything for you?"

"Why should it?"

"You're a man."

I thought about Wesley, watching the shadow on the inside of her thigh.

"I've seen it before."

She left the room. I dragged on the smoke, knowing I was there for a reason. Not her reason.

When she came back in, she was naked. This time she had on a fluffy blond wig piled up on top of her head, soft tendrils framing her face. Lavender eyes. Black spike heels, no stockings. A black garter banded her left thigh. Her right hand was full of leather and steel.

"You don't trust me?"

"No."

"I need you to trust me. I can be whatever you want. Any woman you want. Just close your eyes and think of it. Tell me. And it happens."

My eyes slitted until she was out of focus, smoke drifting past my face. Her purring voice was background music.

Belle. The big girl twirling before me in her new outfit, pretty-proud, prom-bound. "Come *on*."

Strega. On her knees but not begging, witch-fire eyes promising threats. "You'll be back."

Flood. The chubby little blonde, scars on her body never reaching her heart. Merry, bouncing flesh. All her debts squared now. "I'm for you, Burke" was how she'd said goodbye.

The music stopped. "You can't be anything I want," I told her.

"Your voice is different. The last time you were here, you said cold things. But they were weak. I know when someone's playing a role. That's what I do. You're not playing now."

"You're a lousy psychologist."

"I know when someone's lying."

"You should."

She tossed whatever she was carrying onto the couch. Bent at the waist, rooted around. She held a circle of chain in her hand for me to see, then she pulled it over her head like a necklace. "You know what this is?"

"No."

She walked over to my chair, hands behind her back. Dropped to her knees on the rug. "It's a choke collar. For dogs. See?" She pulled the ring and the steel noose tightened around her neck.

I waited.

Her other hand came from behind her back. Handcuffs. She tossed the key in my lap. Snapped one of the cuffs on her wrist. Reached her free hand behind her. A leather leash. She snapped the hook onto the collar ring. Put her hands together behind her back. I heard the other cuff click home. She turned on her knees, back to me. Held out her cuffed hands. "See?"

"See what?"

She turned again to face me. "Take the leash. Hold it in your hands. There's nothing I can do. Tug on the leash, I come along. Like a dog. Pull too tight and I can't breathe. Try it."

The leash curled like a snake on my leg. I didn't touch it. "What's this supposed to mean?"

"There's more straps on the couch. You can do whatever you want. There's no way I can hurt you."

"You couldn't hurt me over the phone either."

"You're afraid."

"Not of you."

"Of *you*. Of yourself. Take the leash. Hold it in your hand. Feel the power."

I took the leash in my hand, watching her eyes watch me. Something stirred. "I don't feel anything."

"Yes you do. Don't be afraid of it."

"Tell me what you want."

"I lied. My daughter went back to him. Train. I want her back. I want you to get her back."

"How?"

"Talk to him."

"It won't work twice."

"Yes it will. Just go visit him again. A couple of times. Watch his office. Let him see you. Elvira will know. She'll know you'll always be around. He doesn't want people poking into his business. Another girl won't be worth it to him. Just be around. You don't have to do anything. Just be yourself. Tell Train you're investigating him or something."

"What if it doesn't work?"

"A couple of weeks, that's all. Just a couple of weeks. If it doesn't work by then, give it up. Okay?"

"You're paying for this?"

"Whatever you want."

"Money's what I want."

"What about me?"

"What *about* you?"

"I lied to you. And now I confessed. Don't you think I should be punished?"

"Not by me."

"Don't be afraid. You feel it, I know you do." She pushed her face closer, dropping it into my lap. My mind saw the message Wesley left on the rich woman's bed. I felt her lips against me. I was as limp as the leash in my hand.

She pulled her head back. "I thought . . ."

I climbed out of the chair. "I'll call you," I said.

She struggled to her feet, following me down the hall, hands cuffed behind her, the leash dangling from the choke collar.

"Burke!"

I stopped in the living room, waiting. "Get me out of these hand-cuffs. Or leave me the key. I don't have another one. I can't stay tied up like this."

Lousy little liar. "Call a friend," I told her.

92

WESLEY would be holed up somewhere in the city. Someplace with no neighbors. He had no baggage, no friends, not even a dog. He could go on the move every night. Carry whatever he needed in a duffel bag. No pressure points on his body—he'd been ready for this all his life. Torenelli's boys didn't have a chance. Trying to catch mist in a butterfly net.

I thought about my office. Pansy. Mama in her restaurant. Michelle in her hotel. The junkyard would be safe, but I'd have to stay once I moved in. Compared with Wesley, I was a citizen.

I called Wesley from Mama's. Worked my way through some hot-and-sour soup waiting for the call-back. He must have been keeping a close watch—the phone rang in twenty minutes. I answered it myself, saving time.

"Yeah?"

"You called."

"I have to go back in. See the man you told me to stay away from. Wanted you to know in front."

"Why?"

I knew what he meant. "It's part of this whole thing—I don't know what yet."

"You're checking on that address for me?"

"Already started."

He hung up.

93

I WENT LOOKING for the Prof. Slipped a roll of quarters in my pocket. Tolls for the turnpike. I found him on Vanderbilt, just before it dead-ends on Forty-second Street. A big shoeshine box in front of him. No customers.

"Let's take a ride," I said.

"I wish I could, but I'm holding some goods."

I glanced at the shoeshine box. He nodded.

"How long?"

"Quarter to a half."

I propped a boot on the metal last, lit a cigarette while the Prof went to work. He knew how to do it. Taking his time, running a toothbrush around the welt, taking the polish directly on his fingertips, working it in, popping the rag. Misted the leather with a little spray can, flicked it off with a buffing cloth. He was finishing up the second boot when two heavyset black guys rolled up. They leaned against the building wall, watching. Chilly young men. Pups from the same litter.

The Prof finished up with a flourish. Tugged at my pants cuff to let me know.

"There's your shine, and it's damn fine."

"How much?"

"Put down a pound."

"Five bucks?"

"The ride is five. You want the honey, you come to the hive."

The two pups pushed themselves off the wall in case I was going to argue. I handed the Prof his cash, moved off. Didn't look back.

The Prof caught up to me around the corner. His hands were empty. He got into the Plymouth and we headed over to the West Side Highway. Pulled over at the Ninety-sixth Street exit, hooked the underpass, and found a parking spot on the river. I popped the hood, hauled a toolbox out of the trunk. We kept our heads under the hood, playing with the tools as we talked.

"I saw him again."

"Keep it up, you'll be draped in crepe."

"I'm in it. He did that job—the one on Sutton Place. Spit in Torenelli's face. Julio met with me too. They want Wesley. Alive."

"And the heat still wants you?"

"That was Julio. The fucking weasel dimed me to turn up the flame. So I got no room to move."

"When the man's got a gun, it's time to run."

"That's what I should've done. If I'd known Wesley was tracking Mortay . . ."

"You know tomorrow's number, we're all rich."

"I know. This is different. I'm in the middle."

"That ain't the place, ace."

"Tell me something I don't know."

"There's no time for that, brother. They're both on the set, so place your bet."

"Wesley."

The little man turned, leaned back against the Plymouth's grille, looking out at the Hudson River. Lit a smoke, taking his time. "It always was him, wasn't it?"

"What're you talking about?"

"In the joint. When you was just a young fool with gunfighter dreams. That's who you wanted to be like, right? Wesley? The ice man."

"He's got nobody, Prof."

"Nobody dragging him down, you mean. Nobody to cry over when they're gone. Traveling light don't make it right."

"He's not a rat."

"This is true. He wanted your head, you'd be dead."

"Wesley wants his money. You know how he is. The Italians made a mistake. Torenelli's hiding. Wesley wants to know where. Settle up."

"It's over, then?"

"That's what he says."

"What do they say?"

"Who? Who should I ask? What they got, it's a big pile of cheese. They don't care which rat gets to eat. Torenelli don't make the count one morning, somebody else'll step in."

He nodded, dragging deep on his smoke. "Somebody knows where he is."

"Yeah, but who?"

"Torenelli. I remember him. A pussy in his heart. He ain't got the stones to go it alone. He was gonna kill *himself*, he'd use pills."

"That's the way I figure it too."

"Wesley ain't no private eye. Who's looking?"

"Morehouse."

"The reporter? That West Indian is my man! You dig his piece on that dude in Louisiana doing life in the box for a lousy stickup? Where the head of the Parole Board ended up doing time?"

"Yeah. I dealt with him before. I gave him some of the inside stuff from the Sutton Place thing. Hard stuff, right from the scene. From the horse's mouth. Got his nose wide open. He knows brass at NYPD."

"He know why you want the info?"

"He don't want to know."

The Prof dropped his cigarette, ground it out under his heel. "What's my end, friend?"

"They think I got no slack, but there's a knot in the rope. I can unravel it, I got room to breathe. There's a little girl. I need to take her to Lily, take her back when it's all done."

"That's it?"

"There's questions only Lily can get the answers to."

"You got the plan, I'm your man."

I lit my own smoke. "I thought I'd feel better after that motherfucker was gone." Belle's father.

"I know."

94

I CALLED the ex-cop who does the phone work. Met him in a midtown restaurant. Gave him an envelope full of cash and some new phone numbers to check. A new address too.

Called Lily. Waited an extra quarter's worth for them to get her to the phone.

"It's me. Could I ask you a question?"

"Sure."

"If a teenage girl had a story, could you tell if it was the truth?"

She knew the kind of story I wanted her to validate. "It depends. I could probably tell if something happened, but not necessarily when. And I might have trouble identifying the source. You have a history?"

"All out of her mouth."

"I'll take a shot. Or maybe Immaculata could do it if you don't want to bring her here."

"It's not a job for Mac."

"Okay."

"Lily . . . I probably won't be able to make an appointment. She might be . . . annoyed. Not want to talk."

I could feel her shrug over the phone. "It happens."

"Thanks."

Called Davidson.

"Anything?"

"Nothing. My prediction? There'll never be a Grand Jury on this one. It's going to be marked 'closed, one arrest' and fade away. They know you had nothing to do with it."

"I owe you any money?"

"I'm good."

That was the truth.

95

I KNOW HOW to wait. When I was in prison, I never thought of going over the wall. I wasn't doing a life sentence, and I wasn't ready to go straight once I was out. I let a couple of days slide by slow. No sense pressuring Morehouse—he'd get it done or he wouldn't.

But if he didn't . . .

The trust-fund hippies who live underneath my office don't stir until midafternoon. I think they call getting high "performance art" now.

Mama answered herself. In rapid-fire Mandarin.

"It's me."

"Letter come for you."

"At the restaurant?" Wesley? Julio's morons telling me they knew where I lived?

"Yes. Last night."

"See you soon."

96

As soon as Mama put it in front of me, I knew it wasn't from Wesley. Or Julio. Thick, cream-colored envelope, felt more like cloth than paper. Nothing on the outside. I flexed it in my fingers. Not a letter-bomb. One sheet inside, matching the envelope.

The words flowed so smoothly onto the paper they could have been squeezed from a tube. Icing on the devil's cake.

"Ask me. I know."

No signature. I didn't need one.

Strega.

97

I smoked a cigarette, thinking it through. Smoked a couple more. It had to be connected—not one of her witchy games.

I'm not sure how I remembered the number. She answered halfway through the first ring.

"I know who this is."

"Okay. What else do you know?"

"I know what you want to know. Come and see me and I'll tell you."

"Say it now. It'll only take a second."

"Longer than that. Come and see me. You want to do it anyway."

"No I don't. We settled that."

"Nothing's settled. If I wanted to talk on the phone, I would have called you."

I bit into the filter of my cigarette. "I'll meet you. Remember where we first talked?"

"You're afraid to come here."

"Yes."

"Afraid of me."

"That too."

"You can't meet me outdoors. You know better than that. You

know what I have to tell you. Make a choice. I'll be here tonight. From when it gets dark to when it gets light."

98

THE CAR radio said it was unseasonably warm. Mid-fifties. I felt the chill coming from her house before I got it in sight. Pulled around behind. Backed the Plymouth into the empty space outside the garage. The connecting door was open. I stepped inside. I knew the way.

She was in her black-and-white living room, perched on the edge of the easy chair, flashy legs crossed, elbow on her knee, one hand cupping her chin. Fire-streaked hair combed back from her little fox face.

"I kept it warm for you," she said, getting to her feet, heels clicking on the marble floor as she closed the distance between us.

I stood rooted. Nothing was going to get me back in that chair again.

She took both my hands, holding them gently, watching my face. She was wearing a white silk T-shirt that came to mid-thigh. The kind women tie a belt around and make into a dress.

"Sit in the chair. Your chair, remember?"

"No."

"No what?"

"No, I won't sit in the chair."

"But you do remember?"

"Yeah."

"I won't ask you again."

"Good."

She led me to the couch, still holding both my hands. Sat down, pulling me down with her. Pulled one of my hands to her mouth, a dark slash in the room, tiny perfect white teeth gleamed. She kissed my hand. Licked it. Turned her face up to watch mine again. Put my hand in her mouth, sucked on my thumb. Bit it, hard.

"You still taste good."

"What is it that you know? That you wanted me to ask you?"

"Julio told me. He tells me anything. He can never pay off his debt. This crazy man—this killer, they want you to deliver money to him so they can grab him. They're going to leave you there."

"You think that's news?"

"They're going to force you. Very soon. They know how to do it."

"What's the hurry?"

"Their little *don*, he's so afraid. Hiding in his little house. In the basement, like a cockroach. He's afraid, so they're all afraid. He can't wait. He wants to go to his nightclubs, ride in his big car, visit his *gumare* . . . big man. Now he can't do that."

"Okay. Thanks."

Her fingers were twisted in my coat. "Julio hates you. Because you know. What he did to me. He knows you know. I never told him, but he knows. He's put it out that you work with this maniac. The one who did the killing on Sutton Place."

"I already knew that. I got arrested for a homicide I had nothing to do with. That was his work too."

"I could have had Julio taken out years ago. I waited. To make him pay. But he could never pay. It's time for him to go."

"Why now?"

"You're *mine*. Remember what I told you? I ate your blood, I swallowed your seed. You're in me."

"I'm nobody's," I told her.

Witches hear only their own chants. "I told that evil old man. I told him I'd never let him hurt you. The last time he talked to me, he whined . . . like the coward he is. Said the don wanted it done. But I know. It's him."

"It doesn't matter who."

"It *does*. If the boss goes down, Julio's still here. And he'll still want you."

"So you want . . ."

"A trade. I'll tell you where the don's holed up. And you do Julio. Yes?"

"I thought . . ."

"Don't you sneer at me! Don't be better than me. You *want* to do it. You think I don't read the papers? I paid you to get Scotty's picture back. You did that. But the man who did it to him . . . that pervert in the clown suit . . . they said they found him with a broken neck. You did that. You're a cold man. A cold man, afraid of my fire."

"You're wrong, Jina. Wrong all over the lot."

Her eyes fired, flickered, glazed over. Singsong witch's chant. "Strega. Strega when you call my name. It's Strega who'll do this for you. Not Jina. Jina's a nice girl. You don't want a nice girl."

"I don't want you."

She licked her lips. "Prove it. Sit in your chair."

"For what?"

"For what you want."

"I want the address."

"Me first."

Bitch. I sat in the chair. Watched her curl herself around my legs, the T-shirt riding up to her waist, strip of blood-red silk between her thighs. She bent forward, the red silk a thong between her buttocks. Her hand on my zipper. Raspy, hard sound. "Mine," she said, thrusting her hand inside. Nobody home. She made a noise in her throat, took my softness between her lips, licking, making sounds to herself, speaking in tongues. A stirring in the softness but . . . nothing. Teeth nipped at the head of my cock, lips sliding over the shaft, sucking. Dead. As dead as Belle. I thought if it ever happened to me, I'd die a bit. It felt like winning.

She gave it up after a couple of minutes. Eyes focused hard now, watching my face. "Why?"

"I don't know—it's just gone."

"Is this the first time?"

I don't know what made me tell the truth. "No."

"Did something happen to you?"

"Yeah."

"You got hurt?"

"Yeah."

"Is it going to get better?"

"I don't know. I don't . . ."

"Care?"

"I don't even know that."

She pulled the zipper up, roughly. "It won't last. I know. I don't care what any doctor says. Don't be . . ."

"Don't be what? Depressed? Depressed is finding out you're a diabetic. I found out I can't get insulin, you understand?"

"You're not scared." It wasn't a question.

"No."

"You were the last time."

"I know."

"You think that's what did it . . . if you were scared again?"

"I. Just. Don't. Know. Okay?"

"Okay." Her eyes looked wet—it must have been the light in that white room.

I got up to go. "Give me the address."

"I don't have it."

"You . . ."

"I *think* I know where he is. But I have to be sure, okay? You can't go twice. Once it happens, they'll know it came from me."

"It could come from anybody. Their own outfit is lousy with rats."

"What about our deal?"

"I sat in the chair."

"I know. I know there's things you can't fake. Especially you. That's not what I mean. Julio."

"Spell it out."

"You have to do them both."

"When will you have the address?"

"Tomorrow, next day. Soon. Couple of days at most. I swear."

"Okay."

She walked downstairs with me, kicking off the spike heels, padding along on the carpet. She stood a step above me. Bent down and kissed me on the lips. Sweet. No biting into me. No witch-fire. She turned to go back upstairs, watching me over her shoulder. I flashed on Candy and years ago. Something stirred. It died when I remembered Candy had never kissed me goodbye when we were kids.

99

DRIVING HOME, my black&white eyes were still working, but the images were reversed. Inside out. Inverted. For me, playing it safe wasn't playing—it was my life. I couldn't find the controls—nothing was where it had been. Terror said it was my partner, but I didn't have my old pal Fear to keep the nerve-endings sharp. Strega the witch was back in my life. Liars gave me their word, sociopaths gave me their trust. Dead people in my zone—some didn't know it yet. Some had my address. Users wanted my blood and vultures waited for my flesh. And I couldn't work up the adrenaline to get off the killing floor. Get off the track before the train came. It wasn't just my cock that wouldn't work. I didn't know if I was lost or gone. In the ground, with Belle.

Freaks use pornography on kids to desensitize them. Break down their natural resistance. Make them think this is the way things are. Drop the thresholds until they can step over them.

Maybe lies and loss work like that too. They don't take your soul, but they made it not worth fighting over.

Like when you're hijacking. You know you're going back to prison, you just don't know when.

It didn't seem so hard to find a way out. Just hard to give a fuck.

100

IN PRISON, I used to make lists. In my head. Draw a bright line down the middle of my mind. Pro and con. The two things I wanted to be.

Some fights you can't get in shape for. I was only in prison with Wesley one time. We kept missing each other on the exchanges. I heard he even went in the Army for a while—when Vietnam was hot and heavy and the judges would give you a pass if you enlisted. There was another guy in the joint with us at the same time. Dayton was his name. A gorilla. Iron-freak. He muscled off the weaker ones, did bodywork for the gangsters. Good time. He didn't seem to give a fuck, but he survived. A life charmed by strength and stupidity. I don't remember how he got into the dispute with Wesley, but I was on the yard with the Prof when it kicked off.

Wesley was standing against the wall. By himself, like always. Dayton rolled up on him. I didn't hear what they said to each other. Dayton grabbed Wesley by the front of his shirt, pulled him close, slapped him hard across the face. Wesley slumped, hands away from his body. Dayton left him there, walking away with his boys.

One of the young Italian guys standing with us laughed. "My man is about to be mondo dee-ceased," nodding his head at Wesley. He said it the same way they say dee-fense at pro football games. The Prof flashed his hustler's smile.

"It won't play the way you say. For one to five, I say my man comes out alive."

Within minutes, we'd booked twenty cartons of cigarettes against a hundred that Dayton wouldn't outlive Wesley.

It was a sucker bet. Dayton was a Dianabol freak. Snarfing the steroids the way other guys in the joint did Talwin, or Valium, or anything else the docs handed out to help you escape for a few hours. They made him massive—bigger than a human should be. When the hacks found him slumped over the pile of weights in the gym, there wasn't a mark on him. But his skin had a nice bluish tone to it. The guys who bet with us thought we got lucky behind an OD. The ones that stayed in prison long enough put it all together. By then, going up against Wesley was an out-bet.

101

MORALES braced me as I was coming out of Lily's joint. It had to happen—a pit bull would drop a bite sooner than Morales would walk away on the losing end. It would have been okay, but Max was with me. About four steps behind, in my shadow. Morales is about my height but he goes about two-twenty—none of it fat. He was a born head-cracker, not a gunman. That saved his life.

He snatched a handful of my jacket, shoved me face-first to the wall, running his rap, telling me if I was carrying I was going back to the joint . . . when he went dead-quiet. I looked back over my shoulder. Max had one hand on the cop's arm, the other at the back of his neck, bending him backward at an impossible angle. I spun off the wall, making a "drop it" sign to Max. Morales slumped to the sidewalk. I jammed my thumb back in a hitchhiking gesture, twirling my hand, telling Max to disappear.

I knelt next to Morales. He was trying to catch his breath and draw his gun off his right hip with his left hand at the same time—the right arm hung limp and useless at his side.

"You want me to get it for you?" I asked him.

"Cocksucker!" Almost sobbing with the effort.

"Take it easy. You're okay."

"You're not."

"I already know that. Am I under arrest?"

People passed us on the sidewalk. Nobody stopped. I tried to help him to his feet. His eyes were somewhere between rage and pain. Rage won. He fired the elbow of his good arm at my chest. I stepped back and he chopped air. I left him there. Went back to the wall. Stood facing it. Waiting.

Heard him get to his feet, muscles tightening over my kidneys. Felt the barrel of his pistol jam me just where I expected it. Didn't hurt any less.

"Get in the car."

I walked in front of him. His car was empty. He opened the passenger door. I got in. Watched him walk around to the driver's side. His gun was back in his holster.

"You're under arrest. Assault on a police officer. You have the right to . . ."

"Save it. Do what you have to do. You know I never touched you."

"Not you. Your pals. Whoever they were. I never saw them. But you . . . you're gonna tell me who they are. Where to find them. Right?"

"I didn't see anything. I was facing the wall."

"That's the way you want it?"

"I don't want *any* of this. It's you who want things. Things happened, they happen. Whatever you think, I didn't write the script."

"I heard things about you," he said. Lighting a cigarette with the dashboard lighter, not offering me one. "From my partner. He said you were a man. That you could be trusted. We go in on a thing with you—and you Pearl Harbor us—leave us with our dicks in our hands."

"You ever rap a guy in the head with your nightstick when you were in uniform?"

He didn't say anything—that was my answer.

"What if the guy had an eggshell skull? What if he died?"

"Never happen."

"You mean it never *happened*. There's a difference, right? It *could* happen. And you wouldn't have meant it to come down like that. But the guy would be just as dead."

"You saying that's what happened with you in the massage parlor?"

"I don't know what you're talking about. I'm just saying . . . you plan things . . . sometimes the wheels come off. You do the best you can with it. Survive."

"We found out some things. Since everything blew up in Times Square. The guy we found in pieces in the construction site—there was a contract out on him."

"I don't know . . ."

"Yeah, you don't know what I'm talking about, hit man. I didn't think that was your side of the street."

"It's not."

"There's a mob contract out on a guy. The guy gets dead. We know you did it. We're supposed to think it was personal?"

"Think what you want—that's what you *been* doing."

"Give it another spin."

"Not a chance. You keep playing me for something I'm not. You pulled my jacket—you know I'm not a soldier. I'm not a hired killer, and I'm not stupid."

"We got you tied into that skell. The one that got iced in the playground."

"That was the charge I was arrested on. So how come I'm on the street?"

"I look like a fucking pansy judge to you? You think I give a fuck about probable cause?"

"You say that to say what?"

"We weren't going to be pals, Burke. But you don't want me for an enemy."

"Amen."

"So give me something."

I lit a smoke. Used my own matches. Watching the color drift back into his face. His right arm still hung limp.

"I'll give you something, Morales. I'll give you a couple of things. On the house. One, your source. The one who you say tied me into some homicide in a playground. And the one who told you about a contract on a guy you found in Times Square. They're the same man. The same *family* man. Two, you fucking *know* he's a liar."

"So you say."

"Save it for the first offenders, cop. You believed this guy, you'd take me down. Like you said, we're not pals. But I know you. You thought it was me, you sincerely thought I burned you and McGowan, you'd flake me with a piece instead of just selling me wolf tickets about carrying one."

A smile twisted on his face. "You sure?"

"Yeah."

"Say you're right . . . just to be saying it, okay? What's in it for this guy who dropped a dime on you?"

I crossed my hands in front of my chest, one finger pointing at Morales, the other to my door. "He did it. Not me."

"Yeah. But we weren't looking at this guy. He wasn't a suspect."

"He would be, you kept at it. A cold wind's gonna blow."

"Torenelli's daughter?"

"I look Italian to you?"

"When I thought you were okay, you looked sorta Spanish to me. Now . . . now you look Italian."

"I never meant to offend you. I'm not against you. I just want to do my time. On the street, in the jail, wherever. Just do my time. Be left alone."

"That kind of privacy . . . it costs."

"I can't pay what I don't have. And I don't borrow."

"You already owe something."

"If I do . . . if I get the chance, I'll pay it off. Square it up. Ask around. I pay my debts."

"I think you paid at least a couple. I find out you did it for cash, I'll get you. That's a promise."

I threw my smoke out the window. "So I'm not busted?"

He didn't say anything when I opened the door and climbed out.

102

I wasn't under surveillance. The cops don't have the manpower for that, and Morales was still with the Runaway Squad anyway. He'd probably been prowling Lily's joint, watching to see if any of the kiddie pimps he hated so much were working the corners. When he saw me, he couldn't pass it up.

The phone man was where he said he'd be. We passed each other on the steps of the Federal Courthouse in Foley Square. A quick handshake and we each had what we came for.

103

I was in Mama's arguing with Max over his stunt with Morales when the phone rang in the back.

"Young girl," Mama said, sitting down.

I picked up the receiver. "What?"

"It's me. Elvira. You said to call today. I told you I would."

"I need to talk to you. About your mother. About Train."

"Go ahead."

"Not on the phone."

"Maybe you can come here. I'll ask . . ."

"Never mind. I can come there, but I want to talk in private. Tell me where you'll be, I'll pick you up."

"I'm not sure . . ."

"Not sure where you'll be or . . ."

"I'm not leaving here."

"Elvira, I wanted you out of there, you'd be out of there. I'm going to talk with you, one way or the other."

"I'm not afraid of you."

"I don't want you to be afraid of me. I want to talk to you."

"And then . . ."

"And then you go back to wherever you want to go. And you never see me again. Okay?"

A long pause. I wondered who else was listening, signaling to her.

"Okay," she finally said into the phone. "Where and when?"

"Tomorrow morning. On the corner of Flatbush and Tillary. The Brooklyn side of the Manhattan Bridge. Ten o'clock."

"How long will I be?"

"Couple of hours."

"Goodbye," she said. Hung up.

104

NEXT MORNING, the Plymouth an anonymous hulk lurking just outside the remnants of the commuter traffic stream. Max in the back seat, black wool Navy watch cap on his head, heavy gloves on his hands. He was only wearing a gray sweatshirt—it wasn't that cold out.

She must have walked from Train's building. I spotted her a couple of blocks away, stone-washed jeans, a dungaree jacket, hair in a pony-tail. A kid cutting school. I stepped out of the car, waved to her. She broke into a clumsy little trot.

I opened the passenger door and she climbed inside, Max moving in behind her like water flowing over a rock. "Huh!" she said, surprised. I was sitting in the driver's seat by then.

"Elvira, this is my brother, Max."

She snuck a sideways look, mumbled "Hi," eyes downcast. I fired up the Plymouth, heading over the bridge.

"Where're we going?"

"To see a friend of mine."

"How come *he's* here."

"Just along for the ride."

"I thought we were going to talk private."

"Max can't hear. He's deaf."

"For real?" An off-key note in her voice.

"Yeah. For real."

We came off the bridge into Chinatown, tunneling through the narrow back streets to Lily's. Elvira fumbled in her purse, brought out a cigarette. Max snapped a wooden match, held it for her. She said "Thank you" in a finishing-school voice. Max bowed slightly. "Does that mean 'You're welcome'?" she asked.

"Yep."

"Can you . . . talk to him?"

"His name is Max. I can talk to him. So can you, you want to bad enough."

"Oh! How?"

"Think of what you want to say, then act it out. Like charades."

"Can I try?"

"Go ahead."

She curled her feet under her, tapped Max on his forearm. Pointed at him, then at me. Pinched her shoulders against her slender neck, spread her hands, palms up. Max pulled off his gloves, tossed them on the dashboard. Watching her face closely, he pointed at himself, then at me. Waited for her to nod. He tapped his chest over his heart. Reached past the girl, tapped me in the same place. Hard. The finger curled into a fist. The fist slammed into his open hand. That hand wrapped around the fist. The two hands twisted together until the fingers were intertwined.

"He *is* your brother!"

"Sure."

Elvira put her two hands on an imaginary steering wheel, pointed to me, pointed out the windshield, made a questioning look at Max. He shrugged his shoulders, pointed at me, nodded.

"He doesn't know where we're going?"

"He doesn't care. He's with me—that's where he's going."

105

We PULLED up behind Lily's. Max got out. He'd go inside, tell them to open the back door for us.

I lit another smoke, offering her one. "There's a woman inside. Her name's Lily. She's a good friend. Of me and Max both. She's the one I want you to talk to, okay?"

"About what?"

"She'll do that part. All you have to do is what you say you always do . . . tell the truth."

"Is she gonna ask me about Train?"

"Not the way Reba asks questions."

I got a blank look back. Train didn't tell all his people how his fleshy polygraph worked.

"Never mind," I told her. "Lily's a certified social worker. You know what that is?"

"Like a shrink?"

"Yeah, sort of. Anyway, the point is that she's not allowed to repeat anything she's told. Anything you say to her is confidential. That's the law."

"But . . ."

"Elvira, listen to me, little girl. You think any of those kids running around in karate outfits could stop Max? This talk with Lily—it's for you. I know you don't understand that. I know you don't trust me. You don't have to. We made a deal. I took you out of Train's joint and I let you go back. He can't stop me and my friends. I have to find out some things and I want Lily to talk with you. You do that and we're done."

"What if I don't?" Not pouting, curious.

"Then I'm going to ask Train."

"He said you'd be back. He's never wrong."

"You think about that. You decide *how* I'm coming back." I'd been searching for the right button. Tried one more. "You want to protect Train, talking to Lily's the way to do it, understand?"

"My mother . . ."

"Is *out* of this."

"She says you're hers. Her old boyfriend."

"What does Train say?"

"How did you . . . ? He said you were nobody's child. That's what he said: 'That man is nobody's child.' "

"You know what he meant?"

"Maybe."

I threw my smoke out the window.

"I'll talk to her," the girl said finally.

The back door opened and I led her inside.

106

INTRODUCED Lily and Elvira. Watched for the hundredth time as waves came off Lily, enveloping the kid, excluding me. "She has a calm center," Immaculata explained it to me once. "Like Max." They walked down the hall together.

Max was probably in the gym, wrestling with the kids. That wasn't for me. I had some time to kill, so I found an empty office, put my feet on the desk, closed my eyes. I had things to think about.

When I opened my eyes, Immaculata was sitting on the desk, her hand on my ankle.

"You're awake?"

"Sure."

"Burke, I don't have much time to talk. You must let Max help you. It is very important."

"Help me what?"

"Whatever it is you're doing. It doesn't matter."

"Yeah, big fucking help *he* is. You know what he did yesterday?"

"He told me."

"He tell you he almost turned a lousy roust into a Class A felony?"

"Max is your brother. He is in great pain. Men don't know how to take some things. Some gifts. He cannot forget what you did. To save our baby. What it cost you. He must believe he is helping you or he cannot feel whole."

"Mac, you know what Max does?"

"I am his wife. He is the father of our child. You remember when we met?"

I remembered. A night subway run. Me carrying the goods, dressed like a bum. The Mole at the other end of the train, a satchel full of explosives. And Max the Silent sitting across from me, looking like a tired, drained old man. Three punks got on the train. Looked me over.

Wouldn't bother with a wino. Started on Max. Asking him for ten bucks for a cup of coffee, shoving him around. No big deal—we only had a couple of more express stops to go. It was going okay until Immaculata saw the action. Dressed like a Vietnamese bar girl, as out of place on that subway as a clock in a casino. She charged the punks, telling them to leave the old man alone. One pulled out a pair of brass knuckles, giggling at the new prey. Max took them all out quicksilver-fast—just flashes and sounds. He shed his filthy raincoat and the tired old man became the Mongol warrior. Bowed deeply to the woman who had come to save him. He signed, I interpreted. She saw past his strength, he past her beauty. They've been together since.

"I don't care what it takes." Her voice soft and relentless. "Is that clear enough for you? I want my husband back. His daughter needs him back. You know what he is. If you tell a true warrior he cannot make things right, his duty is to die trying."

I lit a smoke, playing for time. Her eyes stabbed. "Don't try and trick me. I know you could do it. For *now*. Max even said so—how you can lie so smoothly."

"How can I . . . ?"

"There is a man you went to see. Your enemy. Max has no fear of him, this little killer with his guns."

"Mac, I'm telling you the truth. Believe it or don't, it's still the truth. The man you're talking about . . . he's not my enemy. I don't know how I know . . . I'm not even sure I knew until I just said it. But I'm not gaming to protect Max."

"You must let him help you." Intractable. No slack in the rope.

"What am I supposed to do?"

"Let him help you find what you're looking for."

"What I *lost*."

"No. What you seek. Please."

She bent forward, kissed me lightly on the cheek. Her perfume stayed after her.

107

MAX WALKED IN, kids hanging on him like amateur mountain climbers. Before I could say a word, Lily pushed past Max, holding Elvira's hand. She gave me a "stay where you are" look. Told Elvira, "Go with Max. I have to talk to Burke for a minute before he takes you back."

Elvira obediently held out her hand. It disappeared in Max's. He went back toward the gym, leaving a wake of rowdy kids running to catch up.

I lit a smoke. Lily sat down. Her voice had that distanced, professional tone she uses when the anger laps at the boundaries of her self-control.

"Post-Traumatic Stress Disorder. Long-standing. Original stressor undoubtedly the mother. Compounded by numerous instances of sexual exploitation so frequent that they merged into a real-world distortion pattern. Amoral, almost sociopathic aura to her productions. She imitates affect, but has very little sense of feeling things. Nerve-endings blunted. Some indication of Borderline Syndrome too. She actually . . . physically feels a void inside of her. Relates to mother almost as a rival. Tested clean on the MMPI Lie Scale. Telling the truth. Guiltless. Heavily bonded to this Train individual. And she's pregnant, maybe two, three months gone."

I let her see my eyes, willing her to relax. "All that means . . . ?"

"I don't have time for games, Burke. You know damn well what every single word I said means. You've spent years studying. Just because it wasn't in college doesn't make you a stupid thug."

I held up my hands. "Okay, okay. I wasn't being cute. I meant . . . what's the bottom line? Where she is: it's better than being with her mother?"

"There's no *better* to any of this. Where she is now is just one of the places kids like her end up. Nobody wants you, so you hit the streets. And there, somebody always wants you. For something. They prove they want you by paying you money. A child like that, she couldn't tell a rescue mission from a cult."

"Is she being abused now?"

"Not in her mind. She's working for this wonderful goal. This island they're going to buy someplace. Where they can all live in peace . . . a big, loving family."

"Yeah, like every pimp is going to let his woman retire someday. Open up her own boutique, right? They have her turning tricks?"

Lily's eyes were dark, soulful. Little dots glowing like plutonium around the iris. Holding something in check.

"No. She was in Germany. Making porno movies. But she's too old now."

"Fifteen."

"Yes, fifteen. All she could bring in as a prostitute would be a couple of hundred a day. And she'd have to work outdoors, take a lot of risks. Train doesn't let his people take risks. No, she's not turning tricks . . . they're breeding her."

"What?"

"Breeding her. Like a brood mare. She told me she was 'mated' to one of the young men in the cult. When she has her baby, Train's going to sell it. You know the going rate for a healthy white baby with a solid medical history, educated parents, the whole works?"

"Fifty K and up."

"Yes."

"Doesn't she want the baby?"

"She doesn't want *any* baby. She expects to have a baby a year for a few years. So Train will love her. He takes the best of care of her. A special diet, exercise, regular visits to a doctor."

"The boys . . . he can't use them all for breeding."

"She's so cold about it, it's frightening. She says boys are worth more than girls. They can earn money even when they're old . . . she means like eighteen, nineteen. They go on the circuit too. The boy she mated with, he was in Amsterdam for a few years, then he came back here to work."

"She told you a lot."

"Don't you get it? She doesn't see anything wrong with it! You know what the words mean. She's not a child in her soul. Hasn't been for a long time. It's *all* okay. Train saved her. He saved all of them."

"She tell you about Danielle?"

"Yes. And she told me you brought Danielle back to her father. Don't blame yourself."

"You think it's true, then?"

"Oh yes. All true."

Wesley's voice in my mind: "They didn't pay me." Somebody owed me too. "Isn't she afraid Train will do something to her when he finds out she talked?"

"She's not afraid. She thinks you're a criminal. She says Train knows you. He's in control. Two of the young men, they're his bodyguards. She says they took one of the girls out of there when the girl went crazy. She wouldn't answer my questions about it—she just assumes the girl is dead. And she says her mother knows you too."

"So she thinks . . ."

"I don't know what's going on in that damaged brain of hers. She thinks you and her mother want to blackmail Train, or that you're going to work for Train, or you have your own organization like Train's . . . or God knows what. It's a simple world to her: the big fish eat the smaller fish. They eat enough little fish, they grow into big fish themselves. Here's what she said: 'Everybody gets used. The way to keep from getting used *up* is to learn to be use*ful*.'"

"That's not her line."

"No. But she recites it like a fundamentalist quoting the Bible."

"You said she was bonded to Train . . . sounds more like bondage than bonding."

"It isn't. The bonding is real. Train is real to her. He saved her.

Remember that. She's a bright girl. She knows her life was short on the streets. Drugs, a trick with a razor, a sadistic pimp . . . it doesn't take much to snuff out a candle in a hurricane."

Homicide danced in my mind. "Rescue me." My blue Belle. That was all she'd asked. I took her off the runway and into the ground. Like I took Danielle from her pimp. I ground out my smoke with the tip of my boot. Lily was too focused to even frown at me.

"What happens to her if Train goes down?"

She shrugged. "Elvira would find another."

"There's no place for her?"

"A psychiatric hospital. A prison, maybe. No place good."

"What should I do?"

Lily's hands went to her hips, titanium threads in her soft voice. "You brought her to me for a reason. To find out some things. Are your questions answered?"

"Yeah. Are you making any calls?" Lily was best pals with Wolfe, the head of the City-Wide Special Victims Unit. Wolfe was part of the tribe of warrior-women in the city. I'd met a few of them over the years. Catherine, the beautiful social worker in City-Wide's office who specialized in elderly victims. Storm, the brand-new head of the hospital's Rape Crisis Unit. Queenie, an investment banker who left her lizard briefcase and upscale outfits at home when she volunteered at Lily's joint on weekends. All of them not taking prisoners, slugging it out aboveground. Where it's legal. Where the light doesn't shine for men like me. Wolfe had crossed the line with me once. Just for a minute in time. Then she dropped my hand and went back to her life. I wouldn't ask her again.

"Should I?" she asked.

"Can you stay quiet for a bit?"

"I'm a mandated reporter. The law requires that I report every case of suspected child abuse that comes before me in my professional capacity."

"You just did."

"I'm calling it into the Hot Line. But I don't know her full name or her address."

"Okay."

"I *will* know, Burke. And then I have to call Wolfe."

"Okay."

"*When* will I know."

"Ten days, two weeks."

I lit another smoke, waiting for her answer. So much for me to carry. Dead weight. Unreasonable anger flared in me. Lily, she could do the right thing, sleep easy. She walked the line. Part of me wanted to pull her over it.

"Lily, can I consult you in your professional capacity? As a client?"

"Sure." Absentminded, still thinking about waiting to call the Hot Line.

"I have a problem that's affecting my mental state."

"What?" Impatiently.

"I'm going to kill someone."

She got it. Never flinched. "Ten days, Burke. It's too late for Elvira, but not for the others . . . not for all of them."

But for my love.

108

ELVIRA WAS quiet, sitting between Max and me on the way back.

"Your friend Lily . . . she was nice."

"But you know it was all game, right?"

She flashed the no-soul smile of a little girl who learned to do tricks too soon. I pulled up outside Train's place. Max stepped out, holding the door for Elvira like a chauffeur.

"Tell Train I'll be around to see him soon," I told the girl. "I won't be taking you back. Just one last talk. I want to part friends. Tell him, he'll know what I mean."

She turned to face me. "Did my mother kiss you goodbye the last time you saw her?"

"No."

She slid off the seat without a word. I didn't look back.

109

MAX DIDN'T react when I passed by Mama's. Didn't change expression when I cruised by his warehouse. I knew the look on his face. Whatever. It. Takes.

I backed the Plymouth into the last slot in the loading bay of what had been a factory years ago. When the landlord rented it out for lofts, he left the last piece to use as a private garage. When I explained to the landlord that his son's identity was safe with me, he gave me a hell of a break on the rent. Free. Threw in the garage too.

We took the back stairs to my office. Max stood well aside as I opened the door. I threw Pansy the signal—she waited patiently to see what I'd brought her. The beast watched Max with her homicide eyes, a soft growl just inside her teeth. Talking about him the way he had talked about Wesley.

Anytime. Anytime you want.

They'd known each other for years. Max never patted her. She never bothered him. He bowed to Pansy, no expression on his face. Pansy watched.

I got her some liverwurst out of the refrigerator, gave her the magic word, watched it vanish. She stretched out in a corner by the couch, bored. I crossed over to my desk, cleared a place so I had a flat, blank table. Gestured for Max to sit in the chair I use for clients.

He made a gesture like he was dealing cards. I shook my head. Our life-sentence gin game wasn't going to be continued tonight.

What was the truth? My promise to Immaculata? Or could Max really know? Why didn't it hurt me more . . . like it should have? How come? Bad pun.

How to explain it? I lit a smoke. Put it on the lip of the ashtray, folding my hands behind my head, looking at the cracked cement ceiling. Max reached over, put the cigarette to his lips, took a deep drag. Smoke fired out his flat nose in two broad jets.

I pointed at myself. Put my hands under the desk, tried to lift it off the floor. Strained. Gave it up. Too much weight for me to lift.

Max hooked two fingers under the desk. It came off the Astroturf I use for carpet like it was floating.

I shook my head. It wasn't a weight someone could lift for me.

He spread his hands. "What?"

I drew an hourglass figure in the air. Made my right forefinger rigid, poked it into an opening I made in my left fist. Again and again. Okay?

He nodded, watching.

I pointed at my chest. At my heart. Stiffened the forefinger. Approached the opening in my fist. The forefinger went limp. Wouldn't go in. Pointed at myself again.

Max pointed at me. Smiled. I was joking, right?

Wrong.

He made an hourglass sign of his own. Made a "no good" gesture. Drew another in the air. Opened his hands. Try another woman.

I drew another woman. Another. One more. Pointed at myself again. Stiffened the forefinger—let it sag limp. It was me, not the women. Me.

He pointed at his groin, shook his head. Tapped his skull. That's where the problem was.

I nodded. Yeah, so?

He pointed at an old calendar on my wall. Since when?

I made the sign of a pistol firing. Looked at the ground. Blew a goodbye kiss. Since Belle.

He made an "it's okay" gesture. Tapped my wristwatch. It would get better.

No.

His face closed. He went off somewhere inside himself, looking. I smoked, watched my dog, let my sad eyes play over this miserable little place I lived in. The last time Belle was there, it had sparkled.

Max got up, went by himself into the back room. Pansy tracked him. Once you got in, you could move around. You just couldn't leave until I told her it was okay. Nothing back there but a hot plate and the refrigerator. Toilet, sink, and stall shower. I waited. He came back with two paper packets of sugar, the kind they give you in diners. Put them both on the desk, side by side. Tapped one closed eye. Pay attention.

He pointed at me. Tore open one of the packets. Emptied it into his palm. Tossed the sugar into the air. Wiped his hands. All gone. Looked at me.

I nodded. Yeah, that was it.

He shook his head. No. Took the other packet and put it in my desk drawer. Pointed at the desk top. Nothing there. Still gone?

I opened the drawer. Took out the other packet.

The warrior nodded. Took it from my hand. Slipped it into my coat pocket. Patted me down like a cop doing a search. Pulled out the packet, held it up to the light. Made a gesture, "get it?"

No.

He took the packet, walked over to the couch. Stuffed it under one of the cushions. Looked around the room, confused look on his face. Where is it?

I pulled it free from under the cushion, held it in my hand.

Watched my brother, watched his eyes. He'd said all he could.

Then I got it. Hell of a difference between something lost and something missing. It wasn't gone—I just didn't know where I'd put it.

I bowed to Max.

He took the packet from my hand. Pointed to my chair. I sat down. He made frantic searching gestures, opening drawers, looking under stacks of paper, rapping the walls with his knuckles, looking for a hiding place. Shook his head. No. Not that way. He leaned back, put his feet on the desk, closed his eyes, folded his hands over his stomach. Pointed at me. I imitated him. It was peaceful lying there. Safe and peaceful. I wondered if the fear-jolts would come back someday too. I hated them so when I was young and doing time. Wished them away. It never worked. Back then, when I wanted to be somebody I couldn't be. Something Candy always knew I wasn't.

Something brushed my face. I opened my eyes. The packet of sugar was lying on my chest. Waiting.

Which is what I had to do.

It would come to me.

I held a clenched fist in front of my face. Yes!

Max tapped my fist with his own.

Sparking flame to light the way.

110

WHEN I got back to the office after dropping Max off, I let Pansy out to her roof. Turned on the radio. A car bombing out in Ozone Park, Queens. A soldier and an underboss splattered. I had some rye toast and ginger ale, thinking I might like to bet on a horse when this was all over.

Pansy came back inside. I worked on her commands for a half hour or so, just to keep her sharp. Like oiling a gun. Then I went to sleep.

The radio was still on when I woke up around ten o'clock that night. Another bombing, this one in Bushwick, Brooklyn. The wise-guys would be paying people to start their cars for a while.

I went into the street. Called Strega. She was right by the phone, like she knew.

"It's me. You find out?"

"I think so. I'll be sure by tomorrow night."

I hung up. Called Mama. Nothing from Morehouse, the lazy bastard.

Dialed the Mole. Heard the phone picked up. The Mole never speaks first. "I need a car," I said. "You got one?"

"Yes." Terry's voice. The connection went dead.

Terry let me into the junkyard. I slid over and he took the wheel, guiding the Plymouth through the maze to a resting place.

"They still fighting?" I asked the kid.

"Mole says Mom has to make her own decision."

"He tell *her* that?"

"No. But she knows."

The Mole was working in one of the Quonset huts he has scattered around the place. No windows, but it was as well-lit as an operating table. A tired-looking Ford four-door sedan was in pieces on the floor.

"What're you doing, Mole?" I greeted him.

"Working." Mr. Personality.

I remembered the counsel the Prof had given me when I was a kid first learning to do time. Watch. Watch and learn. Pay attention or pay the price. I sat down on an old engine block, lit a smoke.

Terry worked with the Mole like gears meshing. Nothing wasted, quick and clean. Each of them took an end of the Ford's back seat. They slid it back into place. I heard a sharp click. The boy shoved harder, using his shoulder. Another click. The rocker panels were off. I saw what looked like a long, thin shock absorber running parallel to the ground. Where the running board would be if they still used them on cars. The Mole fitted a short length of track between the back and front seats. Fiddled around in the trunk. A sound like something being released. I went closer, peered over his shoulder. The back of the front seat was a solid-steel plate, ugly welds slashed across the corners. The front seat was welded to the chassis around the bottom seams. A brick wall.

The Mole signaled to Terry. They each took an end of the back seat, slid it back and forth on the runners. It reached all the way to the welded steel plate. Terry sprayed the runners with silicon.

"We'll test it," the Mole said.

Terry pointed to a pile of green plastic garbage bags stacked against the wall. "Give us a hand, Burke."

I picked one up. Heavy. Maybe sixty pounds. "How many you need?" I asked.

"Six?" the boy said, looking at the Mole. He nodded, absorbed.

I took a sack in each hand, brought them over to the car. Terry wrapped both arms around one sack and followed me. The Mole watched. One more trip each and we had them all.

"What now?" I asked.

The Mole pointed at the back seat. "Four there, two in front."

I loaded them in. Terry struggled until he had one sack on top of another. Two big lumps in the back, one in the front, behind the wheel. Driver and two passengers.

The Mole threaded a wire from the dashboard through the open car window. Backed up until we were against the wall. He stripped the wire, wound it around a terminal on the workbench.

"Stand back," he said.

The back seat shot forward like it was fired from a rocket launcher, slamming into the steel wall. The car rocked on its tires. The back seat bounced off the steel plate, floating listlessly on the siliconed tracks. We went to take a look. The four green plastic bags were plastered to the steel wall like paint on canvas. It smelled of old smeared death. In the front, the top bag had hit the steering wheel and ripped open. White suet mess inside, blood-streaked.

"It works," the Mole said. "We have to tighten the front seat braces."

I stepped outside to get away from the smell. Waited for the Mole and Terry to join me.

The kid was first out. "What was that mess?" I asked him.

"Just fat they slice off the sides of beef in the meat market. They throw it out in big tubs. The Mole says it's pretty much like people, only without the bones."

Michelle would love it. The Mole lumbered out into the night air.

I looked over my shoulder at the car. "How does it work?"

"Two hydraulic pumps. Compressed air. When you hit the trigger, the back seat releases from the catches and slides forward on the tracks. Very fast. Into the wall behind the front seat."

"So if anyone's sitting in the back seat . . . ?"

"Crushed. No escape."

"And the driver."

"Once it's strengthened, no problem. If you wear a seat belt."

I dragged deep on my cigarette, thinking about what my family had been telling me. About not acting like myself. Thinking about insurance. "Mole, could I borrow that car?"

"It has to be cleaned. Then we have to reset the trigger, wire it to a button on the dash, put slipcovers over the front seat. A lot of work. This was just an experiment."

"But you could do it."

"Yes." He hesitated. "The car, it's a killing machine. For Nazis."

"Mole, you know about Wesley. You know he's back and . . ."

"I know."

"Well? Can I . . . ?"

The Mole's lumpy body stiffened as he looked up into my eyes. "Wesley's not a Nazi, Burke."

"Mole . . ."

"What he does, it's not for freakish fun. Not like them."

"You're saying he's like . . . us?"

"More like us than them," he said as he walked away, the kid trailing behind.

I left the Plymouth in the junkyard. Switched it for a dark blue Buick sedan with clean plates.

By the time I stashed the car in my garage it was four in the morning.

I let Pansy out to her roof one more time. Then I went back to sleep.

III

I WAS IN the restaurant early the next morning. Mama brought me a copy of the *Daily News*. The headline said "Sniper Killing on Staten Island." A middleweight mobster had been shot late last night in the living room of his home in Todt Hill. Watching television with his wife. All she heard was glass breaking. A neat hole in his head, right at the hairline. Police said the sniper must have worked his way onto the grounds, lain prone, and fired at a slight upward angle. There were a half dozen pieces about who the guy was, speculation about what it all meant.

Morehouse was on the money with his column. All the Strike Force charts and graphs don't mean a thing when there's a wild card in the deck. He ended it nicely: "Once the feeding frenzy starts, it doesn't matter where you rank in the food chain."

112

THE REPORTER finally called. Mama took the message. I rang him back.

"You got it?"

"Sure."

"Meet me . . ."

"Oh, man. Why can't you be civilized once? You know my address, come to my house."

"Not tonight."

"Okay, man. Talk to me. Be quick now, I got work to do."

"Tomorrow morning. Eleven o'clock. You know where the guys work on their cars under the FDR? Like around Thirty-third?"

"Sure."

"I'll be there."

He made a disgusted noise. Hung up.

113

NIGHTTIME. Strega's time. Could there be a good witch? Compared with Candy, Strega was as pure as driven snow. The kind they drive across the border in ten-kilo shrink-wrapped packages. Ice-pure.

I drove into Queens. Dialed her number from a pay phone.

"I'm waiting for you," was how she answered.

The empty spot in her garage was like the impression your body leaves when you get out of bed. The Buick fit.

She stepped into the garage as I closed the car door. Wearing a steel-gray seamless sheath that stopped at mid-thigh. Matching spikes. A single strand of black pearls. Her hair was wild, face scrubbed clean. Not quite ready to go out on the town. She took my hand, pulling me up the stairs. "Let's tell secrets," she whispered.

The living room was dark, pierced by thin beams from the track lighting mounted on the ceiling. The smoke from my cigarette spiraled up into the light.

She took my coat, slipped it off my shoulders, tossed it on the couch. Sat next to me.

"You don't carry a gun anymore?"

"Julio fixed that. I'm out on bail. I can't afford a fall."

"It doesn't matter. You don't need a gun here—it's safe."

"No man's safe around you."

She smiled a witch's smile—rheostated. "You're mine. I never hurt what's mine. Remember Scotty? Remember why I needed you? I never let anyone hurt what's mine. You wouldn't let anyone hurt me either. I know you."

Yeah, everybody knows me. "We had a deal," I said. "I kept my piece, you kept yours. This is another. Another deal."

"I know. I found him. The compound in Sands Point. It's out on the Island. It's a fortress, soldiers all over the place. Dogs. Electronic stuff. He stays in the basement. Julio said even if you dropped a bomb on the place, the don would be okay."

"Great."

"He can't even talk on the phone. He's too scared. He told Julio this man . . . Wesley? . . . is the devil. The real, real devil. He's going mad in his stone basement. He won't watch television—he thinks this man can see him through the screen. Julio, he thinks it's funny—the don would pay a million dollars for Wesley's head, but he doesn't even know what he looks like."

"Julio saw the don?"

"Oh yes. At the compound. Julio's got his own plan. He's going to make Wesley dead. Do what the don couldn't do. Be the *boss*. He'll never be my boss again."

"So he wins no matter what happens?"

"That's what he thinks. Ugly evil old man. He feels strong when he thinks of the don cowering in his basement, afraid of the dark. But when he thinks of me, his strength is gone. That's why he has to go. He thinks it's my time. Time to free himself. But it's *his* time. I waited long enough."

"He's got to leave that basement sometime." Thinking of Train, safe in his house. With his human polygraph and his bodyguards who made little girls' bodies disappear.

She leaned into me, head against my chest. I'd never seen a black orchid, but then I knew what one smelled like. Her hand went to the inside of my thigh. "I'll tell you a secret now. In the chair."

"Jina . . ."

"Please."

Such a strange word from a witch. I sat in the big chair. She squirmed into my lap, lips against my neck. I heard every word, like she was talking into my brain.

"The don can't stay in the basement. He'd lose it all. The others, they'd know. And you know what happens then. When you drop the leash, the dog bites. So every Monday night, he meets with his captain. On the Fifty-ninth Street Bridge."

"How do they work it?"

"The captain's boys park on the Manhattan side. The don's boys park on the Queens side. Then they *walk* across. Soldiers in front, soldiers behind. They do their business and they go back."

"Every Monday night."

"At one in the morning."

She turned sideways so her thigh was across my lap. "I'm a good girl," she whispered in that witchy little girl's voice. Reaching for my crotch. Nobody home.

"Let the beast out," she said. "I know what to do with him."

"Ssssh," I said in the darkness. Patting her just above her hips, stroking her back. "It doesn't matter. There is no beast. You *are* a good girl, Jina."

Her hand came away from my crotch, pulled gently at a button on my shirt. "Sleepy," she said.

I shifted my weight. Her skirt rode up. A faint trail of light on her stockings. I wrapped my other arm around her, rocked her gently. "It's okay, girl."

She took my thumb into her mouth. Didn't bite it this time, or suck on it. Just left it there, touching it with her tongue. Made a quiet noise in her throat.

I held her for a long time while she slept.

114

"WAKE UP," is the first thing I heard. She was still there, face softened by sleep, hair tousled.

"I'm awake."

"It'll be light soon. Time for you to go."

"Yeah."

She got off my lap, pulled her skirt down. Shook her hair loose. The sleep fled her eyes. She bent forward, face inches from mine. The witchy hiss was back. "Julio goes too."

I nodded.

115

I WAS AN HOUR early to the meet with Morehouse. Pansy prowled a tiny circle in front of the car while I was doing something under the hood. Nobody came close enough to find out what.

Morehouse pulled up in his Datsun, fifteen minutes late.

"I was looking for your other car, man. Been cruising the area for a half hour. I . . . what the fuck is that?"

"Pansy!" I snapped, throwing her a hand signal. She hit the deck, watching Morehouse like a Weight Watcher about to jump ship.

Morehouse's lip curled. "Was that a dog once? Before it swallowed a car?"

"I thought all West Indians loved dogs."

"No, man, you got it wrong. All West Indians *are* dogs. Just ask my girlfriend. Anyway, I got what you wanted."

"I just hope it's not that fairy story about the old man being holed up in a fortress in Sands Point."

Morehouse was too cool to give it all away, but his eyes slid away from me just far enough to let me know I'd hit the target. "Well, that's what's on the street."

"Yeah. And Donny Manes stabbed *himself* to death."

"Hey, man, that was the word. *Is* the word. From on high."

"From on the pad."

"I didn't say that."

"Okay. Thanks anyway."

"That's it?"

"What else is there?"

"Our trade, man. What is wrong with you? I'm not done—I can still come up with the winner. Italians dropping like World War II out there. You were right. Something's coming. And I want to be in the paper with it first."

"I get it, you'll get it, okay? I may have something else for you too. Interested in a cult that traffics in babies?"

"Adoption ring?"

"No. A breeder farm. Using little girls just about old enough to bleed."

"You know I am."

"Want to help out?"

"How?" Suspicion all over his face.

"Switch cars with me."

"What would you want with this old wreck?" he asked, waving his hand at his city-beater.

I pointed at his license plates. NYP. New York Press. Everyone in this city has special plates: doctors, dentists, chiropractors. Everybody but lawyers—it wouldn't be safe for them. "Your plates go anywhere. And even the Italians won't dust a reporter."

"What's this got to do with the baby-seller?"

"Everything."

He reached in his pocket. Tossed me his keys. "Registration's in the glove compartment."

"Mine too."

Morehouse was born to be a reporter. He walked to the Buick, opened the door, one eye on Pansy. He pulled the papers out of the glove box. "Who's Juan Rodriguez?"

"Quién quiere saber?"

He laughed.

I snapped my fingers, opened the door to Morehouse's wreck. Pansy launched herself into the back seat. "I'll call you," I told him.

He stood close to me, voice low. "Burke, there's one thing they say about West Indians that *is* true. We *do* love children."

116

I PARKED Morehouse's car behind the restaurant, let myself in through the kitchen. Stashed Pansy in the basement. Grabbed the pay phone. Rang Wesley's number. Three times. Hung up.

I was on my second helping of soup when the phone rang.

"What?"

"Time to meet."

"You got it?"

"Yeah."

"Tonight. Same deal."

"Right."

"Bring the Chinaman."

When Max came in, I was working on a plate of fried rice with Mongolian ginger-beef. I told him we had a meeting that night. He had his own sign for Wesley: an X drawn in salt spilled on the table.

Mama gave me a gallon container of steaming meat and vegetables to take down to Pansy.

Max showed me a copy of the racing form. I shook my head. No. Not yet. But when he dug out a deck of cards, it was okay. We played gin until it got dark. Immaculata came in with Flower. Max took the child from her, parading into the kitchen to show the assorted criminals working back there his prize.

"Hi, Mac."

She leaned over. Kissed me. "Max is back, Burke. I don't know what you . . ."

I held up my hand. "It's not over yet."

"It doesn't matter. Whatever happens." She bowed. As if to fate.

I took Pansy back to the office. Showered. Changed my clothes. Lit a smoke and watched the darkness outside my window.

117

MAX RAPPED a knuckle against the windshield as I pulled off the road. I looked where he pointed—a tiny Day-Glo orange dot glowing to the side. It blinked off as I watched. I braked gently, waiting. The light glowed again. Okay. We left the

Datsun by the side of the road, walked in the direction of the light, Max first.

Under the network of girders the wind made hunting sounds. The light didn't go on again, but Max walked like he was following a neon strip in the dark. He stopped when we came to a clearing in the jungle. Broken glass on the ground. Tire carcasses. Rotting pieces of car upholstery. Discarded furniture. Shipping crates. A bicycle without wheels. Max slapped his hand lightly against my chest. Stop. Here.

I lit a cigarette, tiny red light of my own. A siren screamed above us. An ambulance—racing the hospital against the morgue.

Wesley was in front of us, just a thin strip of his face showing.

"How's he do that?" he asked me.

"What?"

"He can't hear, right? But he don't make a sound when he moves."

"I don't know," I told him. Not blowing him off—it was the truth. "That's the real reason they call him Max the Silent."

"That isn't your car."

"Julio, he knows my car."

"Okay." Wesley sat down on one of the crates. I sat across from him. Max stayed where he was. Not watching Wesley, eyes sweeping the area.

"Tell him it's safe here," Wesley said. "I got trip wires strung all around except for the way you came in. And you're sitting on enough plastique to knock down the bridge."

"That's your idea of safe?"

"The cover's too thick. And if they charge, we all go together."

"Great."

Sarcasm is wasted on machines. "You got it?" he asked.

"The don is holed up. They have a compound of some kind in Sands Point."

"I know where it is."

"Yeah. But he never leaves the basement. And the place is set up like a bomb shelter."

"You sure?"

"Sure. He's scared to death. Won't even talk on the phone."

Wesley went as silent as Max. Time passed. Finally he spoke, voice just past a whisper but with no breath in it. "Fire fixes it."

"What?"

"The place burns bad enough, he has to come out."

"If he has it right, he won't have to. The place could burn to the ground, he'd still be okay in the basement. He has the cash to fix it that way. Some of those rich geeks, back in the fifties, they fixed up their basements like the Russians were going to drop the bomb any day. All the survival-freaks aren't living in the mountains. It wouldn't work."

"Yeah. Maybe you're right. I saw one of those basements once. Guy even had the place soundproofed."

"I got one more thing. The don, he has to meet his underboss. And he won't talk on the phone, remember? So every Monday night, he meets. On the Fifty-ninth Street Bridge."

"Out in the open?"

"Yeah." I told him what Strega told me. He made me go over it twice more, taking each word in a single bite, chewing it slowly.

"He probably stands behind the pillars . . . so even if we drove by in a car, there'd be nothing to shoot."

"Sure." Thoughts flashing. Who'd *drive* the damn car anyway?

His voice was calm, talking about the weather. "This was another time, it wouldn't matter. I got him in a box. I got nothing to do but wait. But I'm in a box too. I got to finish my work."

"And get paid?"

"They'll pay me. When my work is done, I'm all paid up."

"Julio, he still wants me to bring money to you. It'll be a trap, but . . ."

"No good. They wouldn't send the big guys. They try something, everybody gets blown up. We don't get to take them with us. Like when I was in the Army. The soldiers die, the generals find new soldiers."

"How come you didn't stay in the Army?"

"When I went in, I did it like doing time, right? Keep your mouth shut, stay out of trouble, wait till they open the gates. I didn't talk, so they figured I was stupid. I was a good shot too. So they make me a sniper. We had this platoon leader, some college kid. He talked to us like we were dogs. Nice dogs, dogs he *liked* and all. But stupid, you know? Especially the blacks. He made things simple for us. Every time we go out there, it's the fucking gooks keeping us from going home. To our *families* and all. One day, we're in a firefight. Charlie's winning—got too much juice for us. Time to split, come back another day. But this asshole, he wants us to hold our position. Wait for the choppers to spray the area. Or until they drop napalm on us. Four of our guys got wasted the last time they did that. It came to me. In a flash-second, didn't even think about it. We was supposed to kill gooks 'cause they was keeping us from going home, right? And now it was this lieutenant keeping us from going home. I put a few rounds into his chest. He goes down, I step up and yell, 'Retreat!' I'm the last one out. I got a Bronze Star for it. I had a good war record. So when they court-martialed me later they let me out with a dishonorable. No stockade time. I stuck up a liquor store the night I got back to the city. Everything went smooth, but the night clerk called the cops when I came back to the hotel. That's when I caught up with you again. In prison."

"What'd they court-martial you for?"

"I was in Japan. On R and R. In a bar. Some Marines got into a fight with some Navy guys. I was halfway out the door when one of them jumped me. I went down. Came back up, chopped the guy in the back of the head with this glass ashtray. He turned into a cripple behind it."

"An accident . . ."

"Didn't make no difference. I was glad to go. I'm not a soldier. Like the scams you run."

"You mean the mercenary thing?"

"Yeah. They talked to me once. Guys with British accents, only they ain't British. Fight communism, right? Sure. I don't fly nobody's flag."

"Does Julio know your face?"

"I don't have a face. I met him once. He gave me the go for this Mortay freak. But it was dark and he was scared—he couldn't pick me out of a lineup. It was like it is out here—you can't see much."

"He's part of this now."

"I know."

"No you don't. I made a trade. For the information I got. About the place in Sands Point. And the meeting on the bridge."

"You got to do Julio?"

"Yeah."

He went into himself. I could feel the edges go soft, merging with the darkness as the center hardened. I lit another smoke, cupping the tip. Max watched. He could feel the changes in the air like a blind coroner doing an autopsy.

"That's the one thing I know. Really know," the monster said. "Murders. In some countries, the leaders get whacked all the time. You know why? 'Cause the people doing the killings, they're not professionals. They're willing to fucking *die* to get something done. Trade their life for another. Over here, we never get *close*, you know. Only lunatics do it that way. Remember that guy who shot Reagan? I was that close to him, I'd have so much lead in his body they'd need a crane to get him off the ground. You kill people for money, you have to live to spend it."

"So?"

"Julio's no problem for me—he's a problem for you. Even if this informant of yours didn't want Julio dropped, you know he's setting you up. So it don't make a difference—he's gotta go. And the don—he's no problem for you, right? He don't even know you exist. And he don't care. You ever think of just taking me out . . . ? Max, he's close enough now. Maybe. You bring the don my head, you're off the hook."

"No. I never thought about it."

"You're a dancer, not a killer. You don't understand the way things work. Death makes it right. Wipes the slate clean."

"I wouldn't know." Thinking of Belle. Death hadn't made it all right. Not because the wrong man died—because the wrong man did the killing.

"I know a way to hit the don," Wesley said. "But I need three, four people to make it work. You got the people. You help me, I'll do Julio for you."

"It's just me and Max."

"He's in?"

"Yes."

"You got more people. More *brothers*."

"I have to ask. They're my brothers, not my soldiers."

Wesley's voice dropped just a fraction. "Here's the way it goes down," he said. I listened to his toneless voice, thinking how easy he would have taken Mortay. How I should have jumped off the track.

It took a while. "Okay?" he asked.

"I'll be there. Max too. And I'll have the other stuff in place. I'll ask, like I said. Maybe I'll have the other people. If not . . ."

"It'll still go. Just won't be as safe."

I took a deep breath. "I'm going back in. To see Train. Speak with him. Just so you know."

"He's last. Before I finish up."

"Wesley, you remember a girl from the neighborhood? Little Candy? From when we were kids?"

"No."

Max led us back to the car in the darkness.

118

On the way back to the city, I called the junkyard. We stopped in, spoke to the Mole. He'd place the cars. I didn't ask him to do anything else.

It took us a couple of hours to find the Prof. He was working Penn Station, deep in talk with a couple of guys stretched out on sleeping mats made from cut-up cartons. A two-wheeled shopping cart stood between them, full of magazines, empty plastic bottles, a Cabbage Patch doll with only one arm on top. As we closed in on him, I recognized the two pups from the shoeshine stand.

They recognized me too. The bigger one snaked his hand into the cart.

"Chill it, fool," the Prof snapped at him. The pup listened to his teacher. The Prof walked over to us. We stood against the corner as I ran it down.

The little man thought it over. "There's always danger from a stranger."

I thought of what the Mole said about Wesley. "He's not us, Prof. But he's not them either."

"I'll drive. From the far side. Couple of hours. You don't show, I go." Dealing himself in. One piece left.

I rang Michelle's room. "Are you decent?" I asked her.

"No, but I'm dressed."

Max and I went up to her hotel room. She was wearing green Chinese pajamas, makeup in place, hair still up. Smoking one of her long black cigarettes.

She kissed Max on the cheek, reached over, squeezed my hand. "What is it?"

"Monday night, late. I need someone to drive me and Max. Wait for us. Couple of hours. We don't show up, take the car and split."

"What's the risk?"

"Not much. The car'll be clean when you're sitting in it. We come back on the run, you can still fade."

"Somebody's paying?"

"Somebody."

"I'm in for a piece?"

"We're not stealing, Michelle. Flat rate. You call it."

"I'll have to take the whole night off. Say, two large."

"Okay."

"You're different now. Different again."

"What?"

"You don't feel like a gunfighter to me anymore. But you're not back to yourself. Something's still missing."

I knew what it was: I didn't feel afraid.

119

I T WAS getting light when I took Max back to the warehouse. I waited while he got my mail from upstairs. Same old stuff.

Always danger from a stranger. Somehow I knew he'd be awake. I dialed the number from the basement. Told the man who answered the phone what I wanted. Waited.

"Mr. Burke."

"Train. I'd like to make an appointment to see you. Continue our dialogue. Tie up the loose ends."

"What loose ends?"

"Questions you asked me. About . . . security. I believe I have some answers for you. And maybe we could do business."

"I see. Around noon?"

"I'll be there."

120

 LEFT Morehouse's car on Remsen Street, where it was legal to park with NYP plates. Max and I walked the rest of the way.

The same young man we saw the first time let us in. No karate outfit this time. The chairs were already in place in the top-floor room.

"My brother will wait outside, with your permission. I don't think anyone needs to hear this."

His eyes were a bright blue. "My staff has rather strong feelings about me . . . about my safety."

"You're safe with me. Sometimes it's safer to talk privately."

"The last time we talked. About security. You said something about me having to leave this place sometime. It seems to me that you're already back inside."

"I'm a businessman, not a kamikaze."

"Very well."

Max stepped outside. We were alone. I rotated my head on the column of my neck. To get the kinks out, break the adhesions. And look around. Glass brick ran in a long loop around the top of the room. I had to play it like they were listening—walk the tightrope.

I lit a smoke. "You have enemies. Personal enemies. I think that's part of the cost of doing business for you. That wouldn't frighten you."

"You think I'm frightened?"

"Concerned, okay? Intelligently concerned. About a problem you have. I think one of your personal enemies realized his impotence. And went to a professional. I don't think your security questions were academic."

"Are you guessing about all of this?"

"No."

The blue eyes honed in. That was his wake-up call. "Are you . . . involved?"

"Not yet. I thought I might be. If we can do business."

"I'm not certain I understand."

"You have a sweet business here. Making wine out of rotten fruit, that's a technique. I admire your insight, your skill."

He bowed slightly, waiting.

"The way it works, you cruise the streets. Look for old furniture that people throw out on the sidewalk. Then you refinish the furniture, remodel it, paint it. You sell the furniture to people who want that kind of stuff in their houses. And it's all profit. Garbage into gold. Dirt into diamonds. Why should anybody be mad?"

"Indeed."

"Once in a while . . . not too often . . . somebody wishes they had their furniture back. But you've got this rule—you won't sell it back to anyone who put it out on the curb in the first place."

"They threw it away. It's not theirs."

"Yes. You're a street-cleaner. A scavenger. But you know how people are—they never miss water until the well runs dry."

"You're a perceptive man. I believe we . . . I misjudged you."

"That happens. You have resources, you can ask questions. You know when the truth is around. When it isn't."

"Yes?"

"The truth is around. Here. Now. One of these people who discarded his furniture, he wanted it back. There was a disagreement of some sort. But this individual, he couldn't go to the authorities. The law's on your side. Once you throw garbage out at the curb, it belongs to anyone who picks it up."

He bowed again. Just a slight movement of his head.

"So this individual, he goes outside the law. To a professional. Somebody wants you. And by now you know it isn't me."

"You came for Elvira."

"And I returned her."

"She told you some things . . ."

"And I brought her back to you. I'm not the man who's looking for you."

"No? Then what are you?"

"I'm the man you're looking for."

"How so?"

"Every profession has competition. You have your work, I have mine. I wouldn't know your competitors, you wouldn't know mine. You thought I was here for a particular reason. You were wrong. But someone is out there. For you. Someone I can deal with."

He made a slight "keep talking" move with one hand.

"I have two professions," I told him. "One of them is finding people. I can find this person."

"And then?"

"My other profession."

"And what of *my* profession?"

"That's your business. It seems you could use a man like me."

"I have people."

"You have children."

His eyes locked in. "*My* children."

"Children deserve protection."

"Yes. I must do what is best for my children. Anything else would be immoral."

"Morality can be costly."

"Whatever . . ."

"Very costly."

"Yes?"

"Fifty thousand."

"All right." Unfazed. "I assume you want some sort of . . . preliminary payment."

"It's not necessary."

"I'm not familiar with these things. I just thought . . ."

"I know where to find you. After it's done."

"How would I know?"

"I'll bring the proof. If you're not satisfied, there's no charge."

He stroked his face, pretending to think about it.

"It's for the children," I said.

"Yes. I have no choice. My obligations. You won't mind if I check . . . ?"

I nodded, knowing what he meant. It didn't matter. Wesley had his work and I had mine. And I was back to it. The day I couldn't scam dirtbags, I'd go straight.

I didn't see the signal. Reba came into the room. A white silk robe with a hood, white sash around her waist. Nothing else. She sat next to me on my left, hooking one thigh over my legs, pulling the robe around her shoulder like she was cold. Her hand found my heart.

Train gazed at the ceiling. His voice went thin, dry-washing his hands.

"Is someone looking for me?"

"Yes."

"To hurt me?"

"Yes."

"You know who it is?"

"Yes."

"You could stop him?"

"Yes."

"Could I stop him?"

"No."

"Would he take money?"

"No."

Reba's hand shifted, shielded by the robe. Fingers trailed across my cock. She wiggled her butt like she was trying to get comfortable. I couldn't see her face.

"Are you the man who is looking for me?"

"No."

"Do you believe Elvira is safe here?"

"Yes."

Reba's hand cupped my balls. A gentle squeeze. Her thumb stroked my cock. It stirred. Stiffened.

"Are you working for Elvira's mother?"

"No."

"Did you ever?"

"When I brought the girl back to her."

"The man who's looking for me . . . is he for hire?"

"Yes."

Reba ran two knuckles of her hand up and down the shaft of my cock. Found the tip with her fingers. Squeezed. It was a piece of steel, threatening the zipper.

"But not by me?"

"Not now."

"Because he's already taken someone else's money?"

"Yes."

"Do you know whose money?"

"No."

"How would he come for me?"

"By fire."

He nodded. Reba slid off me, gathering her robe, whispering, "It's all the truth." I crossed my legs as I reached into my coat for a smoke. Lit it, waiting. Reba padded out of the room.

"You'll tell me when it's done?" he asked.

"I'll show you."

Max was outside, standing alone.

121

ALONE IN my office, I stroked Pansy's soft fur the way the New Age lunatics rub crystals. Getting apart from myself, wrapping what was left in my own fear. Letting the core speak to me.

Being the answer.

"Nobody knows where Wesley's going, but everybody knows where he's been," the Prof said.

I lit a smoke, replaying every square inch of the chameleon's apartment. Everything I'd seen. Waiting for it to kick in. It would come. Reba knew.

122

CANDY answered her phone.

"It's me," I said quietly. "You were right. I want to get it back. Hold the leash in my hands."

"I don't like the way you left me the last time."

"I did. That's how I knew you were telling the truth."

"That's my baby. Anytime after three, okay?"

"I'll be there."

123

THE DOORMAN was sneaking a smoke just outside the building. The Prof yelled "Yo', Roscoe my man!" at nobody and the doorman turned. Max and I went inside. I took the elevator to the top floor.

The wig was strawberry blond this time but the yellow cat's eyes were her own. Wearing a white terry-cloth bathrobe. "It all starts back there," she said. "Come on."

We went to the last bedroom. She dropped the robe to the floor. The choke collar was around her neck, leather leash dangling to her knee. I sat on the psychiatrist's couch, pulling hard on the leash. She came to the couch obediently, eyes dreamy. I pulled again. She sat on the couch, slipped onto her hands and knees. I stood up. "Stay there," I told her.

I walked behind her. She dropped her shoulders to the couch, her round butt seemed to shimmer in the dim light. "Stay the way you were," I said.

She pushed herself back up on her hands, saying nothing.

"I know where the stuff I want is. Stay there."

I went to her closet. Found what I needed. When I walked back, she hadn't moved.

"Put your hands behind your back."

The handcuffs were leather-lined. I snapped them home. Looped the leash through one of the rings in the floor.

She licked her lips. Cold cat's eyes. Feral and fearless.

I knotted the leash. Her shoulders came forward, bent, touched the couch. I stepped behind her. Her slim ankles were close together, muscles bunched on the backs of her thighs. I cuffed her ankles together. Held a length of chain in my hands. She crooked her feet back over her butt in an arch, holding her cuffed hands back toward her ankles, waiting to be hog-tied the way another woman would wait for a bus. I linked the chain to the cuffs holding her ankles. But then I pulled back, hard. The front of her calves hit the couch. I tightened the chain around one of the couch legs. She was spread out, on her stomach, chin on the couch. The way I'd been on those subway tracks.

Her body was faintly coated with sweat, like she'd been oiled. I put a tube-shaped leather pillow under her hips.

"I can't move an inch," she purred. Like it was magic words.

I put one knee on the couch next to her. Patted her butt lightly. Slid my hands up to her shoulders.

"There's a mirror. Behind the screen. If you want . . ."

She was still talking when I pushed the ball gag into her mouth, slipped the elastic over her head.

Then I went looking for what I'd come for.

There had to be another room someplace. I found it off the dressing room. A butcher-block desk with one of those tiny designer lamps. A high-tech phone with a row of unmarked buttons down one side. I wrapped a handkerchief over my finger. Pushed each button, watching the stored number come up on the liquid crystal screen. I filed the numbers in my head, hanging up before they could ring even once. Ten buttons. Only four had numbers stored.

I stepped into one of the bathrooms. Flushed the toilet. Candy had it backwards. It wasn't her who knew me. Now.

I was back inside the last bedroom in a couple of minutes. Slipped the elastic off her head. The ball gag popped out.

"You okay now, baby?" she asked.

"Not yet."

"I thought . . ."

"I'm not finished," I said, unlocking the cuffs from her ankles. She wiggled her hips. It wasn't to get the feeling back. I unlocked the cuffs from around her wrists. She waited. I unknotted the leash. Pulled her to her feet.

"Get dressed."

Her eyes were downcast, voice soft, feeling her way. She wasn't good at ad-libs. "Tell me what to wear. Tell me everything—I can't get dressed unless you tell me what to put on."

"A sweater and a skirt."

"Should I wear a bra, honey?"

"Yeah."

"Panties?"

"Yeah."

"What color?"

"It doesn't matter."

"I . . ."

"Pink, okay? Do it quick."

"Should I wear stockings? Heels?"

"No."

"How old am I?"

"You'll see," I said, pulling hard on the leash. "Hurry up."

I pulled her down the hall to her dressing room. Watched as she dressed.

"Where's the key to this place?"

She handed it to me. I put it in my pocket. "Come on," I said, bunching the leash in one hand, holding it behind her neck. Even when we were kids, that was the way I held her—never her hand.

I led her to the front door, opened it, pushed her outside. She didn't say a word. The hall was carpeted. I took her to the stairwell door. One short flight to the roof. Twenty flights below us. A naked red bulb was the only light. Emergency Exit. I prodded her forward. Pulled the leash. She stopped. I was one step behind her.

She knew what to do. Grabbed the railing with both hands as I lifted her skirt from behind. "What if somebody comes?" she whispered. Making it come back.

"Too bad for them." Max one flight below us. Only one person was going to come.

My zipper rasped. Her hands went behind her, thumbs hooking the waist of her panties. She had them down just before I slammed into her.

I felt the muscles inside her grab and hold. I never touched the silicone.

It didn't take long. She made a greedy noise as I shot off inside her. Pulled up her own panties. Never turned around. Like old times.

124

B ACK IN her apartment. Candy sitting on her couch, the leash a dark line between her breasts inside the bright yellow sweater.

"You'll get her back for me now?"

"Yes." I took her key out of my pocket, running my fingers over it, rubbing hard. I tossed it to her. It bounced off her shoulder. She never took her eyes from me.

"I always loved you," she said.

125

I TOOK THE stairs down with Max. The Prof was waiting in Morehouse's car. I handed him the soft plastic block from my pocket. The key to Candy's apartment was sharply outlined on its face.

"Tell the Mole I need two, okay? He can leave them in one of the cars for Monday night."

"It's done, son."

126

Monday, midnight. Max and I pulled off the FDR, leaving the car to the darkness. Michelle was in the back seat. Max waited while I walked along the riverbank with Michelle. She leaned into me, her hand on my arm.

"Here's the papers you wanted," I told her.

"This is pretty thick for just a passport," she said, putting the packet into her purse.

"The rest is from the Mole."

She stopped in her tracks. Slit the envelope with a long thumbnail while I lit a smoke. I saw a wad of greenbacks. And a note on the graph paper the Mole uses for stationery. I left her to herself, smoking in silence. When she turned her face to me, tears streaked the perfect makeup.

"After tonight, I'm gone from here."

"I know."

"When I come back, I'll be me."

"Yeah."

"I love you, Burke," she said. Pulled my face down to kiss my cheek. "You watch out for my boy—you take care of him."

I didn't ask her who she meant. "Come back at one, okay?" I told her. "You'll hear some kind of a big bang. Wait five, ten minutes. We're not here, go. If we're coming, we're coming fast. You see us coming toward you, just walk away, leave the keys in the ignition."

"I'm not running around in this mess in my good shoes."

"I mean it, Michelle. Don't wait. We don't need a driver."

She gave me another quick kiss. "Take care of Max," she said.

The ground felt squashy under my boots as we made our way down to the river. Manhattan is a big island; the East River separates it from Queens, dotted by smaller islands. Welfare Island. Roosevelt Island. Once they used them for insane asylums, hospitals, leper colonies. Now they use them for luxury co-ops. Other islands too. Real small ones. Just clumps of dirt and trees sitting in the river. You could get a good view of the Fifty-ninth Street Bridge from them.

Michelle would wait on the Manhattan side. We couldn't just stash a getaway car in that neighborhood—it wouldn't be there when we needed it. The Prof was in place on the Queens side. When the pressure came, we'd move away from it. If we could.

Wesley was waiting. A darker-than-night shape near the water. He handed me the Uzi. A soft hiss as the rubber boat inflated. He pointed to a pair of duffel bags and a large tool chest with a handle on top. Max took the two duffels in one hand, the tool chest in the other. Wesley didn't seem surprised. We boarded the boat. Wesley sat in front, steering. Max and I alternated strokes with the paddles. The river's only about a quarter mile wide where we were working, with the island sitting in the middle. It didn't take long.

We beached the boat. Wesley set up a pair of tripods in the soft ground, pressing down hard to make sure they were firmly seated. He bolted a spotting scope on top of one, a rifle onto the other. No talking—sound carries over water. No smoking. He pointed to the sniperscope, pointed at me. Blew a sharp puff of air. I nodded. Wesley settled in behind his rifle, making himself at home. He swept the bridge with his scope, nodding in satisfaction. He pulled a bullet from his jacket pocket. Long, slender bullet. A soft snick as he chambered the slug. I was inside his mind. Target rifle. One target, one bullet.

Wesley sat behind his rifle, eyes somewhere else. Nothing to do but wait. A foghorn sounded far down the river. The Harbor Patrol had passed almost half an hour ago. They hadn't even swept the island with their searchlights.

I saw the line of humans moving. Walking the bridge. The spotting scope picked them out. Three up front, a man in the middle, three behind. I swung the scope to the Manhattan side. Four men, walking together. I blew a sharp puff of air, imitating Wesley. He settled in behind the scope, moving the barrel in tiny circles. A snake's tongue. Testing. Waiting. Fangs sheathed.

The two groups came together. The man who'd been in the middle from the Queens side stepped forward. One of the men from the Manhattan side detached himself. They walked on the outside of the bridge, safe from traffic. The two men met near the middle of the bridge, slightly to the Queens side. They stood with their backs to the girders. Then they switched places. I blew another puff at Wesley. "I saw it," he whispered. So low it might have been only inside my head.

I saw what Wesley saw.

The target's eyes were shielded by his hat. I zeroed in on the lower cheekbone—the bullet would travel up, climbing all the way till it met his brain. And blow it out his skull.

They were talking. I heard Wesley take a deep breath. Let it all out in a smooth stream. Felt him go coma-calm. So he could squeeze the trigger between heartbeats. The don's lips stopped moving. He cocked his head slightly. Listening to the underboss.

The don fell forward a microsecond before the earsplitting *ccccrack!* ripped my ears. The underboss ducked.

Wesley was on his feet, breaking down the tripod. Max grabbed my scope and tripod in one scoop. Wesley pointed to the Queens side— standing dark and quiet in the distance. No time to argue. We threw everything in the boat. The muscles in my back screamed trying to match Max's strokes. Sirens shrieked somewhere behind us. I knew Wesley would be working the spotlight in front of the boat, watching for the answer. The boat veered left toward my side, where Max's strokes would do most of the work. We ran aground. Wesley popped the release. The air hissed out of the boat as Max made the run to the car.

I took the wheel. Wesley and Max loaded the stuff into the trunk, climbed into the back seat. I pulled away smoothly, heading for the empty factory district of Long Island City.

"Thanks, Prof."

"It's been fun, but my piece is done," the little man said. Meaning he didn't want to stay along for the ride. I stopped within sight of the IRT. Held out my hand. He grasped it, let go. Opened the door and split. Never looked into the back seat.

127

I FOLLOWED Wesley's directions to an abandoned factory building off Meserole Street in Brooklyn, not far from the Queens border. Wesley got out, unbolted a heavy padlock. I drove the car inside. Pitch-dark. It even smelled empty.

Max reached into the trunk. Held the stuff up for Wesley to see. Wesley made a "put it down right there" gesture. "I won't be here tomorrow," he said to me.

The freight elevator was a bombed-out void. Wesley walked in the darkness like he could see. We followed the sounds he made. Found my hand on an iron railing. Staircase. Wesley walking ahead. Three flights. The top floor was only half there. No glass in the windows. Light from somewhere came through them. Boxes piled up, some covered with a tarp. Cans of food against one wall. Rats made their scratching escape noises.

I lit a smoke. So did Max.

Wesley sat on one of the boxes.

"No doubt in your mind?" I asked him.

"I hit him. With those bullets, I hit him anyplace, his head's in pieces."

"They'll go crazy looking for you."

"Crazy . . . you ever have a suicide dream, Burke?"

"What's a suicide dream?"

"Where you dream of killing yourself. You ever dream of killing yourself?"

"I did once."

"What happened?"

"I dreamed I was real depressed. Sad like there wasn't any reason to keep on. So I made a list. Of all the people I wanted to take with me. Figured I was gonna die anyway, I'd just start blasting everyone on the list. Sooner or later, one of them would get me. Save me the trouble."

"Did it work?"

"No." I felt crazy laughter bubble in me. "I got through the whole list. Then I didn't want to die anymore."

"My list is too long. Yours too?"

"Not anymore."

"You all settled up?"

I thought about Train. Julio. "Just about."

"What'd you use on that Mortay?"

"Use?"

"To off him."

It was like talking into a machine. But not a tape recorder. "A .38 Special. And I dropped a grenade on his face after he went down."

The machine's voice lightened. Wesley's laugh. "A fucking .38? A pistol? Why didn't you just throw rocks at him?"

"I got it done."

"He was supposed to be real good. Like Max here. You got him with a pistol, he must have been close."

"He was."

"Chump."

"I know. Now. Now's too late." For Belle.

"Anything I can do for you?"

"You mean . . . ?"

"What I do. I'm almost done."

"Just Julio. And Train."

"So I was right. From the beginning. You were on his case."

"No I wasn't. Things changed. I learned something."

"Something about a kid?"

"Yeah."

"That soft spot—it's like a bull's-eye on your back."

"Nothing I can do."

"It's not your problem, right? Not your kid."

"I didn't want it like this. I wanted to be . . . something else."

"What?"

I dragged deep on my smoke, looked into the monster's eyes. "I wanted to be you," I told him.

"No you don't. I'm not afraid. Of anything. It's not worth it."

"Wesley, what do you know about Train? What made you think I was on his case?"

"The guy who hired me. I figured it had to be something like that. He knew your name."

And then he said the man's name. Danielle's father. The man with the special basement on Long Island.

I threw my cigarette on the floor. Ground it out.

The monster knew. "There are no good guys, Burke. You're a thief—go back to stealing."

I didn't like the sound of my voice. "Not just yet."

He read my thoughts. "He's on the house. Keep your list short. I'll meet him after Train's done. To get the rest of my money. I'll leave him where I meet him."

I lit another smoke. "I told Train I'd take care of you."

"Good. They're easier when they're sleeping."

"You need a ride anywhere?"

"No. I got a car stashed just down the street. I'll get rid of the stuff first, then I'm gone."

Max bowed to Wesley. The monster moved his head in return. Stiffly, like he wasn't used to it.

I followed Max down the stairs.

128

THE ALL-NEWS station had nothing about the killing on the way back to Manhattan, but it was all they were talking about by the time I got up in the morning. Ghost stories. The one I liked best had Colombians blasting the don from a speedboat passing under the bridge.

129

I DROVE OUT to the junkyard. Sat down with the Mole. Told him about a girl named Elvira. About selective breeding, supervised by slime.

I drove back to the city in a black Ford four-door sedan. Max followed in Morehouse's Datsun.

130

IN MY OFFICE, I went over the Ma Bell printout the ex-cop had gotten for me. One of Train's six numbers had no long-distance calls at all. Never used up its message units either. A dead line. For incoming.

It was one of the numbers stored in Candy's phone.

131

Julio left a message for me at Mama's. I called him at his club.

"What d'you want, old man? You think I'm setting up a meeting now, you're crazy. You got nothing to threaten me with."

He sounded strong, alive. In control. "Who said anything about threats? Cut that out. Talk sense. We're on the same side. Your problem disappeared with my problem, okay? I'm gonna make some moves of my own now. There's one little thing . . ."

"What?"

"The bitch, she has something for me. Something I wrote down once. She says she'll give it back, I give her a present."

"Why tell me?"

"She's a crazy woman, you know that. She has something stuck in her head, there's no talking to her. She wants to give it to you. You bring it to me, you take the present back to her. Then it's done."

"Get somebody else."

"I would. It's *her*, okay? You know what she's like."

"I'm not going to see her."

"Hey! Somebody's gotta do it. I'll take care of you, don't worry."

"And then we're quits."

"On my honor."

132

I CALLED STREGA. "You called him?"

"Yes."

"You couldn't leave it alone?"

"Don't be mad. You know I told you the truth. And he wants the letter. It's in the way now. The little man has big plans."

133

I HEARD the slug muffle the phone with his greasy hand. "The guy wants Don Julio."

"I'm here," he snapped into the phone.

"She says she'll hand it over to me. Out in the open. She wants to see it happen."

"What's that mean?"

"It means you come. Alone. I come. Alone. She drives up. Hands me what you want while you watch. Goes back to her car. I give you the letter for the present you have for her. You wait while I take it over to her. I get in my car and we all go home."

"My boys won't like me going anywhere alone."

"You're the boss, right? Who cares what they like."

"All right. Where?"

"You know her. Queens it's got to be. You're coming from Shea Stadium, okay? On the Grand Central. Just before La Guardia, there's a gas station. You pull over there, where there's a railing. You can park the car, walk down to the water. Where guys fish in the summertime. Got it?"

"Yeah."

"She says tomorrow. Eleven o'clock in the morning. You park all the way to the right. She'll be there, parked to the left. I pull in between you. Get it done."

"I'll be there."

I called Strega. Told her what tomorrow was going to be.

134

WESLEY said Julio was on the house. A trade for the don. But the don had been Wesley's killing. All his. Danielle's father had turned me into a dog. A hunting dog that fetched his raw meat back. He had to pay. Wesley said he'd do that freak. In his soundproof basement. Train was a trade. Not all mine, but enough.

I couldn't let Wesley within shooting range of Strega—the monster might feel the heat. And strike. Strega. The witch-bitch. She'd set it up this way. "You wouldn't let anything happen to me." Wesley was out.

At eight-thirty, I swung into the gas station. Told the guy to fill it up. Max got out to go to the men's room. The pump jockey filled the tank, took my money. I drove off alone.

A couple of minutes after eleven, I backed into the lot. Strega's BMW on my left, Julio's Caddy on the right. I swung the Plymouth between them. Got out, opened my trunk, left it open. Walked to Julio's car. His window snicked down. I put my head inside, checked the back seat. Empty.

"Get out, Julio."

He showed me a thick envelope. "I thought you were supposed to get the letter first."

"I am. I want you to open the trunk. Make sure you came alone. Mine's already open, you want to look."

He got out, a sneer on his face. Unlocked the trunk. Empty.

"I'll be right back," I told him.

"Burke, wait a minute." His gloved hand on my arm. "I got no more troubles, you understand? Except her. Crazy people, they're always trouble. They *stay* trouble."

"Why tell me?"

"I know you can get to Wesley. I'm going to make some arrangements. I want to pay him for the last job. The old don, he was a fuckin' idiot. No trap, no games. I give you the cash, you deliver it to Wesley. I don't gotta be around. I just want him to know . . . no hard feelings . . . it's a new regime, like they say. You could do this?"

"Maybe."

"Yeah, you always say 'maybe.' I ask you if you get up tomorrow morning, you say 'maybe.' You can do it. When you see Wesley, you tell him he's all right with me. Aces. I even got a nice easy job for him. Cash up front, how's that?"

"I'll see."

I left him standing there. Walked over to Strega's car, feeling his eyes on my back. She stepped out of the little sedan, wearing a black coat, black scarf over her red hair. She handed me a thin envelope.

"I was right," she said.

"Yeah, you were," I said. "Now get out of here."

"I want to see it." Witchy eyes, even in the sunlight. "I was right . . . about everything."

I walked back toward Julio. The old man came forward, one hand reaching into his pocket. Highway traffic hummed to my right, planes thundered to my left. I held out Strega's envelope to Julio. With his confession inside: how he made a little girl-child dance for him. The child he just sentenced to dance again under Wesley's bullets. He took his hand out of his inside pocket, slipped what I handed him into his coat. Reached back inside. A fat envelope. I took it. Closed my hand over his. He pulled back. "What . . . ?" Max launched off the railing in a dark blur. Julio twisted his neck sharply just as I heard the snap. He fell into me. I slipped his dead arm over my neck, walked him to the railing. Propped him on the bench, emptied his pockets. An old man, sleeping in the sun. Until you got close enough to catch the smell.

I walked back to my car. Closed the trunk on the dark bundle of blankets back there. Followed the BMW out of the parking lot.

The Plymouth shot past Strega, heading for the Triboro Bridge. I thought I saw her wave something at me but the windows of her car were very dark. I couldn't be sure.

135

I CHECKED my list. I had to spook him, not tip him off. Called one of the six numbers on the printout. Not the dead line. Asked for Train. He came, quickly.

"It's me," I said.

"How did you come by this number?"

"From the man we discussed."

"A shot was fired through my upper window last night. Nobody heard it. There was a little round hole in the glass. A big chunk of plaster torn off the wall."

"I'll have him tomorrow. If I thought you knew what he looked like, I'd prove it to you."

"I know what he looks like."

It would have chilled me, but I knew how he knew.

"If I can pull it off, I'll call tomorrow night. Take you to him."

"You mean . . . ?"

"Yeah. COD."

136

CALLED Morehouse. Got him live, no machine.

"Stay by your phone tomorrow night. Keep the line clear. All night."

"Sure."

137

CALLED CANDY.

"Hello, baby," she said into the phone. Breathy. Knowing how old she was supposed to be.

"I want to do it again," I told her.

"Anytime, honey. Just tell me."

"There's something I have to do first. Something real important."

"I know you'll be okay."

"Yeah. I'm just a little nervous."

"Anything I can do?"

"No, I'm covered. He doesn't know . . . oh, never mind. It's too complicated. But when it's done, I'll bring Elvira back."

"Are you going to have to . . . ?"

"No. I'm going to do something for him. Something he really wants. He'll *give* me the kid. No problem."

"Oh, I *knew* you could do it. Didn't I tell you?"

"Yeah. I'll call you soon."

"I love you," she said. Like she had before.

138

"I'M ON MY WAY," I told Train over the phone.

"I'll be here."

They let me in downstairs. Two of them went with me, close enough to touch. The two Elvira said had made the crazy girl disappear.

He was standing this time. By the window. The one with the little round hole in it. The monster's word was always good. I stepped close to him, keeping my voice down.

"He's dead."

"You're sure? Who is he?"

"Wesley. I'll take you to him—you said you'd know his face."

"How can I be sure?"

"You'll see for yourself."

"Sure of *you*."

"Ask Reba."

His blue eyes blinked rapidly.

"I don't know how you'll know him," I said, my voice soft, slightly awed, "but I know you will. You can go in my car. Take a couple of your men with you. Hold a gun to the back of my neck all the while, if you want. This is the truth—Wesley is a dead man."

"Where?"

"I left him on Wards Island. I'll show you. I've got a flashlight in the car."

He gestured to the two men. Left me alone in the room. Reba came through the door. I stayed against the window, tapping the ashes from my cigarette onto the sill. She walked against me, wrapping her arms around me, grinding her hips. I slid my hands inside the robe, cupping her buttocks. The globes seemed to swell in my hands.

"Can you work your trick standing up?" I asked her.

"The man is dead?"

"The man is dead."

She pressed against me, a fleshy heat-exchanger. "Will you come back? After you show him?"

"What for?"

"For me. I'll tell *you* the truth."

"Then I'll come."

"Yes," she said, promising.

Train came back in with the same two men who'd taken me upstairs. "I'll go with you. We all will. When we come back, you'll have your money."

I nodded.

"And whatever else you want here."

"Let's go," I said.

139

THE FORD was half a block away. I unlocked it. The overhead light went on. The front seat sagged badly on the passenger side, upholstery ripped, a sharp spring showing through.

"It doesn't look like much," I apologized. "Where we're going, a nice car would stand out."

I climbed in behind the wheel. The damaged front seat hadn't been necessary—the bodyguards played it the right way—their bodies pressed against the one they had to keep safe. One of them got into the back. Train next. Then the last man.

I buckled my seat belt. Pulled away from the curb. Drove past the House of Detention. Took the Brooklyn Bridge to the FDR, heading north.

I glanced at the rearview mirror. Train was sitting quietly in the middle, hands on his knees, staring straight ahead at nothing. The two guys on either side of him were in their early twenties. Looked enough alike to be brothers. Close-cropped hair, flat faces, hooded eyes. The first generation of the breeding program? As I hooked onto Wards Island, I heard the sound of a round being chambered. Felt the pistol nestle into the back of my neck.

"You know what that is, Mr. Burke?"

"Yes."

"No matter what happens, Tommy can do his job. The pistol has a hair trigger."

"Tell him to be calm. We're almost there."

I lit a cigarette, leaning back, pressing my head into the gun. Amateurs.

I pulled over under the girders. "Okay," I said, turning sideways to speak to Train, voice low and conversational. "We'll have to walk from here. I'm rolling down my window. Why don't you have Tommy get out and hold the gun while . . ." I pushed the switch in the middle of the last word, ducking my head. The train hit the wall.

The gun never went off. My breath was gone. The windshield was splattered with flesh and fluid. I let air seep in through my nose until my lungs started to work. I didn't look in the back seat.

Unbuckled my seat belt. Stepped outside. My legs wouldn't work. I sat down outside the Ford, waiting. It would come back.

In a few minutes I started walking. By myself. Fingering the little transmitter in my pocket.

The Plymouth growled alongside me, running without lights. The passenger door opened. I climbed inside. Hit the switch. The window went down. Max drove slowly. The Ford was in sight. I held the transmitter out the window, as high as I could. The Mole said it had a quarter-mile range. We were much closer than that. I pushed the button. The Ford exploded. Flames filled the rearview mirror as Max hit the gas.

He dropped me off where I'd left Morehouse's car.

140

I CALLED MOREHOUSE from a phone on the West Side. "You know the Yacht Basin?"

"Sure, man. Where you think I keep *my* yacht?"

"Fifteen minutes."

"I'm rolling."

141

HE PULLED IN. Seemed relieved to see his car still in one piece. "What's on?"

I handed him his keys. "There's gonna be an explosion tonight. Somewhere on Wards Island. Off the approach road to Kirby. The cops'll find bodies inside. They won't make a connect. You know McGowan and Morales?"

"The Runaway Squad? Sure."

"You call them. You got a tip, right? The connect is to a man named Train. He's running the baby-breeding operation." I gave him the address.

"They'll need more than that for a search warrant."

"Save the bullshit for your column, pal. Let them get a warrant the way they always do. You know that Anonymous Informant? The one they use on every search warrant since the Supreme Court told them they needed one? Time for another guest appearance. Tell them to run it through Wolfe at City-Wide. She'll know what to do. Besides, the joint'll be full of victims, not perps."

"Right on, man. When do I know?"

"You got nothing else to do tonight, right? Maybe you're working on that movie script you're always bullshitting about writing someday. So you're monitoring the police band—I know you got a scanner. You get a call a few minutes after they get theirs."

"I'm off."

"Hold up. There's one more thing. A little girl inside the joint. Her name's Elvira. Or Juice—I don't know which name she'll use. Don't let SSC put her in a shelter or a foster home—she'll run. She knows how to do it. She needs a psychiatric hospital. And she's pregnant."

"Okay. Anything else I should know about her?"

"Yeah. She knows my name."

"Crazy people say all kinds of things. 'Specially on the psycho ward."

"Your car sucks," I told the West Indian, not saying the rest—that his word was good.

We shook hands.

142

It DIDN'T hit me till later. Alone in my office. No lights. Pansy's dark shape on the couch. When Flood had killed the sadist Goldor in his fancy house . . . killed him to save me . . . she almost came unglued. Got off the track. Shaking so bad. Throwing away the clothes she'd worn like they were diseased. I'd held her to me. Rosie and the Originals on the cassette. Angel Baby. "Remember reform school?" I'd asked her, dancing so slow we weren't moving our feet. Until she came back to herself.

She couldn't come back to me that night.

Not Strega's fire, not Wesley's ice.
I found my way.
Survive.

143

I WOKE UP the next morning by myself. The way I always do. Belle was still gone. The pain in my chest was still there. But now I recognized it for what it was—a tourniquet around my heart, not a stranglehold.

The Plymouth found its way over to Mama's. Judy Henske on the cassette. Singing just to me. An old gut-bucket blues number came through next. I didn't remember the man's name but I know he died young. And hard.

> *Too sick to go to the doctor*
> *Too tired to go to sleep*
> *Too broke to borrow money*
> *And too hungry to eat*

And then a sweet girl singer, fronting off some doo-wop group that never had a hit record.

> *Your tears in my eyes*
> *Your heart in my heart*
> *Defeat and disguise*
> *Can't keep us apart*

The weight wasn't off, but I could carry what was left.

Mama had the *Daily News*. The story about the bombed-out car on Wards Island was buried on page six. The paper had it down to more mob homicides. Couldn't find a word about Julio. It would take a day or so for the Queens cops to run his prints. And they'd throw the body into the same garbage bag with the rest of the mess Wesley made. Morehouse's column would be out tomorrow.

Max came in. I showed him the story about the firebombed car. He drew his X on the table. Wesley's work. He made a questioning sign. I pulled an imaginary cord a couple of times, made the sign of something rushing past. Train. He bowed.

My brother was right. I'd pulled the switch, but it was Wesley's work. Mine was done.

Almost done.

144

MAX PULLED the racing form from his pocket. I kicked back to read. The horses' names all looked unfamiliar to me. Soon I was lost in a stakes race for three-year-old trotters. There was a shipper from Illinois. Gypsy Flame. An Arsenal filly out of a Noble Hustle mare. Good lines. Her trainer was bringing her along slowly, but she was tearing up the home tracks. A 2:01 at Sportsman's Park in Chicago in the cold weather—that was flying. I went over her last eight races. She always ran off the pace, charged hard going home. She'd be at a disadvantage at Yonkers with the tight turns and the short stretch, but she always ran clean. No breaks on her record. Morning Line had her at 8–1. Yes.

I looked over at Max, to tell him what our selection would be. His seat was empty. I glanced at my watch. Damn. I'd been lost for almost two hours.

Mama was up front, by the cash register. I went back to the pay phones. Dialed my broker. Maurice snatched it on the first ring.

"What?"

"This is Burke. Give me the four horse in the second race at Yonkers. Two to win."

"Horse number four, race number two. Yonkers. A deuce on the nose. That right?"

"Right. You miss me?"

He hung up.

145

THE PHONE RANG before I could go back to my table. I picked it up myself.

"Yeah?"

"Friday, be sure you're watching TV. It don't matter which channel long as it's a network. Try NBC. They got the fastest crew. 'Live at Five.' That's the best show. Don't wait for the late news—watch it go down."

"All right."

"That car. Last night. In my spot?"

"Yeah, the papers made it sound like a train wreck."

"I'm gonna take a trip. Out to the Island. Pick up my money. Then Friday. Watch TV. I'll wave goodbye to you."

"I . . ."

"Don't say my name. I'm leaving you something in my will. Remember what I said. About kids. Don't let the hunters see the soft spot."

"I won't."

"Goodbye . . ."

The machine sputtered—I couldn't make out the last word as the phone went dead.

146

"THIS IS real nice, Burke. Just like the joint, except for the food," the Prof said, sneering.

We were in Mama's basement. At a long table we made out of an old door. I was playing gin with Max, the scorepad to his left. He owed me almost twenty grand. A nineteen-inch color TV stood on top of a couple of barrels we had piled up. Max brought it with him that day, carrying it in one hand like an attaché case.

Max reached for a card. "Nix on the six, chump," the Prof barked, slapping the Mongol on the arm. Max ignored him. I grabbed it. Turned my hand over. Gin.

"Why you waste time playing cards with this fool, Burke? Just take out a gun, tell him to empty his pockets."

"He wins sometimes."

"Yeah. Whenever a cop gives mouth-to-mouth to a guy who faints in a gay bar."

I lit a smoke, sipped at the cup of clear soup standing next to me. Pansy snarled in the corner—she wasn't used to color TV. And she wanted pro wrestling, not soap operas. She's only a dog—she thinks she can tell the difference.

Max took out a racing form, still pumped up with our last success. Gypsy Flame had destroyed the field, powering overland on the back stretch, clearing the others by the paddock turn, driving home with room to spare—$17.20 to win, more than seventeen hundred bucks to the good on our first bet in months. I waved it away—I couldn't concentrate. Max had picked up the cash from Maurice. Like old times. Moving money, not bodies.

"When's this gonna go down?" the Prof asked.

"I don't know, brother. I told you a dozen times. He called, said to watch the tube. So I'm doing it. You don't have to stay."

"He wasn't my friend, but I'll see the end."

"Okay, then. You want to sit in for Max?"

"No way. Fucking Wesley. You always could pick 'em, Burke."

He acted it out for Max—some of the characters I'd hooked up with in the joint. The Prof had a gift for it—he used to be a preacher.

Time passed. Like it does inside the walls. Except it was safe where I was. Working on my alibi. Mac was upstairs. Lily was going to drop over later. Hell, I was hoping the cops rolled by too. Whatever Wesley was up to, I wanted to be on another planet.

147

Max saw it first. Rapped the table to get our attention. A trailer running at the bottom of one of the soap operas. HOSTAGE SITUATION IN RIVERDALE SCHOOL . . . ARMED TERRORISTS SEIZE ST. IGNATIUS . . . POLICE AND FBI ON THE SCENE . . . STAY TUNED.

"No way," the Prof said.

But I knew.

The soap opera played on. At two-fifteen, they broke in for a live report. Guy in a trench coat, hand-held microphone, sound truck behind him.

"We have no details yet. Apparently, an armed team of terrorists has captured the school. The doors and exits are blocked. The terrorists arrived in a rental truck and entered the school disguised in some way. The police were alerted by a phone call from inside. There was machine-gun fire. If the camera will just pan over . . . you can see the truck on the edge of the school yard. This is as close as the police will allow us to go. We understand there has been a telephone hookup to the terrorists, and the Hostage Negotiation Team is in place."

The anchorman from "Live at Five" cut in. I guess they told him to report to work early. Wesley would have been pleased. And the anchorman asked the right question. "Tom, you say shots were fired. Were they fired by the terrorists?"

"We just don't know. The police have a tight ring around the school."

"Tell us something about the school."

"St. Ignatius is an exclusive private school here in Riverdale. One of the oldest prep schools in the area. Grades nine through twelve. Some of the most prominent families in the city send their children here."

I clicked on the radio. They had a crew at the scene too. The reporter said something about a media demand, whatever that meant.

Back to the TV. The field reporter was on camera. "It seems that the terrorists have herded the children into the gymnasium. One of them just broke a window. We can see somebody attaching a bullhorn of some kind. I think they're going to make their demands . . ."

A cop's voice. "You! Inside! What do you want? You can't get out!"

The bullhorn fired back. A measured, unexcited voice. A machine talking through a machine. "I want a helicopter to take us to the airport. I want a fucking 747 to take us to Cuba. You got that, pigs?"

"Crazy bastard thinks it's 1969," the Prof said.

"Let the kids go!" the cop shouted back. "Let the kids go and we'll get you the plane."

"Dumb-ass motherfucker forgot the ransom." The Prof shook his head sadly.

The camera held steady on the school. The field reporter read from a list of famous people whose kids were inside. Tomorrow's judges, politicians, mobsters. The seeds Wesley wanted to burn out of the ground.

"You! Inside!" The cop on the bullhorn again. "We've got the plane for you! Waiting at the airport! Let the hostages go and we'll send in some police officers to take their place! Unarmed!"

The monster's voice cracked back. "Bring more cops! You need more cops! Lots of cops!"

"Oh shit!" the Prof muttered, no questions left.

Camera panned to the SWAT team. Riflemen with scopes. Cops in riot gear—helmets with faceplates, flak jackets, pump shotguns. A cauldron coming to a boil.

The announcer's professional voice came through, just the trace of a tremble inside.

"There's a man on the roof! Get the camera on him."

A man standing there in jungle fatigues, field cap hiding his eyes, gloves on his hands.

The rented truck exploded. A greenish cloud filled the screen. Bursts of machine-gun fire ripped. Screams and shouts from everywhere. The announcer held his ground.

"The unknown man on the roof has apparently detonated the explosion in the terrorists' truck here on the ground . . . the crowd is taking cover. A squad of policemen has gone around to the back of the school to try and gain access to the roof. The darkness you see on your screen isn't your picture . . . apparently some type of gas has been released from the truck . . . we're about five hundred yards from the scene . . . the gas is lifting . . . we don't know how many terrorists are left inside."

The camera focused on the lone madman.

"The man on the roof is lighting something. It looks like a torch. He's holding it high above his head . . . he . . . oh my God . . . he looks like some bizarre Statue of Liberty . . . he's . . ."

The dynamite exploded in Wesley's hand and the screen went blank.

148

WE STAYED THERE until late that
night. Flipping channels, checking the radio. Every report made a liar
out of the previous one. Seventy-five kids dead. A hundred. Two
hundred. School security guards machine-gunned. Grenade tossed into
the administration office. One of the surviving kids said he heard
explosions, gunfire. Then a voice on the PA system telling all the
students to get into the gymnasium. A man was standing at the podium,
dressed in military fatigues. They all filed inside. The man put some
stuff around the door seams. Dropped duffel bags in all the corners.
One of the kids screamed. The man raked the row with the machine
gun. The kids shut up after that. The ones still alive. The man was
shouting at the cops through the bullhorn. Then he ran out. Everything
started to blow up. The kid talked in a mechanical voice from his
hospital bed. You could hear his doctors arguing with the cops in the
background.

The cops were combing through the human wreckage. So far, they
hadn't found a single terrorist.

"You think Wesley's going to Hell?" I asked the Prof. He believes
in that stuff.

"If he is, the Devil better be ready."

"Amen."

149

THE COPS HIT Train's operation. Found what they were looking for. Morehouse broke the story. Lily led the team of social workers debriefing the kids. The FBI Pedophile Task Force was in on it. Even Interpol.

I called Morehouse.

"Congratulations on your scoop."

"Yeah, man." He sounded sad, the sun gone from his voice.

"What's wrong?"

"The little girl? The one that needed to go to the psycho ward?"

"Yeah?"

"She went out a window. While the cops were breaking down the front door."

"She's on the loose?"

"It was the top floor, man."

"It's not your fault—she was gone anyway."

"Sure."

150

THE PACKAGE arrived a couple of weeks later. A nine-by-twelve flat envelope. Thick with paper inside. Routed from my Jersey PO box, the one I use for mercenary stings. Max handed it to me in the warehouse.

I slit it open. A single sheet of paper. Neatly typed letters. "Put on a pair of gloves before you open the next envelope. Burn this part."

I did.

A dozen sheets of single-spaced typing. On a typewriter they'd never find. Each page numbered. Written in blood so icy it ran clear. My hands trembled. I lit a cigarette.

My name is Wesley. You never knew me. None of you did. But you know my work. I killed my first human in 1967.

He gave the lieutenant's name. Where it happened.

Four rounds in the chest. M-16. I killed two men in that prison you put me in.

Dayton and another guy I hadn't known about.

When I got out of prison, I started killing people for money.

Names, places, dates, calibers. The dope dealer even the Marielitos and Santeria couldn't protect. A blowgun with a poisoned dart. An ice pick in the kidney in the middle of a racetrack crowd. The list went on for pages.

Marco Interdonanto. Car bomb. Carlos Santamaria Ramos. At La Guardia. A spring bomb in a coin locker.

The one where the whole crowd died along with him.

Tommy Brown. I cracked his skull with a lead pipe and set fire to the house.

Near the end, I got to the part he left me in his will.

I killed somebody named Mortay. It was a contract from a man named Julio. He works for Don Torenelli. I shot him with a .38 Special, then I dropped a grenade on his face. I killed a man named Robert Morgan. In a playground in Chelsea. A rifle shot from the roof. The same contract. Julio wouldn't pay me. He said it was the don's orders. So I hit Torenelli's daughter on Sutton Place. I cut off her head and stuffed it in her cunt. I wrote 2 on the wall. It was a message. They didn't listen.

Then he listed the other hits. Queens, Brooklyn, Staten Island.

Torenelli put out a contract on me for revenge. I shot him on the Fifty-ninth Street Bridge. A .220 Remington with a night scope. Then I killed Julio. I killed a man named Train. I blew up a car on Wards Island with him in it. A man named Morrison hired me to do it. On Long Island. He tried to get out of paying me, so I killed him too. With a .357 magnum, wad cutters. Two in the chest, one in the face. He owed and he had to pay.

All my life, I worked for the same people. They had different names, but they were all the same. All bosses. Generals. I was a soldier.

I have no love in me for any of you. You have no love for me. You don't need my story. Why doesn't matter. What I did, you did it. You did it to me, I did it to you. I'm tired. I'm tired of all this. I'm not a man. I don't know what I am, but I wasn't born to be it. So I'm dying to be it. What I am.

I have no friends and I have no fear. I only stopped because I got tired. You could never have stopped me.

I worked for my money. That's what I did. They didn't pay me. So I made them pay. They didn't listen to my warnings. So I'm leaving them one last warning. I don't know where I'm going and I don't care. But they better not send anyone after me.

If you're reading this, you're a cop. Some kind of cop. I'm not leaving you this as a favor. It's my last chance to tell you how much I hate you.

Pray to your fucking gods that I'm the last one. But you know I'm not. There's more coming. You do things to us, we grow up and we do things to you.

I'm signing this with the only name you ever cared about.

His dark thumbprint was at the bottom of the last page.

151

I READ IT through twice. He wasn't just getting me off the hook, he was warning me. For the last time. Never show them your soft spot. Everyone in the street knew mine.

Wesley checked out and took a bunch of kids with him. Seeds. Cards in a stacked deck. They dealt them—the monster played them.

I held the pages in my gloved hands. Knowing the last word Wesley never said to me.

Brother.

I waited until my hands stopped shaking. Then I called Morales. "It's Burke. Let's play some more nine ball."

"I get off at four."

152

I WAS AT MY TABLE when he walked in. In the middle of a rack.

"Take off your coat," I said under my breath. "Just do it, you're not the only guy in the room wearing a gun. When we're finished, go someplace private and read what you find in your pocket."

His mind wasn't on the game. I was up a yard and a half before he split.

153

WHEN I called Mama's the next day, the message was waiting for me. I met Morales on West Seventeenth, just off Twelfth Avenue. Whore corner. We watched the girls jump into cars for a while.

"What do you want . . . for what you gave me?"

"To get square."

"Most of it's the dead truth. *Most* of it. We checked it out. He knows things only the killer would know. Why would he take you off the hook?"

"I don't know what you're talking about."

"We can clear a couple of dozen unsolved homicides behind this. It means a gold shield for me."

"And for McGowan."

"He's my partner," he said, insulted.

"I'm not."

"No, you're not. But we're square. There was no paper on you anyway."

"I know. It's over."

He held out his hand. I took it.

154

IT WASN'T OVER.

Just Wesley's killing was.

Candy let me in. Wearing a man's button-down dress shirt over toreador pants. Like a hundred years ago. "You want to play?" she asked.

"Not today, outrider."

The cat's eyes narrowed. "What?"

"It was always you and Train. From the beginning. Elvira didn't run from you—you dumped her. Into Train's net. You knew Train was on Wesley's list. You thought I killed this Mortay freak. Thought I was a killer too. You knew Wesley was coming, so you put me on the same track. Facing him."

"I had to find out. I just watch—I don't risk. I didn't know how to find Wesley, so I sent you after Elvira. I knew there was a contract on Train—I knew Wesley was holding it. I know how he works. He watches. He waits. And then he does his work. It was all a play, and

I wrote the lines. Wesley sees you hanging around, he figures you're with Train. Then he comes. You get in his way, somebody goes down. Not me. Never me."

"And you fuck the winner," I said. Remembering the subway tunnel, the kitten in the basement.

"Sure. That's the way it works. But I never thought you'd win. And you didn't."

"How long have you been with Train?"

"Since I was nineteen. I was one of his first. His very first. But I'm no outrider. That's a game. For the kids. Nobody leaves. I'm a partner, not a soldier. I made him . . . all that mumbo-jumbo bullshit. He tell you the one about truth?"

"No."

Her voice changed the way her face could. Train's voice: "If there is no truth, saying it *is* the truth. So there is always truth."

She watched my face, smiling. "Pretty good, huh? I gave him that one. He works the place in Brooklyn, I work here."

"Your partner's gone. So's Elvira."

"I'm still here. I know how to do it. There's plenty of kids. I'll always have me. I don't need anybody else."

"You're garbage."

"Am I? You think I loved you? Even when we were kids? It was Wesley I loved. He had the power. You . . . you're a weak, soft man. You were never hard. Me, I *made* you hard. I can do it again. I'm the one that's hard. Like Wesley. You should see your eyes . . . you want to beat me to death right here. But you can't do it. You can't hurt me. I know you. We can go in the back room right now. Tie me up so I can't move. And I'll still be in control."

I didn't say anything, watching her. The love Wesley never knew he had. He was better off where he was.

"You won't go to the cops either. That's not your way. The secret is to *know*. Like I know you. You could never hurt me. Wesley won. He's out there someplace. And I'll find him. I know you. If you were really a killer, you'd kill me."

She turned her back on me, walked out of the room, leaving me alone. Giving me a choice.

I closed the door behind me.

155

As I walked down the carpeted hall, a puddle of shadow moved. I nodded. Max drifted silently back the way I came, a key in his hand.

.

A NOTE ON THE TYPE

This book was set in a digitized version of Granjon, a type named in
compliment to Robert Granjon, a type cutter and printer active in
Antwerp, Lyons, Rome, and Paris from 1523 to 1590. Granjon, the boldest
and most original designer of his time, was one of the first to practice the
trade of type founder apart from that of printer.

Linotype Granjon was designed by George W. Jones, who based his
drawings on a face used by Claude Garamond (ca. 1480–1561) in his
beautiful French books. Granjon more closely resembles Garamond's own
type than does any of the various modern faces that bear his name.

Composed by PennSet, Inc., a division of
Maryland Linotype Composition Company,
Bloomsburg, Pennsylvania

Printed and bound by R. R. Donnelley & Sons,
Harrisonburg, Virginia